BURIAL GROUNDS

An absolutely addictive and heart-pounding crime thriller

BILL KITSON

DI Mike Nash Book 14

JOFFE BOOKS

1·80

Joffe Books, London
www.joffebooks.com

First published in Great Britain in 2022

This paperback edition was first published
in Great Britain in 2022

ISBN: 978-1-80405-299-0

For Val
My all-round superstar

CHAPTER ONE

The pleasant summer's evening was ignored by the couple in the car. They had been arguing since they left Netherdale on the journey to Bishopton. The driver's complaint, although it highlighted the strength of his feelings for his companion, nevertheless irritated her.

'I hate these snatched meetings. Most of the time, we've to settle for a quickie, and even worse, nothing more than a bit of slap and tickle. Just for once, I'd like to be able to take you to bed and make love to you all night — or even longer.'

Her response was a reflex, and she regretted it almost as she spoke. 'There's a simple way to remedy that. They call it divorce.'

'You know damned well that's not possible. If I was to leave her, that would mean walking away from the company I helped to create. In turn, that would leave me jobless and penniless. And if she found out I was shacking up with you, that would put you in the same boat.'

They had never discussed finances before. There had been much greater priorities to concentrate on.

As they neared the sharp bend that marked their final approach to Bishopton, she asked, 'Are you totally dependent on her money?'

As he swung the wheel to guide the vehicle, following the curve in the road alongside the wall of the cemetery, he glanced sideways at his mistress. The bitterness in his voice was evident as he replied, 'Too bloody right I am! The bitch has got her claws in too deep for me to carry on the business without the funding she supplies.'

'She couldn't divorce you if she was no longer alive.'

He was too astounded by the implication of her statement to believe it at first. 'Are you suggesting I kill her? The law takes a very dim view of murder.'

'I wasn't proposing you strangle her. I was thinking more of an accident, something that they couldn't blame on you. There are all sorts of ways and means.'

The driver almost lost control of the vehicle as he turned and stared at his companion. 'You actually mean I should—'

Her scream cut him off.

There was a figure directly in the car's path. He yanked at the wheel in a desperate attempt to avoid the oncoming runner. It was far too late. The impact flung the jogger violently against the sign that read, "*Bishopton Welcomes Careful Drivers*".

A split second later, the car came to a halt against the sign, pinning the unconscious woman between an unstoppable force and an immovable object. The passenger's scream died away into an empty silence.

They clambered from the car to look at the motionless form.

The passenger suggested they should call for help.

The argument preceding the accident was nothing compared to the row that followed. 'We can't do that,' the driver snapped. 'Besides the trouble we'd be in, it wouldn't do any good. She's past help.'

He glanced at the deserted road, the wall alongside it providing excellent cover. 'We're just damned lucky it happened out here in the wilds, where there's nobody about. Let's get out of here sharp, before somebody sees us. There's nothing we can do for her now.'

The driver's last sentence was wrong on two counts. Although the jogger was unconscious, she wasn't beyond help — yet.

His other error was in believing the incident had gone unwitnessed.

The man, who was standing in the shade of an ancient yew tree at the perimeter of the cemetery, had begun recording the scene on his mobile phone before the couple got out of the car. As he filmed them driving away, he smiled. There was a certain irony in what had just happened, given that the cameraman had been in the process of poaching when he witnessed the incident.

That didn't worry him. He'd recognized the driver instantly — knew the woman alongside him wasn't his wife. The witness had committed a minor offence. The accident would give him the opportunity to commit a much graver crime. One that could prove highly lucrative.

Once the car was out of sight, the witness walked across to where the victim was lying slumped against the signpost. He pointed the camera towards her, ensuring he got both her face, and the sign, in the shot. Like the car driver, he believed the woman was beyond help. Even if she had not been, it was doubtful he would have summoned assistance. He turned away, and began walking home, whistling cheerfully as he went.

* * *

The funeral, held at St. Giles Church in Bishopton, was a simple but dignified tribute to a young woman cut down in the prime of life. There were few mourners in the ranks of pews as the vicar led the congregation through the service.

At times, the attention of the dead woman's husband strayed to a memory, a conversation a month ago, when he'd said, 'I wish I didn't have to go. I know that sounds weird, but it won't be the same without you there.'

3

'And I wish I could come too.' She'd smiled. 'If only to keep the hordes of admiring females at bay, but you know I can't go — for two reasons.' She'd patted her tummy, before glancing at the photo on the dresser.

He'd followed her gaze and nodded, appreciating her meaning. The sincerity in his voice was evident as he'd replied, 'You don't have to worry about the adoring females. There's never been anyone else for me since the day we met, and that's the way it will remain as long as I draw breath.'

She'd put one hand on his cheek, stroking him gently. 'This is the biggest opportunity of your life. You can't afford to pass it up,' she'd said. 'You've worked so hard for this, improving until you're now at the top of your game. Your dogged determination and outstanding talent are about to pay off — big time. So go out there, and knock 'em dead.'

He remembered his reply, and wished he'd acted on his words. 'There's been times when I've felt like chucking it all in, times when I seemed to be getting nowhere. It's been your support, and belief, that kept me going. This is as much your triumph as mine. That's why I want you to be there with me.'

'Don't worry, there are sure to be plenty more opportunities. Especially if this Las Vegas thing comes off.'

He'd looked at the photograph on the dresser. 'You'll keep me posted about Mum, even if it's . . .' he'd balked at saying the words. Her mother had become as much his parent as hers, from the day she had taken him in as an adopted child.

'Of course I will,' she'd assured him. 'And from what I learned yesterday, the oncologist is confident that the chemotherapy is beginning to work. If he's right, she should be well again, possibly even before Junior arrives.' She'd patted her belly again, and added, 'Speaking of him — or her — I'm determined to keep up my fitness regime. I've read recently that the fitter and stronger the mother is during pregnancy, the healthier the developing foetus will be. It's taken so much for us to achieve this, and I don't want to leave anything to chance.'

'You read too many books,' he'd teased her. 'But I appreciate the importance of fitness. Let's face it — keeping fit is an essential part of my work.'

The sound of a car horn had interrupted them. She'd looked out of the window and seen the taxi parked by the kerb. 'Time to go, darling. Break a leg, as the actors say.'

He'd gathered his luggage and kissed her goodbye. It was the last time he'd seen his beautiful wife. Now he was a widower, divided between his own grief and the need to support the ailing lady alongside him. The disease she thought she had overcome had returned, and was now slowly, but inexorably, claiming her life. Added to that distress, the heartbreak of losing her child, and of being unable to hold a grandchild, had placed an intolerable burden on her.

Several neighbours, a small group of former schoolmates, and one or two other acquaintances also attended — mostly out of respect, but in one or two cases because it was the done thing. There was one attendee who didn't fit into any of these categories. The mourner remained in a pew close to the rear of the nave, seemingly unmoved by the tragic event, and the feelings of the mourners in the church.

When the service ended, the final piece of music began to play, the one that would accompany the pall bearers as they carried the coffin to its final resting place in the nearby churchyard. As the strains of the stirring anthem *Hymn To The Fallen*, composed by John Williams for the film *Saving Private Ryan*, filled the air, the occupant of the pew slipped quietly out of the door.

Such was the distress of the bereaved husband, he hadn't even noticed the presence of a stranger. It was only much later the reason for the mourner's attendance became clear. And with it, he learned the shocking answers to the questions that flooded his mind, clouding every minute, every waking hour, of his suddenly meaningless existence.

* * *

Before then, however, he had to revisit St. Giles Church again, where he acted as chief mourner for the second time in as many months. Although the autopsy findings merely recorded the cause of death as cancer, he was convinced that the disease had returned following the tragedy of his wife's death. There was no scientific proof to support his theory, that the dreadful loss of her child had accelerated her decline, but he felt certain the disease's effect had been compounded by heartbreak.

It was a cold, raw day, with a sharp easterly wind blowing, driving squalls of heavy showers almost horizontally across the moorland towards the cemetery, but the bleakness of the autumn weather was as nothing compared to the bleakness in his soul.

As he'd stood between the graves of the only two people he cared about, watching the coffin being lowered into the final resting place, he'd remembered her final words in a letter left him. "*You must not allow this to ruin the rest of your life. You have achieved so much already it would be a shame to throw all your hard work away. Don't let what has happened to us claim another victim.*"

Whatever ambitions he had cherished had now disappeared, to be replaced with another, darker motive. Somehow, whatever it took, he would find the person responsible. Only when he had avenged the callous act that had deprived him of all he loved, could he consider what to do in the future.

For some time, it looked as if he would be unable to find the person who, in his mind, had murdered the only two people he loved. Although neither death certificate contained the word *murder*, he knew that the person who left his wife to die on the roadside had killed her as effectively as if they had shot or stabbed her. The pathologist had said that her death would have been avoidable had she been taken to hospital earlier. Learning this merely compounded his misery, and awoke the burning desire for justice. Then her mother's illness had returned, the poison as lethal as arsenic.

Despite all the police enquiries about the vehicle, nothing had emerged to give him the slightest hope of achieving his objective.

The depression that beset him was intensified by his inability to change the situation, until a month later, as he was wondering what to do with yet another day of frustration, the doorbell rang.

A woman of about his own age was standing on the doorstep, a woman he failed to recognize as the stranger from the church. When she revealed the purpose of her visit, it changed every aspect of his life.

He invited her in. The extent of her knowledge astounded him. Whereas he had previously considered only one person the target for his vendetta, he now had to revise that figure. It was over an hour later that the woman left, her final comment providing him with *carte blanche* to act on the information she'd supplied, its accuracy confirmed by the flash drives she handed him.

'I've given you all you need to deal with the matter as you think fit. How you act on it is entirely up to you,' she'd told him. 'I am going away in the next week. I will be out of the country for two months, maybe longer.' She'd handed him a slip of paper. 'That's my mobile number — or one of them, at least. If you need help with *anything*, you can contact me. If you listen carefully to what I've given you, I think you'll understand why you can count on my assistance.'

He'd sensed the hatred she bore from her expression, and tone of voice, as she'd added, 'If it was my decision, I would want to make them suffer as much as you have. As I said, whether you're prepared to go to such lengths, or not, is entirely up to you. By the way,' she'd added, 'the number I've given you is for a pay-as-you-go mobile. Before I return to England, I will dispose of the device.'

After the woman left, he'd returned to the sitting room and stared for a long time at the photograph on the shelf. What he had learned during the woman's visit made what he wanted feasible. Planning was the next stage, but that was something he excelled at. It was part of his stock-in-trade, something that had contributed to his success. How long ago that seemed, almost as if that had happened to someone else.

He knew, without openly admitting as much, that his recent visitor would provide assistance, should he require it. The knowledge that he was no longer alone, and had an ally in his quest, comforted him slightly. But it was exceedingly cold comfort.

CHAPTER TWO

Three weeks later

The sexton at St Mary's Church in Netherdale glanced at his watch. His wife had given him strict orders to be home by 6.30 p.m. otherwise his dinner would be ruined. She'd added, 'And if you're not home by seven o'clock, the dog gets it.'

He had sufficient time to check the gravesite ready for the following day's interment, and still get home in time to avoid her wrath. He hurried across the cemetery, and after a brief inspection, decided all was well. It was only as he headed home, his thoughts on the lamb casserole he would shortly be enjoying, that, out of the corner of his eye, he noticed something odd.

He turned and glanced in the direction. The glance became a stare, and he approached the grave, his footsteps slow as he concentrated his gaze on something that should not have been there. 'Oh, Dear Lord,' he muttered. The headstone showed the occupant of the grave had been laid to rest a year earlier. He remembered the funeral.

He had passed the grave a few days earlier, and everything had been normal. So why was there now a naked body laid on top? Even as he summoned the emergency services via his mobile, he realized the dog would definitely get his dinner.

* * *

DI Mike Nash was at home, about to open a bottle of champagne, when his mobile rang. He glanced at the screen and grimaced. 'It's Jack Binns. That can't be good news.' He pressed a button and listened.

'Sorry to disturb you at home, Mike, but they've found a body in Netherdale Cemetery.'

Nash's buoyant mood was reflected in his flippant response. 'This might come as a surprise to you, Jack, but I already knew that. In fact, I'll let you into a little secret, as long as you keep it between us, that place is actually full of bodies. It's what a cemetery is for.'

'Yes, Mike, but they're usually inside a coffin. This one wasn't.'

Nash listened as Binns gave more details. 'Clara is already at the cemetery.'

'I'll head straight there. Have you alerted Mexican Pete?'
'Yes.'

Nash turned to Alondra, smiled, and shrugged. 'It's comes with the job. I'm sorry.'

'Don't be. I understand.' She hugged him. 'Just hurry back,' she said, with a twinkle in her eye.

As Nash was leaving Smelt Mill Cottage, Jack Binns was ringing DS Clara Mironova at the site. 'Clara, I've told Mike, and he's on his way.'

'Did you tell him everything? I mean did you explain exactly where the body is?'

'No, I chickened out. He sounded to be in such a good mood, I didn't want to spoil it.'

As she waited for Mike and the pathologist to arrive, Clara stood still for several minutes, staring at the grave directly in front of her. She wondered how Nash would react when he saw where the body had been placed. Clara knew better than most that beneath his calm, professional attitude, Mike was highly sensitive. The significance of what she considered to be a dump site might prove highly disturbing to him.

Her thought process was interrupted when one of the uniformed officers, who had been the first to attend, approached her. 'The sexton has returned and brought the vicar with him. They're both waiting to be interviewed when you're ready.'

'I think we should wait until DI Nash arrives. Any sign of Mexican Pete yet?'

The officer winced at the mention of the pathologist's nickname. 'No, and I'm hoping to be away from here before he arrives.' Professor Ramirez, nicknamed after a rude rugby song, had a reputation for being short-tempered, and expressing his anger in the bluntest of fashions.

* * *

As he drove from Wintersett village to Netherdale, Nash thought briefly about the recent telephone conversation. There had been many occasions over the past decade when Sergeant Binns had phoned to report an incident that needed the attention of the area's senior CID officer. Today's looked like marking the end of an era. Jack Binns had served the force with distinction for many years, long before Nash had returned from the Met. Now, with little more than a month remaining before Binns took his well-earned retirement, the last thing he would want was an unsolved crime on his patch as a final memory.

However, the major part of the journey was given over to thoughts of the unopened champagne, and his conversation with Alondra. He wondered what Daniel would think when he heard the news. It had been Nash's eleven-year-old son Daniel who had been instrumental in persuading Alondra Torres, a renowned landscape artist, to return to England from her home in Spain, and to resume her relationship with

Mike. They had done that, he thought with a smile. Her acceptance of his proposal and the engagement ring she was now wearing, was evidence of that. He also had to tell his team. He shuddered inwardly at the thought of the ribbing he would have to suffer — the great Lothario settling for married bliss!

It was heading towards twilight as Nash brought the Range Rover to a halt outside the cemetery gates. The last rays of light, as the sun dipped towards the western horizon, cast elongated shadows, making the uniformed constable standing guard by the entrance appear like a giant. Getting out of the car, Nash thought briefly of the previous time he had entered this place. That had been a sad occasion for him, as he had mourned the girl who had given her life to save him. Now, he wondered how much grief would be caused by the discovery of this body.

He walked through the wrought-iron gates, acknowledging the officer who entered Nash's name on the incident log, and saw DS Mironova in conversation with two men. She had obviously been watching for his arrival, because she signalled for him to join them, and introduced the vicar and sexton. 'I thought it better to wait, so they won't have to repeat what they know, which I'm afraid isn't much,' Clara explained.

'Would it be too much trouble to wait a while longer?' Nash asked. 'I'd rather look at the site and the body first.'

The men agreed, and as Clara escorted Nash towards the scene, she said, 'I hope this isn't going to be too upsetting for you.'

'Upsetting? Why would it be upsetting?'

As Clara guided him past rows of neatly trimmed graves, he realized the significance of the location protected by incident tape. 'The body wasn't on—?'

Clara interrupted before he could finish his question, 'No, it was on the one alongside hers.'

Nash stood by the tape, where his attention wandered to the grave immediately to the right. The lettering of the inscription on the headstone was already beginning to weather, but the message was still legible. Not that he needed a reminder. '*In loving memory of Samantha (Stella) Pearson. She gave her life that others might live*'.

Fourteen years ago, Stella had been Nash's long-term girlfriend. Despite being confined to a wheelchair, she had intervened in an incident that led to her death, and saved Nash from a ruthless killer. The guilt he felt over her sacrifice had never completely gone away. He had learned to live with that guilt, and the sorrow had eased with the passage of time. He glanced at Clara, who was watching him, her expression reflecting her anxiety.

'Don't worry about me. If they'd chosen a different site, they would have upset someone else. Do we know anything about the murder victim?'

'Nothing at all. I think you'll see why when you look at the body.'

Nash looked at the grave closely. His glance went to the headstone before returning to the corpse, which was naked, clearly male, and had been placed on the grave face down. Was that significant? Nash wondered. Or had the killer been in a hurry?

'I think we can rule out suicide. I suppose it's just possible that the man died of natural causes and someone decided to avoid the cost of a funeral, but I think it's highly unlikely, don't you? That only leaves us with murder.'

Despite the silence of their surroundings, the detectives were so engrossed in their examination of the scene that they failed to hear the approach of Professor Ramirez, until he spoke.

'How appropriate to see you in your natural habitat, Nash. Tell me, which grave did you emerge from? By the way, it isn't dark yet. Isn't it a bit early for you to be out and about? And how do you cope, being faced with all these signs of the Cross?'

'Sorry to disappoint you, Professor, but I drove here — and before you ask, no, it wasn't in a hearse.'

Ramirez gave up on his attempt to taunt Nash. 'OK, so what have we got?'

He underestimated Nash's ability to retaliate. 'It's a dead body, Professor. That's why we called you. I assume it's still in your remit.'

'The scene looks trampled. Was that you?' He looked directly at Nash.

'You can blame the sexton who found the body for that. I usually hover above.'

Ramirez shook his head in disgust. 'No sense, some people. I'll wait for the photographer to record the scene before I examine the cadaver.' He couldn't resist a final dig. 'Do you want copies of the photos for your scrapbook?'

Seeing Nash about to reply, Clara, who was used to the exchange of repartee between the two men, sighed, and interrupted. 'We should go and talk to the sexton and the vicar. We've kept them waiting long enough as it is.'

'Very well. Post-mortem at nine o'clock tomorrow morning,' Ramirez said.

As they returned to the entrance, Clara asked again if Nash was OK.

'I'm fine, Clara. I was a bit surprised, but nothing to worry about. In fact, I've got some news for you, but it can wait until we've finished up here.'

Their talk with the vicar and sexton yielded little that they didn't already know.

'I'd been checking on a site for an interment that's due to take place tomorrow. As I returned, I noticed something on that grave,' the sexton explained. 'When I got closer, I realized it was a body. That's when I called the police, and contacted the vicar.'

The clergyman took up the story. 'I was concerned that someone had vandalised the grave and disturbed the rightful occupant, so I got the sexton to take a closer look.'

Clara winced at the possible tampering of a crime scene, dreading Nash's reaction.

Oblivious, the vicar continued, 'Once we saw that it was a man's body, we knew it had to have been placed on top of the grave, not taken from inside it. I went straight back to the vicarage and rang the bishop. He confirmed what I thought. Once this is all dealt with, we'll have to hold a short service to re-consecrate the grave.'

'So the area does not look as it did when you first spotted it?' Nash turned to the sexton as he spoke.

'No, sir, it doesn't. But I was very careful. I watch a lot of crime series, and I knew to preserve the scene.' He almost smiled as he produced his mobile phone and showed Nash the photographs he'd taken before he got near the grave.

'Well, thank you for that. I'll get you a number to send them to. Clara, can you deal with it? Now, did either of you touch the body? Lift the head, perhaps, to see if you could identify him?'

Both men looked appalled by Nash's question. Their expressions, as much as their response, told him they hadn't interfered with the corpse in any way.

'Was he . . . ?' the vicar balked at the last word, fingering his dog collar as if he needed air.

'Murdered? Let's just say that until we get the results of the autopsy, we're treating the death as suspicious. The post-mortem will establish C.O.D, and we'll be better able to judge once we have that.'

'What's C.O.D?' the vicar asked.

The sexton answered, 'Cause of death. You can learn a lot from those programmes.'

Nash glanced at Clara, who was trying not to smile.

'There will need to be a forensic examination of the crime scene. That comprises the grave itself, and a search of the surrounding areas, including anywhere the person who brought the body here might have parked their vehicle.'

'Sorry, Inspector, they can't have used a vehicle. I keep the main gates to the drive locked — it keeps out the undesirables.'

15

'Then how do you account for those tyre-tread marks?' Nash pointed to the indentations in the turf alongside the row of headstones.

'Sadly, there have already been two interments this week,' the vicar told him, 'and the gates are opened to allow the hearse and cortege access.'

'I can vouch for the fact that they were locked when we arrived,' one of the uniformed men interjected. 'We had to wait for this gentleman to open them before we could enter.'

'Well, until the examination of the site is complete, the cemetery must remain closed. I'm afraid the interment planned for tomorrow, and any in the next few days, will have to be postponed.'

Nash and Mironova watched the two men leave. 'I don't see there's any need for me to remain here,' Nash said. 'As it's your weekend on duty, I think you can deal with Mexican Pete and Forensics. And you can also have the pleasure of attending the post-mortem. I don't see why I should have all the fun.'

'Thanks a lot, Mike. You certainly know how to give a girl a good time.'

Nash grinned as he turned to walk to his car. He had only taken a few strides when Clara called after him. 'What was it, Mike?'

'What was what?'

'That item of news you were going to tell me.'

'Oh, that.' Nash tried to control his expression. 'Do you remember when Alondra was here the first time, and I told you Daniel had asked me if she was to be his new mother?'

'Yes,' Clara said, her eyes widening in surprise. 'Does that mean what I think?'

'Yes, it does, and tomorrow we're going to visit him at school to give him his answer.' He got into the driving seat, smiling happily.

Clara stared at the back of the Range Rover as it drove away. 'At last,' she muttered to herself, knowing that if anyone deserved some happiness, it was her boss.

CHAPTER THREE

When DS Mironova pulled into Helmsdale police station car park on the following Monday morning, she was surprised to see not only Nash's distinctive Range Rover, but also the Audi she knew belonged to their acting chief constable, Superintendent Ruth Edwards. The chief, Gloria O'Donnell, was away on compassionate leave, caring for her husband as he recovered from major heart surgery.

She expected to find Ruth Edwards in the CID suite talking to Mike, but the offices were empty.

As she placed her handbag on her desk, Nash emerged from the kitchen and greeted her. 'Morning, Clara. Coffee?'

'Yes please, Mike.'

He brought the mugs through and perched on the corner of Clara's desk. 'There is a distinct lack of paperwork on my desk,' Nash commented. 'Which suggests you either had a very quiet weekend, or you have it in your bag. The other alternative is that you've suddenly been struck down with writer's cramp, or typist's wrist.'

'Neither of those, Mike, it was exceedingly quiet. There was a minor disturbance outside one of the pubs on the Westlea estate, but, as usual, uniform dealt with that.'

'Hardly surprising. That's a normal Saturday night for the Westlea.'

'I saw the chief's car outside and expected to find her in here, so where is she?'

'She's closeted with the first of the interviewees from the shortlist for Jack's job. The other two candidates will be here soon, after which, she wants a word with everyone. Before you ask, no, I don't know what it's about. So, given that there was no other excitement, how did the post-mortem on our grave-yard victim go?'

Clara reached forward and removed a notebook from her bag and flipped it open. 'The victim is male, and the professor estimates he's between thirty and forty years old. Reasonably fit — apart from the fact that he's dead. His fingerprints aren't on the PNC, and we're awaiting DNA results.'

'OK, what about cause of death?'

'That's where it gets a bit more interesting. Other than abrasions on both wrists and ankles, suggesting he'd been restrained, there were no obvious signs of injuries. And by the severity of the marks, the professor thinks he was held captive for quite a long time. He'd struggled to escape from the restraints — obviously without success. The actual cause of death was drowning.'

Clara saw Nash's eyes widen, and nodded agreement. 'Yes, that took me aback, too. Not only was he drowned, but the substance used was tap water, not sea, or river water.'

'Did our worthy pathologist establish when the victim died?'

'He gave a rough estimate, but warned that it might be inaccurate, because the body had been moved. His guess is that the man had been dead for about three or four days before he was found. Lividity suggests the man had been kept upside down.'

'That does seem odd, to put it mildly. As things stand, we're not much wiser than we were on Friday night. Without establishing the man's identity, I can't see how we're going to make much progress.'

Nash thought over what Clara had told him, and then said, 'When Viv arrives, get him to look through our MISPER files, and see if he can come up with anyone matching the victim's description. Failing which, I reckon we're snookered.'

Their discussion of the post-mortem findings over, Clara changed the subject. 'How did Daniel react to your news? Was he pleased?'

'Remember how excited he was when we got the puppy?'

Clara nodded.

Nash grinned. 'Then double it! He's appointed himself my best man.'

'Are you planning to tell the others?'

'I am, but I'll wait until everyone's here. If it's appropriate, that meeting might be a good opportunity. Now, as there seems to be little else to do, I'm going out. I have an important errand to run. I'll tell you about it when I get back, if I'm successful.'

* * *

Clara was at her desk when DC Viv Pearce, their resident IT expert arrived. Born of Antiguan parents, Vivian Pearce, like his father and uncles, had been christened in honour of great West Indian cricketers. He had continued that tradition by naming his young son Brian Charles, after the superb batsman Brian Lara.

'Morning, Clara, where is everybody?'

Having explained Nash's absence and the reason for Ruth Edwards' visit, Clara told Pearce about the body found in the graveyard. 'Mike wants you to work your computer magic, see if there's anyone in the missing person files who matches the corpse.' She passed him a sheet of paper. 'There's a description. It's as close a match as we have — minus the marks on his wrists and ankles, of course. While you're doing that, I'll do a background check on the sexton and the vicar.'

'The vicar? You don't think . . . ?'

'Anything's possible, Viv. And the sexton, well, he seems to think he's knowledgeable enough to take over Forensics.'

She turned to her screen. Both she and Pearce had been scanning the computer files for a while when Nash returned.

'Morning, Viv. Any luck?' he asked, seeing the open file on the screen.

'Not so far, Mike, but I've a lot more to go through. It's staggering how many people are reported missing. Unless we can think of a way to narrow the search parameters, it's going to be a while before I know one way or another.'

'I'll leave you to it, then. Just keep me updated.'

Clara added, 'I can't find anything regarding the vicar. The sexton had a speeding ticket once, if that helps,' she said, with a grin.

Nash smiled and wandered over to Mironova's desk. 'I managed to get a result from my errand.'

'Where did you go?'

'La Giaconda.'

Clara blinked in surprise at Nash's mention of Helmsdale's only Italian restaurant. 'Blimey, Mike, it's a bit early in the day to be gorging on lasagne or spaghetti bolognaise, isn't it?'

'I didn't go there for food. I went to book the restaurant for a private function.'

'Don't tell me you're booking a party for all your friends, because a couple of tables would be sufficient for that.'

Nash ignored the insult. 'The party will be to mark Jack Binns' retirement. I'm picking up the tab in order to say thank you for his enormous contribution to the work we've done here. If it's practical, I'll start issuing invitations at the meeting, when everyone else is here. Speaking of which, where's Lisa?'

DC Lisa Andrews worked out of HQ at Netherdale, and had been on loan recently, helping to cover a heavy workload. She was usually among the first to arrive, so her absence was puzzling.

Clara reminded Nash of the reason. 'She's helping take witness statements in Netherdale about that spate of shoplifting.' She glanced across at Pearce, who was preoccupied with his study of his computer screen. 'She did tell you about it on Friday, but doubtless you've had more important things on your mind.'

* * *

It was late morning before Lisa Andrews reached Helmsdale. No sooner had she entered the CID suite, greeted her colleagues, and accepted the offer of coffee made by Nash, than the door opened again, and the visitor requested another mug.

Nash blinked with surprise before greeting Chief Constable Gloria O'Donnell. 'Good morning, ma'am. Are you here to sit in on the interviews with Superintendent Edwards, or to endorse the successful candidate?'

'No, Mike, that is nothing to do with my visit. I'll explain in detail when everyone's here. In the meantime, white with one sweetener — in case you've forgotten.'

'Yes, ma'am.'

Nash was heading for the kitchen when the door opened yet again, to reveal O'Donnell's stand-in, Ruth Edwards, accompanied by Sergeant Jack Binns. 'That'll be two more, Mike,' Ruth told him.

'I didn't realize when I left home this morning I'd end up working as a barista,' Nash muttered in feigned annoyance.

'Everyone has their uses, even you,' O'Donnell retorted.

Nash co-opted Lisa to act as waitress, and when everyone had their drinks, Ruth Edwards addressed them. 'Turn your back on that computer, Viv, and pay attention.' She turned to Gloria O'Donnell. 'Ma'am, the floor is yours.'

O'Donnell began. 'I asked Superintendent Edwards to call this meeting on my behalf. Firstly, I have to congratulate all of you on the way you have handled the past couple of months.'

As the team members nodded their thanks, she turned to Lisa Andrews. 'I am aware you have been here more than at your post in Netherdale.'

Lisa looked a little concerned.

'Am I correct in assuming that you have been happy with that arrangement?'

'Er. Yes, ma'am,' Lisa stammered in response.

'Good. Because, as of next Monday, you will be here permanently. I decided CID would be better housed in one location. A lot of money was spent when the station was moved to this site, merging with the other emergency services. And I don't think it's being put to full use.' She smiled at Lisa before looking directly at Nash.

'You asked if I was here to deal with the question of Jack's replacement, but that is no longer my concern. As a result of my husband's illness, he is having to retire on health grounds. I have opted to follow suit, and take early retirement. We both realized there are many things we want to do together, places we want to visit, and we've decided to make the most of the opportunity, while we can. In normal circumstances, my successor would be appointed by the Police and Crime Commissioner, but following the death of the office holder, that position remains vacant. In the meantime, there has to be a permanent incumbent for the role of chief constable, and I'm delighted to inform you all that the Home Secretary has accepted my recommendation. With effect from the beginning of next month, my successor will take up the role.'

'Who is it? Do we know them?' Nash asked, beating Mironova to the question by a split second.

'You certainly do. In fact, you're looking at her. The Home Secretary agreed that everything has run so well while Ruth has been in charge, he has ratified her appointment. I am also pleased to say that Superintendent Fleming is intending to return to work when she has her medic's approval.' O'Donnell paused before adding, 'I'm going to take my leave of you now, because I have to visit Netherdale, give the staff there the news, and clear my office.'

Jack Binns spoke up. 'I wish you well, ma'am, and I shall inform my officers. Now if you'll excuse me, I should get back downstairs.' He nodded and left the room, clutching his coffee mug.

Nash waited until the door was closed before he said, 'Before you go, ma'am, there are a couple of things you need to be aware of. The first is that in four weeks' time there will be a party at La Giaconda restaurant. The celebration is being held to bid farewell, and express our thanks, to Jack for his years of service. That has now been extended to include you — as long as you don't mind sharing with Jack.'

Gloria nodded and smiled. 'I'm more than happy to do so, Mike, and thank you. Now I really must go.'

'I did say there were two things you should know.'

She turned to face him and sighed. 'Yes?'

'The second is that I'm delighted to inform you all that next spring you will be receiving a wedding invitation.' He switched his gaze to Ruth Edwards. 'And I will be applying for leave to take my bride on honeymoon.'

Mironova, knowing what he was about to say, reckoned you could have detonated a hand grenade in the room with less effect.

* * *

Two days after Nash's announcement, DC Lisa Andrews arrived at Helmsdale with another surprising news item to reveal. The only occupant of the CID suite was Clara Mironova, who listened with interest to what Lisa had learned.

'I've just been talking to Tom Pratt at Netherdale, and he told me about the guy they've selected to replace Jack Binns. I've no idea where Tom gets all his info from.'

Clara laughed. 'Tom was a detective superintendent, remember. He's bound to have his sources.'

Tom Pratt had indeed been a senior detective. Having taken early retirement following a heart attack, he had rejoined the force to work as a civilian support officer.

'Go on then, Lisa. Who is it?' Clara asked.

'His name is Steve Meadows. He's from Bishopton originally, but when the station there closed, he moved to West

Yorkshire. He's only recently got his sergeant's stripes, and when he learned there was a vacancy, he applied immediately. He's joining us on Monday to work with Jack for a month and learn the ropes.' Lisa lowered her voice slightly, 'Apparently, the reason he's so keen to return is that he had been in a relationship with a young woman from Leeds, but that ended suddenly, and now he's seeing a girl from Kirk Bolton and wants to be stationed near her.'

Clara groaned. 'Not another one.' Seeing Lisa's puzzled frown she added, 'We've only just got Mike's convoluted love life sorted out, and now we're going to be faced with another hyperactive Romeo on the premises. What is it about this place that attracts men who over-produce testosterone?'

She thought for a few seconds, her brow knitted in a frown of concentration. 'Steve Meadows . . . I seem to recall that name.' It took a moment or two before she said, 'Got it! Wasn't he the young constable who found the missing journalist's car in Helm Woods some years back? That reporter who was murdered.'

'I think you might be right, but it is a few years ago, so I can't be sure.'

'If it is the same guy, I remember Mike was impressed by his ability, and the way he worked things out.'

Clara had just finished speaking when Viv Pearce walked in and announced, 'I've just found out who Jack's replacement is.'

Clara groaned again. 'If the *Netherdale Gazette* decides to run a gossip column, I'm going to put you two up for the job.'

CHAPTER FOUR

When Viv Pearce answered the phone, he wasn't to know that it would provide the first clue to the identity of the man they referred to as the Cemetery Corpse. He listened for several minutes, making one or two notes, and replaced the receiver. 'Where's Mike?'

'He said he was calling in at HQ on his way in,' Lisa told him.

'Why do you need him? Is it something urgent?' Clara asked.

'It could be, but I'm not sure. Netherdale have just had a call from Skipton police. A woman there has reported her brother missing.'

'Skipton? That must be over fifty miles away. Why are they involving us?'

'Apparently, they have a missing man, Andrew Derrick. He lives in Gorton village and works as a mechanic for Helm Logistics in Netherdale. His description matches the one we put out over the region, of the corpse in the cemetery. They've taken a DNA swab from the sister and sent it for analysis, but the photo she supplied is very similar.'

* * *

Next day, Nash hoped that his, and Mironova's, meeting with Andrew Derrick's sister, when she travelled through to Netherdale for the formal identification, might shed more light on the victim.

'We need to find out all we can,' Nash said as they drove to the mortuary at the rear of Netherdale General Hospital. 'If it is a positive ID, she promised to bring a spare set of keys for his house. That will save us having to break the door down. To try and speed things up, I've got the boffins on standby. We'll need Forensics to go through the place to determine if he was killed there. The house might provide us with some evidence. Although we may confirm his name, apart from trying to find out if his sister knows a motive for his murder, we're still only marginally better off than when they found the body.'

'Is she coming on her own? I'd be surprised if she's in a fit state to drive,' Clara asked.

'No, the victim support officer is driving her over.'

'Isn't she married?'

'Yes, her name is Mrs Barbara Jackson, but I believe her husband works away.'

When the formality of identification was over, and the professor said he would inform the Coroner's office, Clara escorted the tearful woman to a private room. She explained they needed to obtain any facts that might help them, suggesting a hot drink to help calm the distressing situation. Nash obtained the house keys and handed them to the waiting officer.

Once the sister had regained her composure, Nash began the interview, while Clara took notes. The support officer sat alongside to provide reassurance. During the ensuing conversation, Nash told Mrs Jackson she wouldn't be able to visit her brother's house until the forensic team had finished. 'They will inform us as soon as they've completed the job. In the meantime, we need you to tell us everything you can about Andrew, even the smallest detail. Things you regard as trivial or unimportant might be useful.'

As was often the case when prompted, memories began to surface regarding many aspects of the victim's life, mostly from their childhood. Nash and Clara listened carefully for anything that might be relevant to the case, before the woman again dissolved into tears.

The officer patted her hand before Nash took control. 'Let's start with the obvious question. Do you know of anyone who might have wanted to harm him? Can you think of anything in his life that might have sparked a motive for someone to kill him?'

The answer to both questions was no, so Nash asked, 'Had he made any enemies?'

Again, the answer was in the negative. 'I spoke to him about a month ago, and he told me everything was going well. He was even hoping for a pay rise at work.'

'You haven't mentioned his personal life? Was he involved in a relationship?'

There was a short but noticeable pause before she answered, the reason for which soon became clear. 'There hasn't been anyone recently — in fact, not for a good few years. Andrew had been involved with someone, but it all went wrong. After that, he didn't seem interested in any romantic commitment. I think deep down he was scared of getting hurt again.'

Nash saw the heightened distress talking about this caused her. He was about to ask why when his mobile rang. It was the forensic team leader, reporting the house seemed to be in order, and there was no sign that anything untoward had occurred. He gave the all-clear for the detectives to visit the property. Nash made a mental note to bring the subject of Andrew Derrick's love life up again, when the opportunity arose.

* * *

As they escorted Mrs Jackson along the short path leading to the house at Gorton, Nash checked the exterior of the

27

building. From the recently painted wrought-iron gates to the neatly trimmed lawn, the weed-free borders, and the clean, fresh appearance of the woodwork on the windows and front door, the property appeared immaculate.

Either her brother had employed a decorator and a gardener, Nash thought, or he had spent much of his spare time on DIY. Once inside, there was similar evidence of cleanliness and tidiness. As they examined each room, Nash suggested to the sister, whose distress was apparent, that she should concentrate on trying to see anything that seemed unusual, or out of place. 'It might seem insignificant, but if you were able to spot anything that seems out of character, it might prove useful in finding out what happened to Andrew.'

Nash continued his inspection of the ground floor, finding nothing unusual in the lounge-cum-dining room, or the kitchen. Meanwhile, Mironova escorted Mrs Jackson upstairs. Nash was in the process of checking the contents of the fridge freezer, when Clara called for him to join them. He closed the refrigerator door, making a mental note to remind the woman to remove the perishable items that were already beginning to smell, and wandered up the staircase.

One glance in the bedroom, where the women were standing, suggested that something was amiss. Whereas the rest of the property, both inside and out, bore evidence of the man's passion for neatness and order, the discarded clothing strewn across the bed and floor told a different story.

Mrs Jackson pointed at the scene. 'This is wrong, Inspector Nash.'

'Was your brother careless about his clothes?' Nash asked.

'Quite the opposite, Inspector, he was meticulous to the point of OCD, even as a child. I remember our mother teasing him when she found him pressing his trousers before going to school. More recently, I rang him one evening, and he had the TV on in the background. I recognized the theme tune from one of the soaps, and teased him about it. He told me it didn't matter what was on the telly, as he only used it as a distraction every evening, while he was ironing his work clothes. Even though I knew of his passion for neatness, I could hardly believe that he was ironing his overalls, but he was.'

She sighed and smiled. 'When he was on holiday he used to take a trouser press in the car, in case the hotel or boarding house he was staying in didn't have one.' She looked at the bed. 'One thing for sure, Andrew would *never* leave his clothing scattered around like this.'

As the woman was speaking, Clara slid open one of the doors to the built-in wardrobe. Sure enough, the contents were immaculate. They checked the other rooms and finding nothing else out of place, returned to the ground floor. Nash mentioned the fridge, before asking, 'Tell us more about Andrew, because at present we don't know anything I would categorize as being useful to our investigation.'

'I've told you everything I can think of. What sort of thing do you want to know?'

'One thing that did strike me as odd was the fact that until you contacted Skipton police, nobody had reported him missing. I'm thinking about his work colleagues and friends.'

'His work at Helm Logistics was mostly confined to the workshop. The last time I spoke to him, he did say he was due to take some holiday. He made a joke of it by saying it was gardening leave, but that didn't mean he'd been sacked, just the opposite. I told you he was in line for a pay rise. As for close friends, I don't think he had any. His social life was almost non-existent. He was always a bit of a loner, but I suppose he had good reason for wanting to keep away from the social scene.'

'Why was that? You mentioned a relationship that went sour. Was that the cause of him becoming reclusive?'

'Andrew wasn't always that way, but after what happened to Dee he avoided people whenever possible.' Seeing the detectives' puzzled expressions, she explained. 'He was engaged to a lovely girl. Her name was Deanna, but everyone called her

Dee. She was in the army and was due to return home after a tour of duty in Iraq. The wedding was only three weeks away when we got news she'd been killed by an IED.'

Emotion was beginning to get the better of her, but she continued, 'Andrew went to pieces. He was in a terrible state. He lived in Keighley then, but he shut himself away and began drinking heavily. That cost him his job with one of the big motor dealerships. Eventually, he got himself sorted out and his counsellor, or therapist, suggested a complete change of scene would help. Somewhere he didn't have to pass places that reminded him of times he'd spent with Dee. That was why he applied for a job with a much smaller company. One based far enough away not to conjure up painful memories all the time.

'I say he'd recovered, but that isn't quite correct. His personality changed after Dee's death. I said he'd always been a bit of a loner, but that isn't strictly true. Before her death he was as sociable as the next man, but afterwards he kept everyone at a distance. He wouldn't go to social occasions, even the work Christmas party. He told me he'd given up on them because there was a risk of getting too attached to someone, and that posed a risk of getting hurt.'

She gestured around the sitting room. 'You must have noticed there are no photos in here — or anywhere else in the house. That's not surprising, given the way he felt. I know he enjoyed his job, but I think part of the attraction was that his contact with people was only fleeting and impersonal. Quite honestly, if he hadn't got that job I think he'd have either ended it, or drunk himself to death long before now.'

'You mentioned gardening earlier, and I noticed the exterior of the property looked very tidy. Had Andrew any other hobbies?'

She smiled slightly. 'I take it you haven't been in the garage yet?'

Nash shook his head.

'You wouldn't be able to put a car in there,' she told him. 'That's because Andrew had it converted into his own private pool hall. He had a full-size pool table and all the accessories put in. It cost him a small fortune, but like he said, he'd nothing else to spend his money on.'

Later, when they briefed the rest of the team, Nash summed up the situation, 'Unfortunately, what little we've learned leaves us no further forward. I'd hoped that once we'd got the victim's ID, and found out something about his lifestyle, it would yield some clue as to the reason for his murder. But sadly, all we've been told suggests a lack of motive.'

Nash asked Lisa and Viv to visit Helm Logistics. 'Find out exactly what he did, how popular — or otherwise — he was, that sort of thing.'

When they returned, they were little wiser. 'Andrew Derrick was in charge of maintenance for the vehicles used by their sales and installation force. The company supply phone lines, broadband and Wi-Fi. He was well liked by those of his colleagues we spoke to,' Lisa told Nash.

'So there was nothing you saw or heard that made you suspicious?'

Lisa paused slightly before answering, 'I didn't, but Viv thought their managing director looked a bit on edge, didn't you?'

Pearce nodded. 'He seemed nervous, but that might have merely been the natural reaction to being questioned by the police. Alternatively, it might have been nothing more than the nuisance of having to replace someone whose work was vital to keeping their fleet on the road.'

That left them no further forward. Without a motive, they were no better off than when they found the body.

CHAPTER FIVE

Jack Binns was in the process of showing his replacement around the station. He was explaining where everything was kept, and how the station operated on office hours unless they had a prisoner in the cells. 'It only happens on rare occasions, but you can always get backup from HQ for overnight cover.'

Nash and the other detectives were looking at all the reports, and discussing the cemetery case, when Binns led Steve Meadows into the CID suite. 'And this,' Binns told him, 'is the leisure centre. It's the place where people with nothing better to do spend hours, sometimes days, relaxing over endless mugs of coffee, pretending to work.'

'There speaks a man whose first task every morning is to attempt to complete every Sudoku or crossword he can lay his hands on,' Nash retorted. Turning to Meadows and extending his arm to shake hands, he added, 'I would listen very carefully to everything Jack tells you — that way you'll learn what *not* to do. Good to meet you again, Steve.'

Steve Meadows was somewhat confused, as both men were smiling during the barbed exchange. After the introductions, Binns took him into the kitchen where he explained the workings of the coffee machine. 'If you're first to arrive in a morning, your first task will be to fill this and switch it on. This is the beating heart of the station. Without it, I don't think anyone would function well. If you notice a shortage of anything, mention it to Mike or Clara, and they'll sort out restocking it. There's a kettle downstairs we use for the prisoners' teas and such, but this makes much better coffee for us.' As an aside, he explained, 'Mike bought it because Clara never got the knack of making instant coffee. She's from Belarus you know.'

Meadows looked at him as if Clara's birthplace held some relevance, but shook his head and asked, 'She's the tall good-looking blonde, isn't she?'

Binns cast him a glance. 'Yes, very good-looking. Some would say striking.' He smiled and nodded. 'Of course, you've yet to meet David Sutton. He's helped us out in the past.'

'Who's he?'

'Army major, SAS.'

'Really?' Meadows looked impressed.

'Hmm, and Clara's fiancé.'

'Right, I understand.' He was grateful for the warning, just in case things didn't work out with his latest girlfriend.

As they were returning downstairs, Binns said, 'Although I tease them all whenever I get chance, I have to admit that this is one of the most successful CID teams in the north of England. They all have exceptional skills. When it comes to technology, Viv Pearce is the equal of many IT experts, if not better. Clara and Lisa are both highly observant and percep-tive. As Mike's deputy, Clara is more than capable of filling his shoes when he's away, as she's proved time and again. To be fair, if she was stationed elsewhere, she'd probably have achieved the rank of Detective Inspector long ago.'

'Hasn't she ever thought of moving to advance her career?'

Binns looked appalled by the suggestion. 'I don't think Clara would take a job if it meant moving from here. The same goes with the others. That's just one of Mike's talents

— he inspires loyalty in people he works with. In addition to that, Mike is far and away the best detective I've ever met. It's been a pleasure working with him.'

'What makes him so successful?'

'It's not easy to explain. In addition to his acute observational and deductive skills, Mike also has the ability to think like a criminal, and from that, to envisage how a crime might have been committed. Clara is beginning to develop something of the same sort of talent.' Binns thought for a moment, then added, 'If you ever see Mike with a faraway expression on his face, gazing in to the distance, don't speak, or interrupt him. He'll be in the process of following a train of thought that might prove pivotal to solving a case. I've seen it happen a few times, and so have the others. Often he'll come up with an idea that might sound far-fetched, but later turns out to be spot on.'

* * *

The following day, Steve Meadows performed his first official duty at Helmsdale. Although the simple task of answering the phone seemed trivial, the information he scrawled hurriedly on his notepad was important.

Viv Pearce had just entered the building, carrying the lunchtime sandwiches, when he was hailed by Meadows. 'Before you go upstairs, you'd better take a look at this. It's the details from a call Netherdale control got. The officers sent in response found a body. The postman was trying to deliver a parcel, and as the door was open, he called out to the occupier. When he got no answer, he decided to leave it inside so it wouldn't get nicked. It's on the estate,' he said knowingly, as if that explained every word. 'If memory serves me right, that's where Cheesy Wilson, real name Charles, used to live. Or still lives. Suspected of supplying drugs, but never proved.'

Meadows passed him the details, and Viv ran upstairs to hand Nash the sheet of paper.

Nash stared at it for a moment. 'OK, Viv, check out this character on the system, see if he still lives there. And get us a photo each, will you? Then go to the address with Clara. I'll follow on with Lisa. I've a couple of calls to make first.'

Moments later, Viv returned, and handed them all a headshot of Wilson, showing an ugly scar across his cheek. 'I had a quick look on PNC. He has a string of convictions for burglary, shoplifting and poaching. He's been investigated for drug dealing, but never charged.' He grabbed his jacket from his chair, and headed for the door to join Clara.

Fifteen minutes behind them, Nash and Lisa had just reached the crime scene when Nash spotted the mortuary van, followed by the pathologist's car, pulling to a halt nearby. He handed Lisa a protective suit. 'Here, put this on and let's get out of Mexican Pete's way before he starts his comedy routine on me.'

The building was one of a row of twelve identical properties, known by the politically correct title as social housing. Although some of them looked in need of renovation, the one they were about to enter appeared far worse for wear than the others.

The interior matched the exterior in this respect, but Nash was too preoccupied to take much notice as he stared at the eviscerated remains on the lounge carpet. Having spoken to the constable leaning against the outside wall, who looked slightly green around the edges, Nash was prepared for what he might find. A sideways glance at Lisa Andrews confirmed that she was as surprised as he was, and — judging by their expressions — how Mironova and Pearce had been a short while earlier. One thing was certain — the victim of the horrific attack was definitely not the suspected drug dealer.

Noticing their astonishment, Clara told them, 'Meet Janet Wilson. She also goes by the name Jade, or Sadie, or Candy, depending on her client's preference. She has, or had, a string of convictions as long as my arm — probably both arms — mainly for prostitution. She worked mostly in Leeds, Bradford, Sheffield, and several other places I've forgotten.

Having checked her on the fingerprint reader, Viv got Tom Pratt to research her on the PNC.'

Nash was still taking this information in and checking the crime scene when their pathologist, Professor Ramirez, walked in. '*Madre De Dios*,' he exclaimed, lapsing into Spanish, 'somebody didn't like this woman much. This has to be one of your gorier cases, Nash. Although I admit there's a fair amount of competition for that honour.'

'I guess so, Professor. We'll leave you to it. There isn't that much space in here, especially when you start juggling intestines.'

Ignoring a muttered 'that's sick' from Mironova, Nash told the team, 'I'm going to have a look round the rest of the house with Clara. Will you and Lisa check the outside and round the back, Viv?'

A swift inspection of the kitchen revealed nothing untoward, so Nash and Clara went upstairs. The main bedroom was reasonably tidy, apart from some clothing strewn across the bed. Neither of them thought much about it at the time, and as they were about to head downstairs, Nash's mobile rang. He fumbled it from his pocket, a task made more difficult by the protective suit, and answered. 'Yes, Steve.'

What's happened now? Clara wondered. It must be something important, as she felt sure Meadows knew better than to interrupt them at a crime scene unless it was urgent. She heard Nash say, 'Sorry, can you repeat that?'

He listened again, then responded, 'That was what I thought you said. I just didn't believe it. OK, Clara and I will go. Yes, he's just arrived, I'll tell him.'

He ended the call, and gestured to Clara to follow him. They met Lisa and Viv in the hallway, and Nash called for the pathologist to join them. 'Viv, Lisa, you two remain here. Clara and I are going to Helmsdale. Professor, I don't know the full details yet, but apparently there's another corpse been found in a cemetery. I'll order up another forensic team en route. It appears to be a repeat of the Netherdale one.'

Ramirez glanced at his watch. 'Two corpses in half an hour — good to see you're not losing your touch.'

* * *

'The body was found by a woman who had been to place flowers on her husband's grave. He only died three weeks ago, so she's understandably distressed,' the officer standing guard over the crime scene explained. 'She's waiting in the patrol car with my colleague.'

Nash looked at Mironova, who nodded, anticipating what he was going to ask her. 'After you've taken her statement, get a WPC to drive her home and ensure she has someone who can be with her. The prime reason for her visit must have been bad enough, without this on top.'

It was only a few minutes later that Mironova returned, telling Nash, 'The lady didn't see anyone else in the graveyard. Her sister is staying with her for the time being, so she won't be alone.'

'Good — have you got your fingerprint scanner handy? We'll wait until the forensic guy has taken his photos of the site. I don't want to wait for the professor. He's busy.'

'It's in my car. Do you recognize him?'

'Take a look, see what you think.'

The victim was lying face down like the previous one, revealing the man's profile. There was a scar across the visible cheek, which tallied with the description and photograph seen earlier of Charles Wilson.

'Do you think that's who I think it is?' Clara asked.

Nash smiled. 'I think so, depending on who you think it is.'

'If you're going to stand there making bad jokes, I'm off to get the scanner.'

'Please bring some gloves back, too.'

The photographer signalled it was OK for them to approach, warning them to avoid stepping on any footprints. Nash lifted the dead man's hand while Mironova scanned the index finger. He carefully released his grip and peeled the protective gloves off, before removing his mobile from his pocket and pressing a short code. 'Viv, can you ask our worthy professor how long he estimates Janet Wilson has been dead?'

As he waited, Nash saw Mironova look up from the scanner and give him a nod of confirmation. A few seconds later Pearce told him, 'He reckons she died somewhere around twenty-four hours ago. Why, is it important?'

'It is in one sense, in that we can rule out her murder as being a case of domestic violence. We can also forget Cheesy Wilson having gone down the pub for a pint.'

'Does that mean . . . ?'

'It means Cheesy Wilson is lying face down in Helmsdale Cemetery. And unless the maggots here are on speed, he's been here for several days.'

'Before you go, Mike, I've got a message from the professor for you. He said to remind you he is the regional pathologist, not your personal butcher. He has other work on the slab, so the post-mortems will be in two days.'

Nash could tell Viv was suppressing laughter and replied, 'Tell him I didn't know he worked on the side, cash-in-hand. I'm really cut up about it.'

He told Mironova what had been said, then asked, 'Did anything strike you about the woman's murder scene at Bishopton?'

'I don't know, to be honest. I haven't given it a thought. Why, is it important?'

'I'm not sure. It could be, but it might not mean anything. I was thinking about the bedroom.'

'Mike, you're always thinking about the bedroom.'

Nash grinned. 'There was clothing strewn on the bed, just like the previous cemetery victim. By the colour of his head and shoulders, my guess is Cheesy Wilson was drowned — and he has restraint marks on his wrists and ankles. I also think the killer undresses them when he abducts them — although why, I don't know.'

CHAPTER SIX

The following day was spent organizing door-to-door enquiries and cross-checking any information that came their way from the foot soldiers. After a long, tiring day, Nash reminded them he would be attending the post-mortems in the morning, though he told Clara, 'I don't suppose the autopsies will prove any more revealing than the one you went to.'

In the event, that statement proved to be highly inaccurate.

He'd anticipated the twin procedures being over by late afternoon. But it was after six o'clock before he emerged from the mortuary, clutching the notebook on which he'd scribbled some of the pathologist's initial comments.

For most of the time spent in the viewing room, Nash had been bored rigid. He knew better than to interrupt Ramirez, or attempt to engage him in conversation while he was performing his gruesome task. Instead, he tried to speculate on the motives for the murders, and the connection between a seemingly respectable motor mechanic, a probable drugs dealer, and his partner. That process led only to mild frustration accompanied by a slight headache.

Next morning, he updated the team, telling them, 'For the most part, I'm quoting Mexican Pete verbatim, omitting only the Castilian swear words. The most significant thing he revealed about Cheesy Wilson's death was that it occurred only forty-eight hours, or thereabouts, before his body was found. The importance of this will become apparent later. But it enabled him to establish certain facts that were not available during the previous post-mortem on Andrew Derrick. Cheesy Wilson's body showed restraint marks around the wrists and ankles, and it's clear that the devices used to hold him captive were neither rope, nor tape, but manacles. This is shown by the absence of fibres on the abrasion sites. Also, the victims were kept in water for a long-time ante-mortem, then they were inverted so they were head-first. That obviously caused the drowning, and the bodies were stored like that post-mortem until being placed on the graves.'

'How on earth did the professor work that out?' Clara asked.

'Good question. It had me curious too. The answer comes via livor mortis and wrinkling.' Noticing their collective bemusement, Nash explained, 'The lividity of the corpse shows that it was inverted, allowing the blood to pool in the upper part of the body. Having established the approximate time of death, the entire wrinkling of the skin suggests there was prolonged immersion in water. Presumably that was deliberate, to enable the torture to take place.'

Lisa Andrews frowned. 'Torture, I don't recall that being mentioned?'

'It wasn't. The professor spotted microscopic fibres in Wilson's lungs and airways, and commented it was the same with Andrew Derrick, for which he had no explanation. He now linked his findings to torture.'

'How is that torture?' Viv asked.

'He referred to it as dunking, with a sack or something similar over their head — possibly to obtain information. Whether that's the reason with our two victims, or whether it's down to pure sadism, it's highly illegal — but then, so is murder. What we don't have at present is either a motive, the identity of the killer, or a connection between the two men.'

Nash suggested a short coffee break. 'I need caffeine before I recall the details of the Janet Wilson autopsy. I definitely don't regard attending such an event as one of the perks of seniority,' he added, staring pointedly at Mironova as he spoke.

Once suitably refreshed, Nash continued, 'If I thought the post-mortem on Janet Wilson would be more straightforward, I was wrong. Not only was it far more unpleasant to watch, but it also threw up a surprise nobody could have anticipated. Had it not been for Mexican Pete's expertise in specific areas, the weapon used to kill her would not have been identified. He told me he'd made an in-depth study of bladed weapons and the wound marks they inflict.' Nash paused and smiled ruefully. 'He said this was due to the mountain of work we give him. He explained the instrument used on Janet Wilson was a short-bladed scimitar, something he referred to as a kilij. This weapon was carried by soldiers from the Ottoman Empire, and other Middle Eastern states, in the past few centuries.'

Nash allowed this startling news to sink in before adding, 'How a weapon such as that ends up in a remote part of North Yorkshire, I've no idea — unless the killer is either a deranged antiques dealer, or a museum curator.'

* * *

While Jack Binns was trying to pacify a local resident expressing her displeasure at the parking ticket she'd received, he signalled to his colleague to answer an incoming call. Meadows picked up the receiver and announced, 'Helmsdale Police Station, Sergeant Meadows speaking, how can I help?'

He listened, making notes on his pad, and told the caller, 'I'll get someone to contact you.'

As Binns was still occupied with the irate visitor, Meadows attracted his attention, pointing upstairs. He entered the CID suite, knocked on Nash's office door, and was told to enter.

'Sorry to interrupt, Inspector Nash, but I've just taken a call from the owner of the *Stop 2 Shop* convenience store in Bishopton. He rang to report a case of pilfering, and said he has CCTV footage of the offender. He was a bit reluctant to report it, because he said the thief appears to be a very young girl, no more than eleven or twelve years old, he thinks. It was only when he took note of what had been stolen, and realized it was worth quite a bit of money, that he decided to ask us to intervene. Do you want me to send a patrol car?'

He handed Nash the notes he'd made and awaited instructions. Nash called Pearce through, repeated what Meadows had told him, and asked him to follow up, ensuring he got a copy of the CCTV footage.

Meadows was about to follow Pearce out of the office when Nash called him back. 'Steve, we don't stand on ceremony here. We're all part of the same team, so from now on use Christian names in the office, that's far less formal. And, if my door's open, you don't need to knock before you come in, OK?'

'Very good, Inspector ... er ... Mike,' Meadows replied.

* * *

When the detectives viewed the CCTV footage they were surprised by both the tender age of the offender, and the amount she had purloined during her relatively short time inside the store. Noting the way she moved from shelf to shelf, darting from aisle to aisle, and the unerring way she selected those items she wanted to steal, Nash said, 'She's not doing it on impulse. She's got a shopping list — or, should I say, a shoplifting list.'

'I think you're right, Mike,' Pearce agreed. 'And if you watch the next few frames, I think you'll see why.' As the image moved to where the girl made her exit from the shop, they saw a young man meet her and shepherd her away from the building.

'See if you can enhance the image of the girl and her companion, Viv, and then circulate the photos. With a bit of luck, someone will recognize one or other of them.'

As Clara was about to return to her own desk, she noticed the copy of the *Netherdale Gazette* that Pearce had brought in. Her attention was caught by one of the articles on the front page. She picked up the paper and began to read the piece under the headline "North Yorkshire Superstar Quits Showbiz."

Nash peered over her shoulder, his curiosity roused by her interest in that piece of news. He chuckled as he read the details.

'What's so funny?'

'The names. It shows our local superstar had a decent education, in Latin, at least.'

'Why do you say that?'

'For an escapologist to call himself Magnus Evadere, which is Latin for Great Escape, shows a good sense of humour.'

'What puzzles me,' Clara said, 'is why he's chosen to retire, just when he was becoming so successful. One of the critics quoted in this article referred to him as a latter-day Houdini, possibly even greater than the maestro.'

'That's some compliment,' Nash agreed, 'but I didn't realize you were such a fan of showbiz.'

'I'm not, really. It's just that I was intrigued because we don't get many famous people around these parts.'

Nash laughed. 'You're dead right there — we're more accustomed to dealing with the infamous ones.'

* * *

Rumours had been circulating for a few months about a drugs operation that centred round the Helmsdale and Netherdale areas. More recently, someone who was arrested after being found in possession of cocaine told the police that the dealer he bought from frequented three sites. One was to the rear of Netherdale Cricket Club, an open area normally used as a car park. Another was in the beer garden of the Cock and Bottle public house, and the third, a bus shelter on the side of Helmsdale market place. The difficulty was that the man varied the day and time he visited each location.

That information puzzled the detectives, but Lisa Andrews, who had interviewed the arrested man, told her colleagues, 'Apparently, he advertises his presence with a kind of make-shift flag — a piece of rag on one of those elongated car aerials.'

'They're called whip aerials,' Pearce told her.

'Thank you, Viv, that's contributed enormously to the investigation,' Nash told him. 'The problem is, according to the statement the user gave to Lisa, the pusher's description is far from clear. We could finish up with half of Netherdale cricket team in the cells and still miss our man. At one point in his story, he said the guy was about five feet six inches tall, but later corrected that to almost six feet. Not only can the dealer expand and contract, he can also change his hair colouring from fair to dark brown, and can grow a beard within seconds.'

'If that's the case, how do we go about catching him, and avoid denying Netherdale CC the services of their opening bowler?' Viv asked.

'I think the best way would be via a sting operation. If Lisa visits each location with a backup team to hand, she approaches the dealer posing as a customer, pays for some cocaine, and then arrests him. Handing over marked bank-notes should do the trick.' Nash turned to Andrews and added, 'Alternatively, if you catch him in the act of supplying to someone else, you can arrest them both.'

'Why pick Lisa for the job?' Clara asked.

'She's done most of the work. It's only fair to give her chance to follow it through. Besides, we've enough to do with the murders.'

'While we're on the subject of drugs,' Viv told them. 'I heard a rumour yesterday from one of my sources. It's purely hearsay, but the word is that someone might have scarpered with over a hundred thousand in cocaine, and the dealer is on the lookout for them. My source said nobody has mentioned the absconder's name, but he reckoned if someone turns up in Netherdale General with his guts hanging out and singing treble, that will be the guy.'

* * *

Two days later, Lisa Andrews' persistence paid off. Sergeant Meadows phoned through to tell Nash that she and her backup officers were bringing in a suspect, having arrested him, together with a client, in the beer garden of the Cock and Bottle.

'Thanks, Steve, let me know when they're here and I'll join them.'

He signalled for Clara to accompany him as they went downstairs and headed for the interview rooms. There followed a short, fairly acrimonious discussion with the customer, who was aggrieved at being denied access to the cocaine he'd purchased in good faith. He was further angered when Nash refused to return his money. They managed to get rid of him when they pointed out he was lucky to get off with a warning, rather than being charged with possession. Only then could the detectives concentrate on the dealer.

Before Nash entered the second interview room, Lisa Andrews told him what little they'd discovered about the suspect. 'His name is Tommy Roberts and he lives in Bishopton. He's twenty-one years old, single, lives at home and has no previous. Roberts didn't tell us any of this. In fact, he hasn't said a word since we arrested him. So I guess he doesn't want a solicitor.'

'How did you find out who he is?'

'Steve Meadows used to live and work in Bishopton, remember? He recognized him as soon as we brought him in. Steve seemed a bit surprised when he learned that Roberts was to be charged with intent to supply.'

'OK, let's see what young Roberts has to say for himself, shall we?'

As he was walking towards the interview room, Meadows called to him. 'Mike, could I have a word about Roberts? It might be important.'

'OK, what about him?'

'I used to know the Roberts family quite well. I got a heck of a surprise when Lisa brought young Tommy in. He's one of the last people I'd suspect of being involved in the drugs trade.'

'That's a good while back, Steve. People can change, particularly if their circumstances alter. If they fell on hard times, Tommy might have seen this as a way to provide for his family.'

'That's the thing — they haven't fallen on hard times. I've just had a quick word with my father. Mum and Dad still live in Bishopton, and Dad told me the Roberts family seem quite well off. That puzzled me, and so did something else. When Lisa brought Tommy in, I realized I'd seen his face recently, on the notice board — the shoplifters.'

'Do you know who the young girl in the photo is?'

'I can't be sure, because she was only a toddler when I left Bishopton, but it could be Tommy's little sister. I think her name is Katherine, but everyone called her Katie. There's something odd about all this, because to my mind, there's no way the Roberts clan would stoop to pilfering from a convenience store.'

'Thanks, Steve. That could be useful. I'll be sure to keep you in the picture.'

Nash followed Lisa into the room. He stopped in the doorway, stared at the morose-looking suspect seated at the table, and then told Andrews, 'Wait there a minute, I'll be back. You can set up the recording, but first I need a word with Viv.'

When he returned, Nash told Lisa to hold off from beginning the interview. 'DC Pearce is popping down with an extra piece of evidence,' he explained.

Viv arrived and passed Nash a stills photograph of the shoplifting from the store's CCTV.

Lisa made the opening announcement, stating who was in the room. The suspect stared at her when she said his name, his face etched with shock.

Nash began. 'Tell me, Mr Roberts — or should I call you Tommy? — why are you peddling drugs? And why you are involved in shoplifting?'

Roberts had remained motionless, his gaze lowered to avoid eye contact, until Nash mentioned shoplifting. It was only then that he looked up, clearly surprised by the extent of Nash's knowledge.

'No comment,' he muttered.

'I'm afraid that's not good enough, Tommy. We have you on video, along with somebody else, stealing items from the *Stop 2 Shop* convenience store in Bishopton.'

Nash placed the image from the CCTV camera on the table. 'So who is this child you're working with, and why do you need the money?'

'No comment.'

'We need to know. And we also need you to tell us who supplies the drugs you're selling.' Nash paused. 'Of course, we could do this the hard way, go and search your parents' house, look for the clothing you were wearing in this image from the store. We could speak to your sister at the same time.'

Roberts shuffled uncomfortably in his seat, fear in his eyes.

'Have you got a drugs problem? Are you doing this to feed your addiction — or is there another reason?'

'No comment.'

'If you were to give us the information we need, I might be able to persuade the Crown Prosecution Service to be lenient with you. If not, you'll get the maximum penalty, and the real villains will get off scot-free. They'll be able to continue their vile trade for the next few years, while you're behind bars. Of course, they'll have to find someone else to do their dirty work, and with you unavailable they might turn their attention to somebody close to you. A friend, perhaps, or even a member of your family. Your younger sister, possibly?'

Nash's final comment was, he admitted later, nothing more than inspired guesswork. It was prompted by Meadows' suggestion of the similarity in appearance of Roberts and the child thief.

While the interview continued, Pearce was returning to the CID suite when Meadows stopped him. 'I know it's none of my business, Viv, but when Roberts was brought in, he had a mobile with him. Nobody's taken a look at it yet. As you're our resident IT expert, I thought you might like to do that.'

'Good idea. And you're right to pass it to me — the others would only do the same.' He laughed, then added, 'A lot of the new smartphones like this can erase all data if they're opened the wrong way, so it needs handling carefully. You were wrong, though, when you said it was none of your business. Mike told you we're a team, whether we're in suits or uniforms.' He turned and looked at the open door to the back office, where Jack Binns was watching them. 'That's right, isn't it, Jack?'

Binns nodded and smiled, knowing Steve Meadows was going to fit in well.

CHAPTER SEVEN

Twenty minutes into the questioning, with Roberts look-ing more and more anxious, and still maintaining his "no comment" routine, Pearce re-entered the room and asked them to suspend the interview. 'There's something you should see upstairs. I think it might prove pertinent to the matter in hand,' he told his colleagues, glancing at Roberts meaningfully.

The detectives followed Pearce back to the CID suite, leaving Roberts to be accompanied back to his cell by the uniformed officer.

'Steve Meadows suggested I should look at the data on the mobile found in Roberts' possession, and when I did, I noticed a lot of calls to and from a landline in Bishopton. I checked it out, and the results are extremely interesting.' Pearce passed Nash a sheaf of papers. 'It's Charles Wilson's house.'

'Really? Well, that's something useful. Perhaps our drug peddler likes playing with knives as well? I think we should find out. We'll let him sweat for a bit while we plan our interview.'

Nash suggested that Mironova join him in a final attempt to persuade Tommy Roberts to say more than "no comment".

'Sorry, Lisa, you can watch on the monitor. Clara has much more experience, and we need to make some headway. We've only got twenty-four hours before he must be either charged or released, and he's managing to waste most of them. Clara, bring the crime scene photos from both Wilson murders with you. If they don't shock him into revealing why he's been selling drugs and shoplifting, nothing will.'

Nash paused before entering the room. 'I want you to keep those photos face down on the table, until I give you the nod, OK?'

Once inside, Nash watched Roberts carefully as Mironova made the announcement for the tape as to the change of personnel, then she asked, 'You refused the option of legal representation earlier, Tommy. Do you wish to reconsider that?'

Roberts shook his head, and Clara chided him, 'I'm afraid you'll have to say it out loud. The tape doesn't recognize gestures.'

'No,' Roberts said.

Nash began. 'We've taken a look at your mobile, Tommy. Now we know who your friends are.' He stared at Roberts. 'We went to your friend's house three days ago in response to a treble nine call. You know Cheesy Wilson, don't you?'

'No comment.'

'When we arrived, we found someone had been murdered in a very gory fashion,' Clara explained.

Roberts looked up, startled. 'Was it Wilson?'

'No, he wasn't home,' Nash said. 'DS Mironova, please show Mr Roberts the photo taken at the house.'

She turned over the image of Janet Wilson's body. Both detectives watched Roberts carefully. For a moment, as the colour drained from his face, Clara thought he was going to faint.

Nash waited until the impact of the photo had taken effect, then asked, 'Do you own a kilij?'

Roberts looked confused.

'Where were you last Monday morning?' Clara asked.

'No comment,' Roberts muttered — staring at the table as sweat began to appear on his brow.

Nash began to gather the paperwork. 'OK. If you persist in saying "no comment", I'm afraid you'll be charged with possession with intent to supply — and your sister will be arrested for shoplifting. That's bad enough, but it would be even worse if she finished up like this.' Nash indicated the photo. 'That's the sort of thing that happens to people who become involved with drugs traffickers, and upset the villains they associate with.'

By now, Roberts was pale and trembling, but Nash continued, seemingly unconcerned about the young man's petrified state. 'It wasn't a good day for the Wilson family, because we got another emergency call. This time it *was* Cheesy Wilson who was murdered. His body was found in Helmsdale Cemetery.'

Nash nodded to Mironova, who turned over the second image.

'Unlike his partner' — Nash got to his feet — 'Wilson wasn't stabbed. However, he was equally dead. Now, while you're awaiting trial on the drugs charges, we'll be investigating your link to these murders.'

Roberts' eyes widened in shock. 'I didn't kill them!'

'No?' Nash turned to face the prisoner. 'Then why not see sense and tell us what you know. That's the only way we can protect you from the evil customers you've got involved with. The best way to do that is to stick them behind bars where they can't harm anyone, especially you — or your sister.'

He sat back down and waited.

Roberts looked from Nash to Mironova and then back. He licked his lips repeatedly, and when he eventually spoke, his voice was little more than a whisper, as if he suspected someone might be eavesdropping on the interview. If he'd been reluctant to speak earlier, once the floodgate opened, there was no holding him back.

'I had to do it. I mean the drugs thing, not the murders, not that!' He panicked again, took a deep breath, then gestured to the photo of Wilson. 'He forced me to do it. He said if I didn't, the people he worked for would take my sister Katie, and do horrible things to her. If I didn't agree to work for them, she'd finish up like Sam's girlfriend. Sam refused to have anything to do with them, and they took revenge on Gemma.'

'Who's Sam?'

'Was, not is. Sam Lawrence was a mate of mine. Just after he told them to get lost, his girlfriend Gemma vanished. Sam was frantic. He'd known Gemma since they were in junior school, and he was certain something bad had happened to her. He searched everywhere, but with no luck. Two months later, her body was fished out of the Leeds-Liverpool canal. She'd been stabbed over and over again. Before she died, she'd been raped — time after time. A week after they buried her, Sam went to the flat in Bishopton they shared. He took her photo out of the frame, tucked it inside his shirt, then slit his wrists.'

Into the shocked silence that followed these horrifying revelations, their prisoner pleaded with the detectives to help. 'Will you protect her, Inspector Nash? Can you make sure those monsters don't do such awful things to my little sister, like they did to Gemma?'

Tommy didn't wait for Nash to reply, he began sobbing, uncontrollably. After a while, when he'd recovered a little of his composure, Clara passed him a tissue, as Nash promised he would ensure his whole family were protected.

'Have you any idea who is behind all this?' Nash asked. 'We know Wilson was involved, but the racket is too big for him to deal with alone. He's no more than a middle man. What we need in order to stop it, is to find out who is controlling the distribution. If we can put them behind bars, it will provide the best protection for you and your family. You must try and think of anything that could give us a clue to their identity, or where they operate from. It could be the most insignificant detail, something Wilson might have let slip, or something he'd done. It might prove vitally important.'

There was a long silence as Tommy thought this over. When he replied, his voice was hesitant, as if he was unconvinced that what he was telling them would be in the slightest bit relevant. 'I don't know much about Wilson apart from the drugs thing. I suppose he had a liking for foreign food, though. I saw him a few times coming out of that kebab shop in Bishopton.'

Roberts was surprised when Nash smiled at him, and said, 'Thank you, Tommy, that's exactly what we need. You've been a great help. One more thing before we finish — was it Wilson who put you up to the shoplifting?'

'Yes, how did you know?'

'Several items identical to those you and Katie took from *Stop 2 Shop* were found at Wilson's house, with the price tickets still attached. It didn't take Sherlock Holmes to work the rest out.'

After ending the interview by assuring Roberts he would be dealt with fairly, Nash and Clara headed for the CID suite. 'We ought to get a copy of the file from West Yorkshire, on that murdered girl Gemma,' Nash told her. 'And now that we know where the drugs operation is based, we can seek out that poor girl's killer, and the man who also murdered Janet and Cheesy Wilson, plus Andrew Derrick.'

Clara stopped in her tracks. 'I must have nodded off during the interview, because I missed the part of the conversation where he identified the source of the drugs.'

'Think back to Mexican Pete's autopsy findings, Clara. He reckoned the weapon used to kill her was a curved-bladed scimitar like those carried by Ottoman and Middle Eastern forces in the past. Who is more likely to own such a blade than someone of similar origin? Perhaps someone connected to a takeaway, selling menu items such as kebabs?'

When they entered the office, Pearce was hovering near the doorway, clearly anxious to speak to them. 'I've been doing some more research on Wilson's landline call history, and I found that he made a large number of calls over the past few years to a particular Bishopton number. That rang a bell, because the number tallied with something I'd seen near the phone in Wilson's house.'

'Ignoring your terrible "rang a bell" pun, don't tell me, let me guess. Was it by any chance the number of a kebab takeaway, and was the item a flyer for the same establishment?'

Pearce stared at Nash for a long time in stunned silence, before he eventually managed to say, 'Yes, it was, in both cases. But how on earth did you work that out?'

'Please don't ask him to explain, Viv,' Clara suggested. 'He's conceited enough already, without you thinking he's some sort of mind reader.'

* * *

Clara Mironova was puzzled, and although she pondered long and hard, she was unable to find an answer to the anomaly that was vexing her. Noticing her distraction, Nash asked what was wrong.

'I've a bit of a dilemma,' she explained, 'I cannot for the life of me work out the reason for the change in MO.'

Nash frowned. 'Sorry, I'm not with you. What change in MO?'

'We know Janet Wilson was stabbed repeatedly, leaving wounds that all but eviscerated her, and from what Tommy Roberts told us, it sounds like the girl found in the canal was killed in more or less the same way. However, both Cheesy Wilson and Andrew Derrick were drowned, and the only marks on their bodies were where they had been restrained. So why did the killer change his MO? Added to that, I still fail to see the connection between our male victims.'

'Maybe Janet Wilson was simply in the way. Perhaps the men were tortured to gain information.'

Clara then added, 'There's something else that's baffling me. From what Viv learned, we believe Cheesy Wilson had stolen a large quantity of cocaine. That would certainly explain the motive for his murder. And possibly that of Janet Wilson, if she was either complicit, or just got in the way. The question is, where has it gone?'

'Where has what gone?'

Clara shook her head and sighed. 'The cocaine! Wilson's supposed to have nicked it. Viv told us about it *after* Wilson's death, which tends to suggest that the drugs were still missing. I could understand the dealer repossessing the cocaine and killing Wilson as a lesson to others. But if he failed to find the drugs, that would be more reason for keeping Wilson alive, surely, at least until he'd revealed where he stashed them.'

Nash had to admit that he was equally baffled by the string of inconsistencies she had outlined. After giving it some thought, he suggested, 'Maybe we should revisit the two houses, and this time take a couple of sniffer dogs with us.' He smiled and added, 'I'd volunteer Teal for the job, but my Labrador only seems capable of sniffing out food.'

The following morning, they travelled to Bishopton, where they met up with a couple of uniformed officers from Netherdale. One was accompanied by a pair of energetic, and enthusiastic, Springer Spaniels. At the Wilson house, the dogs found a hiding place containing several small wraps of cocaine, a disappointing quantity compared to the amount they'd hope for.

'That's hardly sufficient to provide a motive for murder,' Nash commented. 'I'd guess there's little more than five hundred quid's worth here.'

Search of Andrew Derrick's house proved even less rewarding, yielding no trace of drugs or stolen property. After ending their futile morning's work, they drove back to Helmsdale. En route, Mironova commented, 'That leaves us back at square one. As far as I can see, today has ruled out drugs being the connection.' She thought for a moment and then asked, 'Have you decided how best to protect Tommy Roberts and his family?'

'Yes, but it's going to need all hands on deck, because it requires a two-pronged attack. First, we should have a highly visible police presence outside their house twenty-four/seven, ensuring all means of entry are covered. At the same time, we'll mount a surveillance operation on the kebab shop. If the latter proves successful, we might not have to worry about Roberts and his family for too long. Given the demand for their products in the area, I reckon we should soon be able to pick up one or two pushers operating like Tommy. From there, we can raid the shop premises and put the distributors behind bars.'

Clara grinned. 'By products, I assume you mean cocaine, not kebabs.'

CHAPTER EIGHT

The first hurdle Nash had to overcome was to obtain authorisation for the deployment of a substantial tranche of their available manpower. Concentrating so much of their slender resources on a single case seemed likely to meet with stiff opposition from their newly-appointed chief constable. Aware of this, Nash waited until later that day, when, armed with the Janet Wilson file, plus that of the earlier stabbing victim, he consulted with Ruth Edwards at Netherdale HQ.

Nash prefaced his request by outlining the advantages, pointing out that if it proved successful, the operation would enable them to arrest a vicious murderer, and at the same time, close down a troublesome source of illegal drugs supply. Having also indicated the potential brevity of both the surveillance and the protection detail, he was hugely relieved when Ruth Edwards gave the go-ahead.

Back at Helmsdale, Nash called his team together, including Sergeant Meadows in the meeting. 'We have a week to wrap this up,' Nash told them, 'so I'm afraid that means everyone has to be on call day and night. Much of the work, particularly watching the kebab shop, will take place between eighteen hundred hours and midnight, so I'm not expecting those who are on that shift to report in at eight o'clock the following morning.' He grinned, and added, 'Eight thirty will be plenty soon enough.'

There was a ripple of laughter.

'Here's how I want to play it.' He turned to Meadows first. 'The bulk of the work is going to fall on you and your guys, Steve. We'll need a car with two officers at Tommy Roberts' house day and night after he's been bailed. That commits six officers on rotation from uniform branch. Plus two officers, in an unmarked car, at the rear of the kebab shop in the evening. However, to cut down the workload slightly, Clara and Viv will man one car at the front of the takeaway. Lisa and I will man a second. That will serve two purposes. Not only will it reduce the pressure on uniforms, but we'll also be able to identify any potential pushers, similar to Tommy Roberts. If we do get anybody, we'll whisk them to Netherdale in one of the cars — the second team can maintain watch. I don't want anyone here in the cells, as it would mean an overnight stay. These youngsters will have been pressurised into working for the suppliers. If we can catch them *in situ*, and in possession, as they leave the takeaway, it will provide sufficient evidence for a search warrant. Watch for anyone leaving without food — I don't think they're bright enough to work that one out. Hopefully, it should enable us to wrap the whole thing up quickly.' He turned to Lisa. 'We need to use your car — mine's too noticeable. Oh, Viv, don't forget the camera.'

* * *

On the second night, the team struck lucky shortly after the takeaway opened, much to the delight of the chief constable at the reduction in overtime costs when surveillance was stood down.

Arriving at Netherdale HQ, Lisa asked how Nash intended to go about questioning the drugs pusher they had detained.

'I'm going to make him a one-time offer. Either he cooperates and gets treated leniently, or he remains stubborn and I throw the book at him. All I really need from him is confirmation that the drugs he was carrying originated from inside, and that he wasn't there for a doner kebab. He wasn't carrying one as he left the shop, so why was he there? That should give us sufficient evidence to obtain a search warrant. If we can nail the source and put the distributors behind bars, that will provide the best possible security for Tommy Roberts and others like him.'

Legal representation was again declined, and when they entered the interview room Nash got his first proper look at the prisoner in a good light. His seemingly casual glance showed him that the young man bore a more than passing resemblance to Roberts, and this decided him on the line of questioning he would adopt.

After the formalities, he asked, 'Who did they threaten to make you carry drugs for them? We know how they operate.'

'No comment.'

'Believe me, the best way to be rid of the danger hanging over you, and to keep them from harming you and those close to you, is to provide the evidence we need to stick them behind bars for a long, long time.'

The prisoner just stared at him, fidgeting nervously on his seat.

Nash paused, allowing his statement to sink in before reinforcing his argument. 'I can assure you that if you fail to cooperate, either because you're in league with these people, or because you're too afraid, you will never be free of them. And while they are still at large, they have the power to do some unspeakable things. How would you feel if someone close to you was to end up like this?'

Nash had taken copies of the evidence photos along, and, as they had done with Roberts, he placed the image of Janet Wilson's corpse on the table. He saw the prisoner's face whiten with shock and knew he was about to crack.

Forty minutes later, with Nash's parting words being, 'Don't worry, this nightmare will soon be over. You'll stay here until we have him in custody.' The interview was ended, and the prisoner taken to a cell. Nash and Lisa headed for home, secure in the knowledge that they had not only the information required to obtain a search warrant, but also the identity of the man they were seeking.

* * *

The raid was timed to take place at 7.30 a.m. Nash was confident that the person identified as the drugs dealer, the man who had threatened at least one of the pushers, would be in the upstairs flat. Although they had initially suspected the proprietor of the establishment, the story their informant had told them painted a totally different picture.

'The owner might still be involved in a lesser capacity, but we can't be certain of that,' Nash told his colleagues, with Ruth Edwards listening in via a computer link. 'The man we're after works there and lives above the shop, which is why the warrant has been extended to cover the entire premises. Viv and I will start in the flat. Clara and Lisa, you check out the shop. This man is believed to be highly dangerous, which is the reason I've asked for armed response as backup. The drugs unit will be on hand with a sniffer dog. Be aware, this man not only serves in the shop, but also delivers takeaways. That gives him ample opportunity to move drugs around without arousing suspicion. It also gives him freedom to threaten, not only the pedlars he has coerced into working for him, but also their families. The only drawback is, although we have been given this man's description, it is by no means complete, and we have no idea of his name.'

During their execution of the warrant, the owner and his wife arrived at the scene to do the cleaning, and were taken to Helmsdale to be questioned later. The search of the shop yielded nothing incriminating. Clara expressed her relief to Lisa as they stepped outside. 'I'm glad to be out of that place. I'm going to smell like a kebab for days to come.'

They headed upstairs to the squalid flat where the occupier, Narek Melikian, had been arrested. Accompanied by armed officers, he was seated on the sofa, wearing only his boxers and a pair of handcuffs.

The first comment, regarding the appearance of the flat came from Lisa Andrews. 'This guy is either bone idle, or he can't afford washing-up liquid,' she said after one glance at the kitchen. Her opinion was based on the mound of unwashed crockery heaped in the sink bearing traces of food residue, and, in some cases, mould.

Nash was more concerned with the actions of the sniffer dog that was showing interest in the contents of a kitchen cupboard. Hidden inside were a dozen large packages of white powder.

Viv Pearce appeared in the doorway. 'I think you'd all better come and have a look in the bedroom. Although I should warn you it's not a pretty sight.'

The disgusting kitchen paled into insignificance. The sight was bad, and the smell was equally revolting — a combination of stale sweat, body odour and other unidentifiable aromas. Clara was thankful that she hadn't bothered with her usual breakfast. Her eyes, like Nash's, were drawn to the double bed, where the posts at each corner had been adapted by the addition of manacles.

The grubby-looking duvet had been twitched back, revealing a lack of sheeting on the mattress. This was discoloured with a variety of irregular shaped stains. Clara refused to speculate as to the source. She turned away, in time to see Viv, who had already opened the ottoman standing against one wall, remove an object from the inside, handling it with extreme care in his gloved hands.

Following her gaze, Nash said, 'That looks remarkably similar to the weapon Mexican Pete described as the type used to kill Janet Wilson.' Glancing back at the bed, he added, 'I think we should beat a retreat and give Forensics the dubious pleasure of conducting an in-depth examination of this luxurious suite.'

Clara muttered something Nash couldn't catch, and when asked to repeat it, told him, 'I was merely saying how thankful I am that I concentrated on the arts, rather than science at school.'

The dog was still searching, and shot past the detectives. It nosed round the room before it stopped, barked, and sat down in the middle of the bedroom floor. There was nothing there. The handler pointed to an unusual break in the floorboards. Twin cuts formed a short rectangle, and he prised at one end with a screwdriver to reveal a cavity containing several items of interest. Among the stash of drugs were several sets of documents, comprising passports and driving licences. Although these were all in different names, the photograph on each of them was of Melikian. Alongside the forged paperwork were bundles of cash amounting to somewhere in the region of £70,000 and, not one, but three mobile phones.

Nash was delighted. 'If they contain what I hope to be in their memories, they could provide links to his source, and other drug distributors operating on a big scale.'

Having said that, even Nash couldn't have anticipated how fruitful their discoveries would turn out to be.

* * *

Jack Binns was on duty and, forewarned by Nash, had called Steve Meadows to assist. Nash and Mironova had just pulled into the car park at Helmsdale behind the police van containing Melikian when Meadows arrived. Nash glanced at his watch and greeted the sergeant. 'That was extremely quick, Steve. I hope you didn't break the speed limit on your way here.'

Meadows smiled briefly. 'I was at home. It is, or was, my day off. Is it always this busy here?'

'Oh no, Steve, sometimes we go for hours without anything happening,' Clara replied.

'Can we get inside and Clara can attend to the coffee machine? On second thoughts, I'll take care of the coffee,' Nash added hastily.

'See, Steve, trivial matters like booking in prisoners will have to wait until Mike's satisfied his caffeine craving. That's how things work round here.'

Suitably refreshed, Nash and Pearce questioned the shop owner, while Mironova and Sergeant Meadows spoke with his wife. DC Andrews remained at Bishopton to liaise with the scientific officers, waiting within the more salubrious surroundings of a police car.

From the woman, Mironova learned the flat was occupied by a distant cousin of her husband's. He covered the opening of the takeaway, alone in the shop for the first two hours, before she and her husband took over. He then worked as their delivery man. She said the man had followed them to England, arriving eighteen months ago. He had begged them for a job and some accommodation, rather than returning to their native country, where his actions had left him highly unpopular. Whereas the detectives had assumed the kebab shop to be under Turkish ownership, the proprietor, his wife, and the cousin were actually from the neighbouring country of Armenia.

Nash and Pearce heard a similar story from the woman's husband, who added that he neither liked, nor trusted, his second cousin. 'The only reason I employ him is because my mother begs me to do this. She asks for this because her uncle has pleaded for us to help Narek, who has troubles in Armenia. I have not knowledge of any drugs. But it is not surprise to me if he is dealing such. I allow Narek to stay in flat because my wife will not have in him our house. Now I see this has been big mistake.'

Having compared notes, Nash, Mironova, and Pearce were all convinced that the couple were not likely to be involved and were bailed under further investigation. The man they had to question next would now be the target of their attention.

Pearce was slightly surprised when Nash opted to take Clara into the interview with him. Seeing his disappointment,

Nash told him, 'I've a shrewd idea this character will need some shaking up, and I want Clara to act as my straight man. In the meantime, I'd like you to check with Border Force — see if they have a record of his entry to the country. Give them all the IDs he's using. They might find them helpful.'

Nash and Mironova were faced with what seemed at first to be an insurmountable problem, when, in response to Nash's first few questions, Melikian merely replied, 'No English.'

Nash tolerated this for some time, even rephrasing his questions, but with no more success. Eventually, he turned to face Mironova, leaving her in no doubt that what was to follow was one of Nash's stratagems. 'At least it's different from "no comment",' he observed.

Ignoring the prisoner, he told Mironova, 'So far we've searched this guy's flat and found a stash of cocaine, worth well into six figures, and loads of cash. In addition, we've found the weapon we're pretty certain was used to kill Janet Wilson and earlier, Gemma, who was thrown into the Leeds-Liverpool canal. Gemma was raped, and I'm sure the DNA on file will match this man's. Then there are the other two murders we're fairly certain are down to him. Admittedly we've no evidence in those two cases, but it will help our statistics no end if we pin them on him.'

Seizing her cue, Clara responded, 'Won't his legal representative object when it comes to court, though?'

'Actually, I wasn't thinking of sending him for trial. That would be a long, drawn-out and expensive process. Even when we've got a conviction, the taxpayers will have for his upkeep for many years. We can see what Border Force have to say. He'll be working without a visa, so we could simply have him deported back to Armenia.'

'You cannot do this,' the prisoner protested. 'I have rights.'

Nash glanced at him before turning back to Mironova. 'It always comes as a surprise to me how quickly people pick up another language.' He looked into Melikian's eyes and told him, 'Now cut the crap, Narek, and tell us the truth.'

Melikian's reaction to Armenia gave Nash an idea. 'We'll leave you to weigh up your options. Interview suspended.'

Mironova puzzled over Nash's sudden decision to abandon the interview. Back in the office, she asked him why.

'When I mentioned Armenia he sounded almost scared, as if he didn't want reminding of his home country. Added to what his cousin said about him, it led me to wonder if there were reasons he was so reticent, and why he might fear being returned. So I thought we should ask Tom Pratt to check him out on the Interpol database, see what he can come up with. If Tom's too busy digging up a golf course, Viv can do it, if he's free. The more ammunition we have available, the better our chances of getting a full confession. We're fairly certain he committed four murders here, and I want to know everything he'll tell us about them. I'm particularly keen to discover why he changed MO between the women he killed and the men, and also where he kept them prisoner. There was no sign of anything capable of holding a body in water in either the flat, or the kebab shop.'

* * *

Melikian was remanded in custody on suspicion of murder, and charged with possession of cocaine with intent to supply. Having gained sufficient breathing space, Nash urged Forensics to process the evidence from Melikian's flat as quickly as possible. Only four days later, with the benefit of the weapon and other evidence from the flat, backed up by the research conducted by Tom Pratt, he was able to confront the Armenian. The case against him had now become a murder charge. He travelled with Clara to the remand centre at Felling Prison.

However, it was elsewhere that Nash concentrated to begin with. 'It seems that you are almost as unpopular in Armenia as you are here. From what we've learned, it isn't only the police there who are anxious to get their hands on you. It seems you're a highly sought-after and valuable commodity, worth more dead than alive, in the eyes of some of the less scrupulous elements there. But both the legal and illegal elements of Armenian society are going to have to wait for a long time to get their hands on you, because you will be spending a long number of years in prison here in England. We now have concrete evidence that you murdered Janet Wilson — traces of her blood were found on the weapon inside your flat.

'Speaking of your residence, we also have definitive proof that you held a young woman there, raped her, and then slaughtered her. Then you took her body in your cousin's van to the outskirts of Leeds, where you dumped her in the canal. You should have paid more attention to cleaning the interior of the van, because we found traces of her blood in it, as well as her DNA on your mattress.'

Nash paused before adding, 'I can also pinpoint the spot where you dumped her lifeless corpse into the water, Narek. You should have erased that journey from the van's satnav memory. With those murders added to the massive haul of cocaine in your possession, I'd say you're looking at several life sentences. As well as all that, I reckon you're shortly going to become extremely unpopular with some of your associates. I'm talking about the people whose contact details we discovered in your trio of mobiles we dug out from under the floorboards, along with the drugs, the cash, and those forged papers.'

Faced with the mountain of evidence against him, and on the advice of his legal aid solicitor, Melikian admitted to the murders of Janet and Gemma, and the drug-running offences. He promised to cooperate with the police by confirming the details of his supply sources for the cocaine.

Despite a long and gruelling interrogation, Melikian maintained his innocence in respect of both the Andrew Derrick and Cheesy Wilson murders. Once again, urged by his solicitor, he admitted encouraging Wilson to recruit the team of young pushers, but strenuously rejected the notion that he had been involved in the man's death. As for Andrew

Derrick, he denied knowing him. His motive for killing Janet Wilson, as Nash had already suspected, was that he had gone to Wilson's house to confront him. Wilson had been absent, so Melikian had gained entry and was in the process of searching for the missing cocaine when Janet had walked in on him.

'So you didn't torture Wilson or drown him?'

'He drowned? I have not seen him before six weeks. Then he took drugs for selling, but gave me no money. This was normal way of business. I could not kill him, because I do not know where he is for this time.'

As Nash and Mironova returned to Helmsdale, Clara expressed her doubts with regard to the Armenian's involvement in the men's murders.

'I agree,' Nash said, 'there is no way Melikian is a good enough liar to fool us for so long. It was obvious he had no idea that Wilson was dead. Let alone how he had been killed, or where the body was dumped. He also seemed genuinely baffled about Andrew Derrick. Above all, if he had tortured Wilson to discover where the missing drugs were, why would he have gone to Wilson's house to search for them?'

'The question is, if Melikian didn't commit those murders, where do we go from here?'

'I think the correct expression is "back to square one", because I'm now convinced that whatever the motive for these murders, it had little, or nothing, to do with supplying narcotics.'

CHAPTER NINE

Helm Woods, on the southern outskirts of Helmsdale, was bordered on one side by the main Netherdale road, and on the other by the river that gave the dale its name. Some of the less densely wooded areas had long been the venue for picnics, barbecues, romantic encounters, and occasionally, campers. Although the latter usually only pitched their tents for a short period of time, there was one whose prolonged stay had attracted the unwelcome attention of a group of less-than-friendly young men from the nearby Westlea estate. A large part of their dislike of the tent's sole occupant was that the man, who their leader categorized as a dosser, was occupying the space they frequented to partake of various substances frowned upon by authorities.

The head of this faction had little time for those he considered to be a worthless drain on society. This illogical thinking discounted the fact that he had himself never done an honest day's work in his adult life. He relied on hand-outs from the government, plus what he could beg, borrow, and occasionally steal, from his parents and others to fund his addiction. Had he been capable of rational thinking, the young man might have seen the absurdity of his reasoning, but he wasn't big on thinking — or rationality, for that matter.

He discussed the problem with several of his close acquaintances as they returned from the public house that had been given the dubious pleasure of their company, until they had been ejected long before closing time. The landlord and other customers had decided to forego the delights of their rowdy, ill-mannered, and uncouth behaviour. The bar owner and several of his toughest clients had surrounded them, and told them, in no uncertain terms, that it was time for them to leave. Knowing the reputation of some of those hard men, the group complied, even leaving their unfinished drinks in their haste to avoid retribution.

Once they had retreated to a safe place, where they frequently gathered in less clement weather conditions, their leader decided to vent his spite at losing valuable drinking time. He soon identified a target for his venom.

'There's this idle, good-for-nothing twat living free in our space,' he told the other members of his clique. 'I reckon it's time he was told to move on. An' if he won't shift his arse from there, I've a way of making him.' He raised his hands, and his small audience saw he was holding a petrol can aloft in one, while brandishing an exceedingly sharp knife in the other. 'I say we shift him, let some other buggers take care of him. You all in?'

His six companions yelled their agreement, mindless of the fact that, like their leader, none of them were gainfully employed. Like him, they saw nothing unreasonable in his argument. 'You gonna burn 'im, or cut 'im?' one of them asked.

'Both, if he gets awkward. But he can't stay if he's nowhere to sleep, can he? If he cuts up rough, then I'll cut him up rougher.' He flashed the knife and laughed. 'Come on, let's do it.'

* * *

It was just after 10 p.m. when the driver, who was returning from his week-long tour of customers in Scotland, passed the fringe of Helm Woods. It had been a successful week, but he was tired and looking forward to the weekend. A keen angler, this was one of his favourite spots, a stretch of the Helm where the fishing rights were held by Helmsdale Angling Club. Tomorrow he would finish off his sales reports, and then head for the river for a pleasant Saturday afternoon. It was time he restocked the freezer with rainbow trout.

Thinking of this made him glance to his right, a reflex action that changed rapidly to a prolonged stare, as he saw the flickering light of flames rising against the dark backdrop of the sky. He pulled to the side of the road, pressed treble nine on his mobile, and requested the fire brigade. Having given his location, he drove forward to a lay-by, to allow the emergency vehicles better access to the scene. For good measure, he switched on his hazard warning lights to guide them. Only then was he able to call his wife and explain he would be even later home than anticipated.

At the same time as he was making the call, at Netherdale General Hospital, a doctor was treating an outpatient for burns to his hand, arm, and neck. When asked how the accident had happened, the patient told the medic that he had been lighting a barbecue and the lighter fuel had spilled.

Although he was by no means an expert on burn injuries, the doctor did not for one moment believe this account of the event. But it was getting late. He'd been on shift for more hours than he cared to think about, and had several other patients waiting for his attention before he could sign off. For those reasons, he didn't question the improbable story, and it was only later, when he was asked by others about the incident, that he gave voice to his doubts.

* * *

In deploying his men, Chief Fire Officer Doug Curran's main concern was that after a prolonged period without rain, the fire might spread throughout the woodland. He surveyed the smouldering remnants of fabric clinging to the twisted framework of what had once been a tent. This was all that remained of what was the seat of the blaze.

His second-in-command asked, 'What do you reckon, Doug? Do you think someone knocked over their camping stove and the tent got barbecued rather than the sausages?'

'I don't think so. From what I can tell, there seems to have been no attempt made to extinguish the blaze. That's always assuming there was someone home when the fire broke out. If that wasn't the case, it raises two other interesting questions. Where is the tent owner, and, if there was nobody in the tent, what started the fire?'

They were standing well back from the area, principally to avoid getting drenched by their colleagues, who were still damping down the surrounding grass, shrubs, and overhanging branches. It was a relatively still, calm night but as Curran finished speaking, a slight breeze ruffled the trees, causing a faint, but unmistakeable aroma to reach him.

He sniffed. 'I can smell petrol. This was arson. And that, in turn, means we must contact our neighbours.'

Curran's deputy smiled, knowing the reference to neighbours meant the involvement of Helmsdale police, who shared their site. 'With a bit of luck, it'll be DC Andrews who turns up,' he said hopefully. 'She's as fit as a butcher's dog, that lass.'

Curran smiled slightly. 'I wouldn't let her boyfriend hear you say that. As I recall, he's more than a bit handy with a .12 bore.'

In the event, the warning was unnecessary. It was half an hour later when Viv Pearce reached the scene and was surprised to find Steve Meadows on site, hauling a portable generator from a police van.

'I brought a set of arc lights, and needed this to power them,' Meadows explained.

'That was smart thinking, Steve. But there is a light on the fire engine.' Viv smiled.

'Yes, well . . . actually, I was simply following Jack Binns' advice.' He grinned. 'I wouldn't want you to be in the dark. Or for him to think I hadn't been listening.'

Having fired up the generator, and switched on the powerful lights to supplement the beam from the engine, Pearce, Meadows, and the fire officers had to wait for a few minutes for their vision to adjust to the illumination, before they began searching the area. They spread out in a semi-circle, walking in a wide radius towards the river. They were some distance from the seat of the blaze when one of the firemen called out, 'Got a body here.' There was a second's pause before his voice became even more urgent. 'The man's unconscious. We need an ambulance PDQ.'

Even as he was speaking, Curran was already on his mobile summoning assistance, as Viv Pearce phoned Mike Nash.

Nash was about to climb the stairs to bed when his mobile rang. He listened for a moment and then replied, 'OK, Viv. I'll be with you ASAP.'

He turned to Alondra and said, 'Sorry, warm the bed for me. I don't know how long this will take.'

He then rang Clara, suggesting she should advise David it could be a late night. 'There's been an arson attack in Helm Woods, and they've found an unconscious man at the fire scene — he's been stabbed.'

* * *

As Nash swung the Range Rover into the nearby parking area, an ambulance's beacons added to the light show as the vehicle reversed to begin its journey to Netherdale Hospital.

Clara pulled to a halt alongside him, leapt from the car and announced, 'One day, I might get a full night's sleep.'

'It would be better to sleep at night, not in the day. Or is it that David's keeping you awake?' Nash responded. Even in the half-light, he knew Clara was glaring at him.

The detectives were greeted by Doug Curran, who began explaining what he believed had happened. 'One of my officers has found a petrol can close to the burnt-out tent. Alongside it is a bloodstained knife, we assume to be the weapon used on the victim.'

'You'd better watch out, Clara,' Nash warned her, 'it sounds as if Doug's hankering after your job.'

'I doubt it,' she responded. 'He must know how tough it is working for someone like you.'

'My lads haven't touched the items,' Doug added hastily. 'We thought you'd want to handle them.'

'We'd better have a look round anyway,' Nash suggested to Clara. 'You never know, Poirot here, and his mates, might have missed something.'

Viv joined them, and their search of the area looked like proving unproductive, until Clara discovered the tattered remnant of what had once been a greatcoat, swathes of which had been burnt completely away. The remaining shreds comprising only a sodden mass of pulped fibres.

The beam of her torch picked up the dull metallic gleam of something she thought at first was a curiously shaped button. Closer examination revealed what looked like an ornately embossed facade.

She peered at it for several seconds, before rubbing at the surface with her gloved finger, and held it up to get a closer look. The metal was cruciform in shape, and appeared to be silver in colour. The engraving took the form of four straight arms ending in broad finials, each bearing a crown. The centrepiece held the Royal symbol, in the letters ER. Although the ribbon that had been attached to the bar was burnt beyond recognition, Clara had no difficulty in identifying the object she was holding.

'Mike,' she called out, 'I think you ought to take a look at what I've just found.'

Nash had just finished placing the petrol can and knife into evidence bags, sealing and labelling them. He and Viv walked across and peered at the item in Clara's hand.

'I don't know the victim's circumstances,' Clara told him, 'but unless this coat was nicked, I'd suggest he's an ex-soldier with a distinguished career.'

Viv was impressed. 'How do you work all that out?'

'Because what you're looking at is the remains of a Military Cross. One of the highest military accolades, awarded for conspicuous acts of gallantry. I recognized it straightaway. David has one, and for some reason I haven't yet fathomed, I get the job of cleaning his ironmongery whenever he has to attend an official event. If this does belong to the victim, it ought to make him easy to identify.'

'We've also got to consider it could be stolen property,' Nash pointed out. 'But there is something that might make his attacker identifiable. I noticed what looked like skin on both the petrol can and knife. My guess is the blaze took the assailant by surprise, and they got burnt. If that's the case, then he would probably need medical attention, and with a bit of luck we should get some prints, or DNA, from the knife. He might already be in our system, but maybe that's asking for too much. Let's try and put a lid on this. We've got enough on our plate at the moment.'

'Should I phone Lisa?' Clara asked.

'No, she's agreed to be on call on Sunday while the rest of us dine out.'

After handing the crime scene over to Forensics, and giving them the trio of bagged items, Nash and Clara thanked Curran and his team. Nash reminded Doug that he was expected at La Giaconda at lunch time on Sunday for Jack Binns' and Gloria O'Donnell's farewell meal.

'I've swapped my shifts. Wouldn't miss that — I've known both Jack and Gloria for donkey's years. It's kind of you to invite me.'

'It's nothing grand. Just a way of saying thanks and goodbye to an old friend, and the chief.'

* * *

Saturday morning, after what seemed a very short night, the three detectives were all in Helmsdale station.

'Viv, we need to establish the victim's ID. Get in touch with Netherdale Hospital, see how he is, and get his details. If you get a name, pass it to Clara. She can work on the military angle, seeing as how she's such an expert on soldiers.' He ignored Clara's scowl and continued, 'And, Viv, while you're on with them, ask if they've treated any burns victims in the past twelve hours. I understand you have a bit of influence there.'

Viv smiled at Nash's reference to his wife, a sister in ICU.

'If you have no success at the hospital, try any GP walk-in clinics. The surgeries will most likely be closed today. If that doesn't work, check with local pharmacies — see if anyone has been seeking medication for burns. From the forensic team's initial findings, there might have been a few people involved, which would explain how they overpowered someone who might have been a soldier. However, there's a fair amount of speculation in that, because the crime scene has been compromised to a degree by Doug Curran and his crew. Their efforts to douse the fire will likely have washed away important evidence, and they've also left a good many footprints in the damp ground. We're relying heavily on what the petrol can and the knife reveal.'

A short while later, Viv reported back. 'The injured man refused to give his name.'

'Really? So, what's his condition now?'

'Well enough, I believe.'

Nash raised his eyebrows.

'He was obviously fit enough to discharge himself from hospital, despite the doctors advising against it. I spoke to the emergency medic who treated him, and he said the knife wounds weren't life-threatening.'

Nash thought for a moment. 'I'm concerned about him. Having lost his only dwelling place, he has few, if any, options open to him. OK, the weather has been fine and mild for a good while, but that won't last, not in these parts. I think it would be an idea to get Steve Meadows to ask his men to keep an eye out for him.'

Clara was next to report. 'I was right. The man is a former soldier, name of Brett Fulton. His rank was Lance Corporal. He was invalided out of the army following the incident that led to him being awarded the Military Cross. Although he recovered from most of his physical injuries, a bullet wound to his right shoulder caused him problems. His right arm and hand are basically useless, except for small tasks. As if that wasn't bad enough, he lost the sight in one eye. He was also diagnosed with severe PTSD.'

'Did you find out how he earned his medal?'

'I did — the army people were only too anxious to help. Fulton took on a group of insurgents who were attacking his patrol with RPGs and sub-machine guns. Despite being hit in the shoulder, he shot four of the assailants, and then sheltered in a disused building. The two remaining attackers launched RPGs at him, but although they almost destroyed his shelter, they only inflicted the eye injury. Fulton shot them both dead.' Clara paused before adding, 'Before he lost consciousness, the building he was in caught fire. Luckily, he was pulled out by his colleagues. Although he didn't get burnt, I can only imagine what horrors the arson attack on his tent must have caused to someone suffering from PTSD.'

'It might have caused him to relapse,' Nash agreed. 'And his physical wounds would have hindered any attempt to defend himself.'

As they were talking, Viv had taken a call in the outer office. He came through clutching several sheets of paper he'd extracted from the printer. 'This is the forensic report on the knife and petrol can found at in Helm Woods. They've identified one of Fulton's attackers, Tyler Watts, who has a fair bit of form.'

'That was quick,' Clara said.

'Yes, I get the feeling they were as unhappy with the situation as everyone else.'

He handed the paperwork to Nash, who scanned the first page. 'OK, ring Netherdale General back and run this character's name past the medics.'

Nash read the file in more detail. Tyler Watts seemed to have been in trouble for most of his young life. A note on the first page referred to his sealed juvenile records. More recent offences showed a propensity for mindless violence, conducted for the most part against property, rather than people. The arson attack and knifing marked a step up for someone Nash categorized as a young thug.

He turned to Clara. 'Liaise with Steve and get a couple of uniforms to act as backup, and then you and Viv can go and arrest Mr Tyler Watts.'

An hour later, they returned, their expressions spoke volumes. 'He wasn't in. His loving mother said she hasn't seen him for a week. Thinks he's gone on holiday with a friend. Yes, really!'

Nash shook his head. 'In that case, get uniform branch on it. Known associates, et cetera. See if they can find him.'

CHAPTER TEN

Alfresco Supplies, on Helmsdale High Street, was a shop specializing in outdoor, camping, and leisure goods. Given the principally rural location of their site, they did a highly successful trade in a range of items from walking and hiking equipment and clothing, to tents and ancillary goods.

On Monday morning, the store manager reached the shop half an hour before opening time as normal, only to discover that the interior of the premises was far from normal. There had been an intruder in the store over the weekend, having gained entry by forcing the back door. The burglar had made off with a tent, a backpack, two sets of outdoor clothing, a pair of walking boots, a sleeping bag, a camping stove, and at least two Thermos flasks. There might have been other smaller items taken, but in his shocked state, the manager wasn't certain.

He called the police, then checked the shop's CCTV. He smiled grimly as he watched the images displayed on screen. With luck, the perpetrator should be easily identifiable. The man had made no attempt to hide from the camera, even turning and facing the lens at one point, as he packed items in the bag. The thief's need for replacement clothing was obvious. The manager couldn't work out why he was wearing a bloodstained sweatshirt, and equally gory-looking trousers. What he also couldn't anticipate was the outcome of his call to the police.

* * *

At the same time as he made the call, DC Lisa Andrews pulled into the car park at Helmsdale police station. She was surprised to see Nash's Range Rover missing from its usual parking spot. When she reached the CID suite, Viv was removing his jacket, and Clara, who was seated behind Nash's desk, explained, 'Mike and the chief constable have been summoned to Scotland Yard. Apparently, the confession Melikian made, together with those contact details we culled from his mobiles, has yielded a lot of names who are already attracting the Met, and other forces' attention. There's a multi-force operation called County Lines in conjunction with the NCA.'

'Remind me . . . NCA?' Lisa asked.

'National Crime Agency,' Clara explained. 'From what little Mike was able to tell me when he rang last night, there could be as many as fifty or sixty "people of interest" on Melikian's contact list, plus others that we don't yet know about. The plan is to mount a long-term surveillance operation, which might throw up a good many more likely candidates for us to deal with. It could mean that Mike and our new chief will be less available than normal. But we've been faced with that before, so if it happens, we'll have to cope without them.'

She turned to Lisa. 'Was everything OK yesterday? No crises we have to deal with?'

'It was a quiet day. Uniforms dealt with it all. I didn't get one phone call.'

Viv looked at her sympathetically. 'You could have come to the dinner with us.'

'I didn't mind. Anyway, how did it go?'

Clara replied, 'We had a lovely meal, nice words spoken, and a few tears.'

'What, Mike was crying?'

Viv and Clara laughed.

'No, the chief and Ruth Edwards,' Clara said.

'Oh yeah?' Viv said, grinning. 'I saw you with a tissue after you hugged Jack goodbye.'

Nash's phone rang and Clara, grateful to avoid embarrassment, answered it. As they headed for their desks, Viv and Lisa could hear laughter in her voice.

She came through to the general office, a smile on her face. 'That was Steve Meadows. His lads have found Tyler Watts.'

Viv looked puzzled. 'But that's not funny . . . is it?'

'No, that isn't! But as representatives of the local gossip column, you two are useless. You obviously didn't know about the party. And you certainly haven't seen Steve this morning.'

Viv and Lisa looked at each other in total confusion. 'What party?' they echoed.

'Last night. After his dinner with us, uniform branch had a leaving-do for Jack. If you speak to Steve, I suggest you do it quietly.'

'Oh, I get it. So why is it so funny?' Lisa asked.

'I told him Jack Binns would never stand for an officer on duty in the state he's in. He's lucky Jack's retired.'

* * *

Clara warned Steve Meadows they would be requiring overnight cover for the prisoners, before she headed for the interview room. Armed with what she had discovered about Brett Fulton, Clara co-opted Lisa to join her in the interview with Tyler Watts. 'I want us to throw the book at him, and we'll start by telling him the calibre of the man he attacked. I'll tell Watts we intend to charge him with attempted murder, and that when the case comes to court the prosecution will demonstrate his victim is a national hero, and will demand the maximum sentence.'

Lisa eyed her colleague for a long moment before replying, 'You've really got the bit between your teeth on this one, Clara. Is that because you relate Fulton to David?'

'I guess so. I did get to thinking how fortunate we are that David recovered fully from his injuries, as bad as they were. He certainly hasn't suffered to the same extent as Lance Corporal Fulton. The comparison is all that much stronger because they were both awarded the same medal.'

As things transpired, the pre-interview disclosure to Watts' legal representative, and his subsequent discussion with his client, did most of their work for them. Having learned of the cast-iron evidence, seen his client's bandaged hands and other burns pointing to his guilt, plus the distinguished service record of the man he had attacked, the solicitor advised Watts accordingly.

When Watts was faced by the detectives, he spoke first, barely allowing Lisa time to complete the opening announcement. 'I got it wrong,' Watts admitted. 'I thought the guy was a loser. He looked like a no-good, a tramp, and I did set fire to his tent. I only wanted to scare him off, get him to move somewhere else. The knife was only for protection. I didn't mean to hurt him. If I'd known about him, I wouldn't have gone near. Do what you like with me.' He hung his head and stared at the floor.

'Do you want to make a formal confession admitting everything you've just told us?' Clara asked. 'If we present that to the court, the judge might look more favourably on your case. You could avoid a heavier sentence.'

Watts didn't need to think Clara's offer over, he agreed immediately.

Half an hour later, as they returned to the CID suite, Lisa said, 'That's another case wrapped up. A good start to the week.'

Clara rebuked her. 'If Mike heard that, he'd tell you off for invoking Sod's Law, as he calls it. Do I have to remind you that we still have two murders on our hands? And the way things stand, we haven't the slightest clue who committed them, or what the motive was?'

'I may have said this before,' Lisa retorted, 'but you're getting to sound more and more like Mike every day.'

Clara smiled slightly. 'That is either a great compliment, or a very cutting insult. I'm not sure which.'

* * *

Nash's phone rang. Clara listened, scribbling notes. She waved for Viv to come through. 'Uniform has attended a break-in at the outdoor supplies shop. I think we can guess the identity of the burglar easily enough. They've got CCTV, and the officer said the thief's face can be seen clearly. I want you to examine the CCTV footage, and, if I'm right, advise Steve Meadows. Ask him to send a couple of his guys to Helm Woods to look for Fulton. You two go with them, and if you a draw a blank, try other similar locations. There can't be too many suitable campsites to choose from within easy walking distance of here, especially if you're carrying a load of equipment.'

Having confirmed Fulton was the thief, later that afternoon they reported that their search had proved successful. They had detained the ex-soldier and seized the missing goods, most of which still bore their wrappings and price tickets. In a final touch of irony, Fulton was placed in the next cell to Tyler Watts, the assailant whose attack had started the whole incident.

Clara informed the shop manager of the arrest, and told the man he would be needed to identify some of the stolen property from which the labels had been removed. 'Unfortunately, he is wearing some of the clothing.'

When she reached home that evening, Clara told her fiancé of the day's events. This was such a normal occurrence that she thought no more about it. David listened with keen interest, but unusually for him, refrained from commenting. Given that the detainee was a former serviceman, Clara found that mildly surprising. She thought David would have been more sympathetic to someone who had suffered so much, but her train of thought was soon distracted by the lasagne he had made for their evening meal.

After the traumatic discovery of the previous day, the manager of Alfresco Supplies was hugely relieved to find everything in order when he opened the shop the next morning. He had barely time to switch on the lighting, put the floats into the tills, and turn the closed sign to open, when the shop bell signified a potential customer. The visitor spoke, and within the first few sentences, the manager realized the man was not there to make a purchase.

Despite that, what he told the shopkeeper was sufficient to command his complete attention. Although he had never been in the armed forces, his father, and grandfather had served with distinction, both involved in battle scenes they had described in harrowing detail. Once his visitor had departed, the manager pondered the information he had been given for a few moments and then picked up the phone.

Brett Fulton was desperate to be in the open air. He had been cooped up in the cell for over fourteen hours and the confinement was beginning to get to him. The fact that he'd been fed and sheltered meant nothing. He acknowledged that it was his own fault he'd been locked up, but didn't care any longer. He could sense the all-too-familiar feeling of depression beginning to wash over him, knowing that nobody cared whether he prospered, or perished.

He was relieved when the woman detective with the foreign-sounding name, who had interviewed him the previous day, opened the cell door and told him he was free to leave — on one condition. 'The manager of the shop you broke into has phoned this morning and withdrawn his complaint. All burglary and theft charges against you have been dropped. However, he has made one stipulation, and I believe it is something you will find is to your benefit. He wants you to go straight to the shop because he wants to talk to you. He is willing to make you an offer that will enable you to remain safe and comfortable. In case you have doubts, this isn't an act of charity, because he believes you can render a more than useful service for the business he runs.'

Clara watched Fulton leave, the erect posture in marked contrast to the drooping, depressed figure of the previous day. She returned to the CID suite, pondering what had just happened. Her suspicions were confirmed almost immediately, when Lisa Andrews asked, 'Are you going on a camping holiday?'

Clara blinked with surprise, 'No, what makes you think that?'

'I saw David coming out of Alfresco Supplies first thing this morning, so I thought he must be buying something for an adventure you're considering.'

'You did, did you? Are you certain it was David?'

'Yes, is that a problem?'

Clara smiled. 'No, just checking my facts. You know how careful we have to be before making an allegation against someone.'

Clara wandered into Nash's office, closed the door, and pressed a short code on her mobile. 'You're a devious son of a bitch. How did you persuade them to drop the charges against Fulton?'

Clara grinned as she heard Sutton gasp with surprise. After a long pause, he stammered, 'How did you know? Did the man at the shop tell you?'

'No, I worked it out. It's what we do here. We're detectives. When the manager revealed he knew about Fulton's distinguished military career, and Lisa Andrews had seen you coming out of the shop, the case against you was confirmed. That's part of our job — we call it deductive reasoning. Speaking of which, how's the great job hunt going?'

Clara was surprised when Sutton replied, 'Quite well, actually. In fact, as a result of this morning's events, I've an interview lined up next week at Catterick.'

Clara's heart sank at the mention of the military base. 'David, you're not thinking of going back in, are you?'

She was immensely relieved when he explained what he actually had in mind.

CHAPTER ELEVEN

There was only one occupant of the second carriage of the train as it approached Netherdale station. Former Petty Officer Warren Peters was returning home after his final tour of duty in the Royal Navy. He had been at sea for nine months on a destroyer, stationed for the most part in the Middle East.

As he stared at the familiar scenery, Peters reflected on the past — and equally on the uncertainty of his future. He had been sorely tempted to re-enlist, but at his age he had decided that was no longer an option, and was only postponing the inevitable. Having left the service without any formal qualifications, he was technically jobless with few prospects.

If that was a problem, his personal life was potentially even bleaker. He had got married seven years earlier, the result of a whirlwind romance while home on leave. Almost as soon as he had installed his bride in the house that had belonged to his parents and grandparents before him, Warren realized that the marriage had been a mistake. He had been attracted to Bridget the moment he saw her in Club Wolfgang, Helmsdale's only nightspot. He visited the place rarely, but on this occasion he had spent several nights there, the attraction being immediate, and deep enough for him to take the plunge.

Warren acknowledged his rash action had been fuelled by pure physical attraction. Once carnal desire had been satisfied, there was little the couple had in common. Thereafter, the marriage went downhill faster than an Alpine skier. This manifested itself when Bridget moved into one of the guest rooms, citing as an excuse his restlessness while sleeping. The last time he arrived home on leave, he found she had gone one step further — the message reinforced by the locked door to that room.

He had considered asking for a divorce. But as Bridget, although by no means a regular churchgoer, came from staunch Catholic stock, he knew this was not an option. His visits home were too fleeting for him to gauge with any accuracy if Bridget had formed any other attachments during his absence, but he suspected that could possibly be so.

The train pulled into Netherdale station, the announcement breaking into Warren's reverie. He collected his kitbag and disembarked, searching the platform for a welcome home party. The concrete apron was deserted apart from a couple of other passengers, and a member of the railway staff, who was wielding a sweeping brush in what could only be described as lacklustre fashion. Warren had sent Bridget a text telling her of the train's arrival time, and asking her to meet him, but received no reply. He took out his mobile and dialled. The call went straight to voicemail. Matters had obviously worsened since his previous home visit. For her to ignore him completely was new. Then he had another thought. Maybe she was waiting in the car park on the far side of the building that housed the ticket office. He hurried to find her.

Warren's disillusion deepened when he emerged onto the concourse to see the car park completely devoid of vehicles. The only taxi in sight was pulling out into the main road, having collected its fare.

The train had been the last of the day. It was now late in the evening, and his choices were stark. He could wait, in the hope that Bridget had been unavoidably delayed, or he could walk across town to the taxi company's offices, and seek a ride to his home in the village of Drover's Halt, the far side of Helmsdale.

Being of sound Yorkshire stock, Warren didn't relish forking out for a taxi fare when there was a possibility of getting a free ride. He opted to wait, and only if Bridget failed to turn up would he activate plan B. Of one thing he was certain; he would wait inside the station building. After a long period in warmer climates, the Yorkshire night air was distinctly chilly. Far worse was the rain, which was lashing the station forecourt, driven by a strong north-westerly wind.

As he sat on one of the wooden benches, which seemed to have been designed by a sadistic carpenter, Warren wondered if his existence could get any more miserable. It was much later when he realized this was only the beginning.

Eventually, having given up hope, he walked across town to the taxi rank, getting soaked through in the process. The driver had been reluctant to accept the fare, knowing the journey would prevent him from getting a share of the lucrative trade available via revellers who were proscribed from using their own transport. It was only the sizeable bonus that persuaded him to overlook his objections.

It was after midnight when Warren reached Drover's Halt. He'd paid the driver, and stood for a moment staring at the large detached Victorian building that had been in his family for generations. It had been his hope that this would be a good place to rear the next members of the Peters' clan, but there was fat chance of that, with separate rooms, and a locked door in the way.

The house was in darkness. That was hardly surprising given the late hour, but it made him wonder if Bridget cared so little that she had gone to bed, ignoring his request for transport. His footsteps were heavy as he walked up the long drive, going automatically to the rear door. The one he had used ever since he could walk. The family tradition was to use the front door only for receiving guests.

As he entered the utility room, Warren glanced automatically to an empty space in the corner, where Bruno's bed had always been placed. Bruno was Bridget's dog, and had been her constant companion for several years. It had been about three months earlier that she had written to him to inform him of the death of her beloved pet. Although by no means the world's greatest dog lover, Warren had come to like the amiable animal. He wondered if the loss of her best friend had caused a further deterioration in Bridget's attitude to him.

Fifteen minutes later, Warren sat in the lounge pondering what he'd discovered, or rather, what he had failed to find. He had searched the house from top to bottom, but had been unable to find any sign of Bridget. The door to her bedroom was unlocked and open, the bed made, clothing stored in the wardrobe. As far as he could tell everything was there, her wheeled suitcase perched on top of the cupboard, the dressing table contained her perfume, hairbrush, and make-up. Warren had then gone out to the double garage, only to find her Mini Countryman parked there.

His rancour about the abysmal state of their marriage was now suspended, replaced by the mystery of her absence. He'd expected to find a note explaining the reason, but there was nothing. So he waited.

By now, it was almost three o'clock in the morning, and he was unable to decide if he should phone the police and report her as a missing person. But she might have gone to visit a friend, and taken only the necessities for a short visit in a small holdall, or even one of her mega handbags. It might even be purely a night out. The only fault with either theory was that it didn't explain how she would travel to such an event with her car still in the garage. The nearest town was Helmsdale, almost twelve miles away.

Eventually, having been travelling for most of the day, and then awake for most of the night, Warren was weary beyond measure. He decided to leave matters until morning to sort out. Hopefully, Bridget would return and everything would become clear.

* * *

Although Nash was usually the first of the detectives to arrive at Helmsdale station, on the morning following his return from the Scotland Yard conference, he was later than normal. On reaching the slip road that bypassed the market place, he found his way barred. He peered through the rain-swept windscreen. The street was completely blocked off, police vans forming an effective barrier to vehicular traffic. To complement these, the pavements on either side of the road were sealed to pedestrians, the streamers of blue-and-white incident tape fluttering in the wind. Nash got out of the Range Rover and heard his name being called. He saw Clara battling with an umbrella, while waving to attract his attention.

Nash pulled up the collar of his Barbour waxed jacket and headed over to her. 'What's going on?'

'Bomb threat,' she replied tersely, her voice crackling with stress. 'When Steve Meadows opened up this morning, he found a package on the reception counter. He knew it wasn't there last night when he locked up. He called for backup from HQ, urgently. Now we're waiting for the bomb squad from Catterick Garrison.'

'Has there been any threats? Any phone calls?'

'Not that I'm aware of. The control room would have notified us by now.' She paused before adding the scariest part of her message. 'The thing is, Mike, the package was addressed for your attention.'

Nash blinked with surprise as he considered the implication. He had made a lot of enemies in the criminal fraternity during his career. There had indeed been one previous attempt to kill him with an explosive device. But he couldn't think of anyone who was at liberty, or who he might have upset recently.

In part to distract his train of thought from the grimmer meaning of what he'd heard, he asked, 'Where's Steve Meadows?'

'He's organizing the evacuation of ambulances and fire engines. If this *is* an explosive device, and it goes off before the UXB squad arrive, he thought it sensible to minimise the potential for a chain reaction, if you follow me. They could be needed.'

'That's good thinking on Steve's part, so I guess we'll have to sit and wait. Who's in charge here?'

'Steve was initially, but as soon as Doug Curran arrived, he handed responsibility over to him. Doug said Steve rang him at home and more or less ordered him here.'

Nash grinned. 'That'll have pleased Doug, being dragged out of his pit, and told what to do, especially in this weather. Has anyone let Ruth Edwards know?'

'Not yet, Mike, we haven't had chance.'

'OK, I'll do it.' Before Nash could make the call, the increasingly loud wail of sirens signalled the approach of a number of vehicles. These, he assumed, would contain the sappers, who had the unenviable task of checking the suspicious package.

Uniformed officers moved pedestrians and other spectators out of the way, while two of their colleagues manoeuvred police vans to allow access. Seconds later, the sirens reached a crescendo as two Land Rovers and a Transit van sped past. With slick efficiency the police officers resealed the barriers. Only when the racket created by the bomb squad's transport ceased could Nash phone the chief. Predictably, Ruth Edwards was appalled by Nash's report of the potential threat and said she would join them.

Standing together in the heavy rain, all the team could do was watch, wait, and hope that the bomb squad would be able to defuse any device inside the package. During their vigil, Nash gave voice to a disturbing thought that had occurred to him. 'One thing that puzzles me is how the person who delivered it gained access to the building.'

Seeing the alarmed expression on Meadows' face, he reassured the sergeant, 'I don't for one minute believe you left the building unlocked, Steve. So we need to work out how this person got inside.'

'I'd like to know as well. The door was locked when I arrived.'

Despite pondering the question, nobody had come up with a potential explanation by the time the army officer in charge approached them, accompanied by CFO Doug Curran.

'Whatever is inside that package, it certainly isn't explosives,' the soldier informed them. 'It appears to be some form of powder wrapped in clear plastic. The powder, the wrapping, and the outer packaging, were all tested and there is certainly nothing that could be used to detonate a device. Inside, there was a message addressed to a Detective Inspector Nash.'

'I'm Nash. What did the message say?'

'Here, read it for yourself.' The officer handed Nash a clear plastic bag containing a sheet of A4 paper.

Nash turned it over and inspected the single sentence. 'It says, "This is a present from Charles Wilson".'

'I'll leave you to puzzle that out,' the soldier laughed.

The chief constable had arrived and apologized for them having to be dragged out on a wild goose chase, to which he replied, 'Don't worry about that, ma'am. We don't mind being called out on false alarms. It's the real thing that gets us twitchy.' He turned and looked directly at DS Mironova. 'Hi, Clara, good to see you. David OK?'

'Er, yes, thank you. He's fine.'

'Good, good.' And with that, he left.

Nash turned to the others. 'This is weird. Charles Wilson was a dealer in cocaine, so I think we can guess the contents of the packet. It's highly likely that the person who delivered this package is the man who murdered Wilson. Not only do we need to identity him, but find out how he managed to enter and leave the police station undetected. Knowing how careful this guy is, I'm willing to bet we don't find any trace evidence anywhere.'

It was lunchtime before any semblance of normality returned to the station and its surrounds. They soon received confirmation that the suspicious package, as Nash had guessed, contained cocaine, with an estimated street value of slightly over £100,000.

'That explains the rumours Viv reported,' Clara commented.

'Yes, but we still haven't solved the problem of how the intruder got in,' the chief remarked.

It was almost by chance that they worked out part of the strategy used, and it was Pearce who made the initial breakthrough.

He reported back to the others, having been detailed to ask the fire and ambulance services if they had noticed anything suspicious overnight. 'One of the ambulance crews got called out in the early hours to Kirk Bolton for a suspected heart attack. The call was a hoax.' Pearce grinned, causing Ruth Edwards to ask what was amusing him. 'When they got to the house, they disturbed a couple of newly-weds in the act of consummating their marriage.'

'Oh dear, not a good start to married life. Have we any idea where the hoax call came from?'

'That's where it gets really interesting. I obtained the number from their control room, and passed the details to Netherdale to be followed up as a matter of urgency.'

At that moment, Pearce's mobile rang. The listeners knew immediately that the caller was their civilian support officer, Maureen Riley, who worked alongside Tom Pratt. When Pearce ended the call, he was smiling again. 'Apparently, the phone was a pay-as-you-go, purchased yesterday from a shop in Netherdale. The buyer paid cash, and gave his name on the receipt as Michael Nash.'

They all turned to stare at Nash, who grinned and said, 'Don't blame me. I was in very dodgy company at Scotland Yard until late yesterday. It suggests the phone was bought simply for that purpose, and then disposed of. My guess is the caller would have been close by when he rang for an ambulance. The crew would have left the shutter doors to their garage open when they left. All he had to do was slip into the compound, avoid being spotted, and make his way to the door connecting their part of the building to ours.'

'He'd still have to get though a locked door,' Clara pointed out.

By common, unspoken consent they all moved downstairs from the CID suite and reconvened at the end of the corridor. Here, the door led to the ambulance depot that occupied the middle sector of the building. Nash tried the door. It was locked. He looked at the empty hook on the wall. 'Where's the key?' he asked.

'No idea, Mike. It was on the hook earlier this week, when I went to talk to the fire brigade guys about the Helm Wood incident,' Viv responded. I put it back.'

'So how did you get through this morning?'

'I didn't. The door's locked. I didn't think about it. I walked round.' Viv looked shamefaced.

'It's a master key that fits both the connecting doors. Each section has one. So how did you get beyond to the fire services today?'

'I had to ask for a key. The ambulance depot copy is kept in a drawer in their office.'

'So whoever broke in must have been equipped to get through a locked door.' Nash paused, and thought for a second.

'Somebody like Jimmy Johnson would probably be able to do it within seconds. I think we ought to get an expert to advise us how the intruder got through, and also suggest ways of tightening our security. I don't relish the idea of people being able to come and go at will. Clara, will you give Jimmy a ring, and ask him to pop round when he's got a spare minute. In the meantime, I think we ought to have a look round and see if we can find the missing key.'

'Shouldn't we get a forensic officer to dust the door for prints?' Clara asked.

'I suppose so, but I reckon it'll be a long shot,' Nash agreed.

'I'll get them to send an officer across,' the chief volunteered. 'I'm going back to Netherdale to deal with what I was supposed to be handling this morning. Mike, you'll keep me up to date with things here, please?'

Later that day, Jimmy Johnson, the former burglar who now ran a locksmith's and security business in Helmsdale, inspected the door and reported to Nash and Mironova.

Before then, Steve Meadows had located the missing key. 'I went round to the ambulance depot,' he explained. 'The key was in the lock on the other side of our door.'

When he arrived, Jimmy Johnson told them, 'It gives me the shivers comin' doon tae a polis station, voluntarily.' He inspected the door closely, even using a magnifying glass to peer at the outer surface of the lock on both sides.

'He only needs a pipe and a deerstalker and he could pass as Sherlock Homes,' Nash whispered to Clara.

Having completed his inspection, Johnson gave his verdict. 'The lock on the ambulance depot side of the door is scratched. Someone with skills like mine has had a go at it frae that side. Then the cheeky beggar's spotted the key on yer hook in here, and locked up as he was leaving. He'd be in and oot in minutes.'

'That's fine, Jimmy. But how do we prevent something similar happening again?' Nash asked.

'If ye want my advice, I wouldnae leave the key on that hook,' he said with a grin. 'Seriously, I'd change tae a security coded lock, on this and any other connecting doors.'

'Send me a quote, will you? Then I'll put in a requisition to the powers that be.'

CHAPTER TWELVE

Warren Peters woke early. In truth, he had hardly slept a wink. He headed straight for Bridget's bedroom. Had she returned late? Was he asleep when she did? The room door stood open as he had left it, with still no sign of his wife.

While he was dressing, he glanced out of the window, and saw the rain hadn't ceased. If anything, it seemed even heavier than the night before. He heard the drops being dashed against the windows to the front of the house. Having spent so long in warmer, drier climates, he would have to become accustomed to the weather prevalent in the north of England. He dug in his chest of drawers and found a thick sweater.

He turned his mind to the mystery confronting him. Of far more importance than the weather was the puzzle of his missing spouse. He could understand her lukewarm attitude to his arrival. Even to the extent of failing to reply to his text messages. But if she had been unable, or unwilling, to meet his train, surely she would have left an explanatory note?

It was only then that Warren was struck by another, far more sobering thought. What if something had happened to her? Could she have been taken ill? Was she lying in a hospital bed somewhere, suffering, while he was castigating her for being neglectful, uncaring? She had no close living relatives who might have claimed her attention, causing her to abandon their home without leaving word. If some crisis had happened, it could only have been to Bridget.

These ideas flooded his mind as he walked downstairs, his footsteps echoing as he crossed the hallway. He knew he would have to try any means possible to find out what had happened to her. Now, his attempts would be focused on the places she might have ended up.

His first call to her mobile was like all his previous attempts, going straight to voicemail. Next, he tried the firm she worked for, but was told Bridget had resigned from her post six weeks earlier. This surprised him. He knew how much she enjoyed her job in an accountant's office in Helmsdale, valued the independence her salary gave her. Now he was faced with another puzzle. Why had she quit so suddenly? Another thing that didn't add up.

What he had learned fuelled his earlier idea that Bridget might have a health issue. His next task was to begin phoning hospitals. He began with Netherdale General. Meeting with failure there, he tried spreading his net wider, but without success. Interspersed with these calls, he kept trying her mobile. He checked the house again, this time concentrating on the kitchen. All the food seemed fresh — there was even an oven-ready lasagne, one of his favourite dishes. This had obviously been purchased for his return.

He realized the only course left open to him was to contact the police. He decided to leave it for an hour or so, and try her phone again. If he still got no response, then he would report her missing. The time dragged by, but eventually the hour was up. Expecting nothing more than the voicemail message, he was surprised when the call was answered.

The conversation that followed was terse, unnatural and surreal, to put it mildly.

'Hello?'

'It's Warren. Who else did you think it might be? What the hell's going on, Bridget? Where the devil are you?'

Again, Bridget's voice was almost robotic, and her question made no sense. 'What do you want?'

'What the hell do you think I want? I want to know where you are. What you're up to? And why you didn't meet my train, or answer my messages and calls? I'll ask you again — what's going on?'

Normally, the anger in his voice would have sparked a vitriolic response, but her reply, which failed to address any of the questions he'd asked, was calm, placid, and toneless. 'I'm sorry, I can't do this anymore. I'm leaving.'

'And I suppose that means you'll be seeking a divorce,' Warren sneered. 'Oh no, wait, you're a Catholic and you can't do that. So why not explain exactly what you *are* intending to do?'

There was another long pause before Bridget answered. This time there was a nervous edge to her voice. 'I have to tell you,' she began, then faltered, 'I have to tell you I'm pregnant.'

Warren was stunned into silence, incapable of responding to Bridget's shock announcement. Before he could gather his wits to demand an explanation, the line went dead.

Despite several attempts to re-connect, each effort ended with voicemail. One thing for sure, his intention to call the police and have her reported as a missing person, was no longer an option. Their first question would undoubtedly be to ask when he had last been in contact with her. His reply of "just over a quarter of an hour ago" would be unlikely to spur them into immediate action.

Although he'd been shocked beyond measure by Bridget's revelation, he began to puzzle over other aspects of their conversation. Her voice had sounded stilted, unnatural, almost as if she was reading from a script. Each question he'd asked had been followed by a long silence before she'd replied, and in doing so, she'd addressed none of the issues he'd raised. Despite pondering it for a long time, Warren failed to come up with any logical explanation.

* * *

It was the first year the gamekeeper had worked on the Layton estate. As the pheasant shooting season was underway, he was keen to present the birds in as great a number, and the most advantageous manner, for his employer and the many guests expected. With that objective in mind, he had constructed several new enclosures at strategic points around the estate, matching the drives, to carry the pheasants towards the waiting guns. That had involved a good deal of extra work, not only in building the pens, but also in visiting them on a daily basis to ensure the birds were fed, watered, and safe from predators.

The breeding and rearing season had been marked by a prolonged spell of mild, dry weather, but that situation had altered dramatically late the previous evening, just as the keeper was downing the last of his night-time cocoa. He'd looked up from the copy of the *Shooting Times*, startled by the rattling sound of the rain being hurled against the cottage window.

'I knew it was too good to last,' he told his wife. 'The pens I'm visiting tomorrow morning are at the far end of the estate, and I've a fair amount of walking to do. Just my luck for it to be raining cats and dogs.'

On reaching the western edge of the estate, close to the outskirts of Drover's Halt village, dawn was breaking. He followed the track as far as his Land Rover would take him. He drove slowly, conscious that the volume of rain cascading down was almost too great for the vehicle's windscreen wipers to cope with. He had equipped himself with waterproof over-trousers, a waxed Barbour jacket, and a rainproof cap. These, he hoped would keep him reasonably dry, despite the undergrowth through which he had to walk.

With a sack of feed over one shoulder and a plastic container filled with water — which he doubted he would need — in his other hand, he set off. He headed for a deer trail he knew would lead to the nearest release pen. He had only taken a dozen steps when he noticed something that definitely didn't belong in the forest.

'Oh, dear God,' he whispered. The sack and small water butt fell from his nerveless hands as he stared horror-struck at the obscenity in front of him. The corpse lying sprawled across the path had died a violent death — of that, there could be no doubt, from the contorted features of the woman's face. It was several minutes before he turned and half-stumbled, half-ran, back to the Land Rover.

On reaching the vehicle, he could use his mobile to phone the authorities. Recovering from what he had just seen would take a whole lot longer.

* * *

'Mike and the chief have been called away to another meeting,' Clara told Lisa and Viv when they arrived at Helmsdale that morning. 'This one's in Manchester, and it's a two-day event. By what Mike told me, this drugs thing has become much bigger than anticipated. He also said he hoped this would be the last time they would be called away for the foreseeable future.'

The two DCs looked at one another before Pearce responded, 'There's not much we can do about that. So I guess we'll have to make the best of a bad job, now that you're acting chief constable and head detective for the area.'

Mironova, who had turned to go into Nash's office to answer the phone, responded with an extremely vulgar two-fingered gesture.

'What did I tell you?' Pearce was undeterred. 'She is definitely getting more like Mike every day.'

The banter was soon forgotten, however, as Clara took a call from Netherdale control room. She listened, scribbling furiously on Nash's jotter before telling the operator, 'Ask the informant to direct officers to the scene, and then wait for our arrival.'

She went into the outer office. 'Get your wellies and waterproofs on. We're going to Layton Woods. A gamekeeper's found a corpse near Drover's Halt. Viv, as you don't speak Spanish, I think you should be the one to phone Mexican Pete — you won't understand when he starts swearing. Lisa, you can have the pleasure of telling our forensic crew they're going to get soaked through. I'm going to bring Steve Meadows up to speed, so I'll meet you downstairs.'

* * *

'Why do people always wait until it's teeming with rain before they report corpses in the open air?' Lisa commented, as they reached the edge of Layton Woods. She pointed along the track towards the body's location, which had already been demarcated by blue-and-white incident tape, adding, 'I don't think there was any need for that. Nobody in their right minds would venture out on a woodland ramble in this deluge.'

She had a point, Clara acknowledged, but the officers were following protocol. 'We'd better stay clear until the boffins have arrived and gone over the ground. We can take a closer look after they've taken photos and given the all-clear. In the meantime, let's have a word with Mellors, not that I think he'll be able to tell us much.'

'Who?' Viv and Lisa asked in unison.

'The gamekeeper,' Clara saw their confusion. 'Mellors was the gamekeeper in *Lady Chatterley's Lover.*'

As she had predicted, the keeper had little information that could prove useful, beyond his answer to her final question, 'Did you recognize the dead woman?'

'I did and I didn't.' He scratched his head, a process impeded slightly by his flat cap. 'What I mean is, I think she might be a local. I've seen a woman similar to her around here, but I can't swear that it's the same person. I don't know her name, I'm afraid. Sorry I can't be of more help. I only started working for the estate this year. Prior to that, I worked and lived in Cumbria, so I don't know many people in this area yet.' He shook his head. 'I've still got to check on the pheasants. Can I go?'

They allowed him to leave, having extracted his promise to visit Helmsdale station so his formal statement could be recorded. As his Land Rover turned into the road at the end of the track, it was replaced by a miniature convoy. This consisted of the pathologist, Professor Ramirez, closely followed by the mortuary van, and the brightly coloured CSI van.

Although Mironova braced herself for an outburst of withering sarcasm from Ramirez, it seemed the rain had dampened his wit. Either that, or he felt it was wasted without his prime target, Nash, being available.

'So, today we have a different corpse,' the professor said, directing the comment at Clara.

'Er, yes, we do,' she replied, unsure of his point.

'Unusual to find one wearing clothing,' he said, as he donned his mask.

For a long time it seemed that the crime scene would yield nothing of importance, until the mortuary attendants were preparing the corpse for transport. As one of them was sliding the black plastic body bag beneath the woman, he stopped, then called Ramirez and the detectives across. 'I think this woman has been here since yesterday, at least. The ground under where she'd been lying is bone dry.'

Their inspection confirmed this, and having searched the area immediately surrounding where the body had been, they retired with little to show for their labours — apart from being drenched. However, the forensic team leader made one observation that later would prove to be of immense importance.

'If you look at the grass near to where the body was lying, you can see it has been flattened, as if a vehicle has driven off the track and across it. There are no tread marks visible — I wouldn't expect to see any after this amount of rain. That would tend to bear out what the mortuary attendant found.'

Mironova thanked him and his men for their efforts, apologizing for having to call them out in such inclement weather.

Ramirez' parting shot was to ask why Nash was absent. Mironova explained, causing the pathologist to shake his head, before saying, 'Our tame vampire won't be happy missing out on this. He won't even get to attend the post-mortem, which I'll be conducting this afternoon. So if you, or one of your deputies, can drag yourselves across to Netherdale, I'll be obliged.'

Mironova told him she would be there, before enquiring as to the reason for the hurry.

'Because I have lectures all day tomorrow in York, I need to be away early.'

The post-mortem was not difficult, nor prolonged. Clara sat in the drab office attached to the mortuary, making notes as the pathologist reported his findings.

'This unfortunate young woman was strangled. There are signs of petechial haemorrhage in both eyes, and the hyoid bone has been crushed. Bruising is beginning to form about the victim's throat, which suggests the killer used his bare hands, rather than a garrotte. I also assume you will want to know when this woman was killed. I estimate time of death as being between twelve and twenty-four hours ago.'

Mironova glanced at her watch, which showed that it was sixteen-thirty. She did a quick calculation. 'I think we can narrow it down a bit further than that, Professor.'

Ramirez looked up, surprised by the interruption, until she explained.

'Very astute,' he commented. 'Almost as good as your boss. Now, there is one other thing, but whether it's relevant to her murder is a question for you and your colleagues to answer. The victim was in the early stages of pregnancy. Around ten weeks, I estimate. I can give you a more accurate date when I've conducted the relevant tests. She had not given birth before.'

* * *

Next morning, Viv Pearce was checking their missing persons' files, without success, when the phone rang, causing him to report to Clara in Nash's office. 'I've just taken a call from the Forensics guy at the murder site. They discovered a woman's handbag, about a hundred metres away from where the body was found. It was in dense undergrowth, and they might have missed it had it not been for the colour, a vivid shade of red. Inside, they found a photo ID driving licence. They also found cash and bank cards, which seems to rule out robbery. The name is Mrs Bridget Peters, with an address in Drover's Halt. I think we might have identified our victim.'

'In that case, I think we should take a ride out to the village and see what we can discover about Bridget Peters. Ask Lisa to man the fort while you and I go snooping.'

At the house, Warren Peters had passed another restless night, unable to snatch more than a few minutes' sleep at a time. Apart from his overriding bafflement as to Bridget's whereabouts, he now had two other factors to bewilder him. One was her statement that she was pregnant. Could her continuing absence mean that she had gone into hiding somewhere, afraid of his reaction to her unwelcome news?

He'd had trouble accepting the truth of that statement, but if it was so, who was the father of her unborn child? The other bewildering fact was the solitary response he got when he did contact her. It puzzled him in two ways. Why had she chosen to accept only that one call out of the countless ones he'd made? Was she too afraid of his anger on knowing she'd been unfaithful? Or was there another reason, one that suggested she wasn't bothered if she spoke to him or not?

Midway through the morning of his second day home, he decided enough was enough. He couldn't stand the torment any longer. He would bite the bullet, contact the police to report Bridget as a missing person, and express his doubts about the strange phone conversation.

He was about to do so, when the doorbell rang. For a moment, he was excited, thinking that it might be Bridget. He couldn't think who else it might be. He had few friends in Drover's Halt, his long absences preventing him from becoming an active participant in village life. The other possibility was that it might be one of Bridget's friends. They could perhaps provide information.

Nothing could have prepared him for the shock the visitors would deliver.

CHAPTER THIRTEEN

When Warren Peters opened the door he saw two complete strangers standing in front of him. The woman, a blue-eyed blonde, was in sharp contrast to her companion, who Peters guessed to be of either African or Caribbean descent. His guess was they might be selling something, or attempting to convert him to an obscure branch of religion, until the woman spoke.

'Mr Peters?' As she asked the question, the woman produced a warrant card. Peters nodded, puzzled for a moment until she spoke again. 'I'm Detective Sergeant Mironova from Helmsdale CID, and this is my colleague Detective Constable Pearce. May we come inside, please?'

Peters gasped, his face reflecting his astonishment. 'I was just about to ring you. Is this about Bridget?'

'I think it would be better if we talk inside, if you don't mind?'

'Yes, of course, come in.' He stood aside to allow them to enter, suddenly afraid that they were here with bad news. While on board ship, he'd watched plenty of movies and TV cop shows, and this was always the way the police approached delivering unacceptable information.

He showed them into the lounge and gestured for them to sit down, but they remained standing. 'What's happened? Is Bridget all right? She isn't in any trouble, is she?'

'Why were you going to phone us?'

'To report Bridget missing. I came home two nights ago and I can't find her anywhere. Please, can you tell me what's going on?'

'You said you came home. Does that mean you've been away?'

'I've been on my final tour of duty. I was in the Royal Navy. We've been at sea for nine months, mainly in the Med and the Middle East.'

He noticed the detectives exchanging glances, and was about to ask why they were questioning him about his movements, when the woman said, 'I'm afraid we've got some bad news for you, Mr Peters. Why don't you sit down?'

'No, I'll stand.' He could feel his heartbeat quicken, scared of what was to come.

'A woman's body was discovered in the woods nearby, and our officers found a handbag at the scene, complete with identification belonging to a Bridget Peters of this address.'

As she was speaking, Clara glanced at the photographs on the sideboard. She gestured towards it, adding, 'That photo together with the image on the driving licence we have . . . I'm sorry to have to tell you that it *was* your wife's body.'

Warren sank onto the sofa. It was quite a while before he recovered sufficiently to speak. 'What happened? How did she die? She didn't kill herself, did she?'

'We have to await the inquest, but the post-mortem indicates that your wife was the subject of foul play.'

It was this final piece of information that broke Peters' calm. He began to cry, his first reaction, a telling one about the state of the marriage. 'Poor Bridget — I know we haven't been getting on well, but she didn't deserve that, whatever she's done wrong.'

He looked at the detectives, tears glistening against the tan on his cheeks. 'Do you know who did this? Bridget was harmless. She wouldn't hurt a fly. Why kill her and leave her out there all alone?'

'That is what we're trying to find out, Mr Peters. Are you certain you've no idea who might have done this to her? Is there anyone you know of who had reason to harm her?'

He shook his head, the shock of what they had told him still failing to register properly. The next questions, although delicately phrased, indicated the way the police officers were thinking. 'What was the state of your marriage, Mr Peters? Were you and Bridget happy together?'

Again, it was a while before Peters replied. 'We got married in a hurry.' He smiled sadly. 'Remember the old saying, "marry in haste, and repent at leisure"? Well it was a bit like that. We both acknowledged that it was a mistake, but we knew we would have to live with it. Once we accepted that, we got along OK.' He grimaced slightly as he added, 'Maybe the fact that I was away at sea for months at a time stopped us from falling out.'

'Do you know if she was seeing anyone else?'

Peters shrugged. Viv Pearce, who was watching the man's body language, later told Lisa Andrews that it was probably the saddest gesture he'd ever seen.

'She might have been, but as I was thousands of miles away until two days ago, how would I know?'

'So you weren't aware that Bridget was pregnant?'

'I . . . er . . . I'm not sure.'

'You're not sure if you knew or not? You're going to have to explain that statement, because it doesn't make sense.'

'I spoke to her yesterday. When I found she'd disappeared I kept trying her mobile, and eventually she answered. It was totally weird, the way she spoke, and then hung up on me. In the middle of it, she said she was pregnant. But it was such an odd call I didn't know whether to believe her or not.'

'Was that why you asked if she'd committed suicide, because she'd told you she was expecting another man's child? Was Bridget so afraid of you?'

'Not likely. She'd be quite ready to stand up for herself.'

'OK, can you give us details of your movements since you returned home?'

Peters had been staring at the carpet, still reeling mentally from the news. His head came up abruptly at Mironova's question. 'You don't think I killed her?'

'It's standard procedure, Mr Peters. We need to know your movements so we can rule you out.'

Or rule me in, he thought. 'I arrived home shortly after midnight two nights ago. I was on the last train into Netherdale, and I'd expected Bridget to be there to collect me. I waited, but she didn't arrive and there were no taxis.' He shook his head as if he needed to explain. 'They never return when they've picked up after the final train.'

Mironova nodded, encouraging him to continue.

'I had to walk across town to the rank. The driver didn't want to take me, said he'd be missing out on a few fares, so I'd to bung him extra. The only time I've been out of the house is to ask my neighbour Mrs Peabody about Bridget. I also checked with Jim at the village shop, but nobody's seen her.'

Clara nodded at Pearce, who put his notebook away as she said, 'OK, that's all for now, Mr Peters. We will need you to come to Netherdale mortuary to carry out formal identification, and also to the police station to make a formal statement. I can arrange that for tomorrow if it's convenient?'

Peters shrugged despondently. 'Why not? I've nothing else to do, nowhere to go.'

'Have you anyone we can call, someone to be with you? What about family?'

'No, no, I'll be OK. There is no one.'

He let the detectives out and closed the door. It was only then, as he trudged wearily back along the hallway he realized how utterly alone he was. Despite their differences, despite everything he'd thought, and sometimes said, about Bridget, she had been a companion. He would miss that, and her, more than he'd ever thought possible.

* * *

Once they were clear of the house, Clara told Viv, 'I'm going to have a word with the neighbour, see if she verifies what he told us. Will you do the same at the village shop?'

'OK, but I think it's fairly cut and dried, don't you? Peters has been away for nine months. He comes home, discovers his wife has been having it off with someone else, and is now up the duff with this other bloke's bar steward. If that's not sufficient reason for him to strangle her, I don't know what is.'

'Viv, how many times has Mike warned us against taking things at face value?'

'I know, I know. But I'm willing to bet I'm right on this occasion.'

Clara stared at him for a moment as she considered what he'd said, then replied, 'And I'm convinced that you're wrong, so why don't we have a small wager?'

'I'm up for that. What's the stake?'

'How about the loser works the next two weekend shifts the winner is on the rota for?'

Pearce, who had a young child hesitated, but agreed, reluctantly. He failed to see Clara's smile as she turned to walk away.

He wandered into the village shop and showed the elderly owner his warrant card. 'I wonder if you know one of the villagers, Mrs Bridget Peters? If so, can you tell me when you last saw her?'

'Aye, I do that. Come to think on it, her husband were in here yesterday, asking t' same thing. I told him just what I'll tell thee. She were in 'ere last weekend getting stuff for when Warren come 'ome. Even got some o' that fancy Eyetalian grub 'e's got a likin' fer. I reckon it's all that travelling 'e does. 'E's in t' Royal Navy, tha knows.' The shopkeeper looked at Pearce, his expression troubled. 'I 'ope nowt's 'appened to 'er. She's a reet nice lass, bonny too.'

'I'm afraid I'm not allowed to divulge anything at this stage.' Pearce thanked the shopkeeper, and as the detective walked away, the old man thought that not being allowed to divulge anything meant that something bad *had* definitely happened to Bridget.

Pearce strolled back to where Mironova's car was parked, his expression thoughtful. Arriving there at the same time as Clara, he listened as she confirmed the neighbour had also been questioned by Peters about Bridget's absence.

'I wish I hadn't taken that bet now,' Pearce said ruefully.

As they were setting off back to Helmsdale, Clara let him out of his misery. 'I'm going to release you from the bet, because what I didn't tell you is that I had inside information that points to his innocence. I only need one piece of corroborative evidence to prove I'm right, and that should be easy to obtain.' She explained her reasoning, adding that it had only been by pure chance that she knew of Peters' likely innocence. 'Now all we have to do is get that confirmation. As punishment for your rash gamble, you can obtain that for us.'

Relieved to be free of the wager, Viv readily agreed, and said, 'I realized I was wrong, when the neighbour and the shopkeeper backed his story about asking after his wife. I don't reckon Peters is devious enough to have thought that up on the spur of the moment. That would argue premeditation. This crime seems to me to be more a heat of the moment act of violence.'

* * *

The next task was to complete the formal identification of the body and take Peters' formal statement. The following morning, having sent a patrol car to collect him, Clara met the bereaved husband at Netherdale General, where the mortuary attendant had prepared the corpse for inspection. Peters took a long, searching look at the woman lying on the table in the drab surroundings of the morgue, and then turned away. 'Yes. That's her,' he told the detective. 'That's Bridget. Can we leave now?'

Once outside the building, he leaned against the wall, breathing heavily as if he'd been running. Until that time, he'd maintained a small, unlikely hope that it had all been a ghastly mix-up of some kind, and that the dead woman might not be his wife, but now even that was gone.

He failed to respond the first time Mironova spoke, so she had to repeat her question. 'Would it be OK for you to go to Helmsdale with this officer?' She gestured to the waiting patrolman. 'We need you to make a formal statement of everything you told us yesterday, plus anything else that might be relevant.' She paused, noting the distress evident from his expression and added, 'I'm sorry, but it would be helpful while it's still fresh in your mind.'

'I'd rather get it over with.'

Mironova was in the process of instructing the officer when her mobile rang. She glanced at the screen, turned away, and greeted the caller. 'Ah, the wanderer returns. You might have been told that some of us have been kept busy while you went swanning off to Manchester.'

Nash calmly responded, 'It makes a pleasant change, because usually I'm the only one to do any work. Viv's brought me up to speed, and on the face of it, it seemed the husband is the likely prime suspect. But I understand you have other ideas. Are you bringing Peters in for questioning?'

'I am, but not as a suspect.' Clara glanced round the car park. 'In fact, he's already en route. I would be too if people didn't keep ringing me. Mr Peters confirmed the body is that of his wife, and I agree it would be easy to think of this as an open-and-shut case. He knew his wife was pregnant with someone else's baby, so he could be seen to have killed her out of jealousy . . . but for one important fact that I hope Viv will have verified by now.'

'Do you want to tell me now, or can it wait until you're back at the ranch?'

'I'll leave it for the time being. I shouldn't be long — provided there are no further interruptions.'

* * *

When she reached Helmsdale, Clara asked Peters if he'd mind waiting until she'd spoken to her boss, and then went upstairs, where Nash waved her into his office. 'OK,' he greeted her, 'what's wrong with Peters as our prime suspect?'

'In the first place, as soon as we spoke to him, I thought he didn't fit the bill. He openly admitted that the marriage was far from perfect, and that he and his wife simply shared the same house. I think the fact that he was away so much might have contributed to that. But if the love was dead, he'd hardly be likely to have strangled his wife in a fit of jealousy the minute he got home. Then, after Peters told us about his return, I realized that as long as he was telling the truth, he couldn't have murdered her. All I need is verification as to when the taxi dropped him off at Drover's Halt. Hopefully, Viv will have got that by now.'

'He has,' Nash agreed. 'He spoke to the taxi driver while you were at the mortuary, and he confirmed that he arrived at Peters' house shortly after midnight, and Peters had luggage with him. Why does that prove he didn't kill his wife?'

'If you've read the autopsy findings you'll have seen that Mexican Pete gave an approximate time of death, but I can narrow that down even further.'

'Explain, please.'

'At the scene when the mortuary attendants moved the body they noticed the ground under where she was lying was bone dry. Meaning she'd been placed there *before* the rain started. I know for a fact that it began raining heavily before eleven o'clock that night.'

'How did you know that? I thought by then you'd have been snuggled under the duvet with David.'

Clara blushed slightly, but explained, 'I was. But the rain was so heavy that it was lashing against our bedroom window, so fiercely it kept me awake. I looked at my bedside clock and it was showing twenty-two forty-five.'

'That sounds fairly conclusive.' Nash noticed the frown on Mironova's face and said, 'Is there something else?'

'There is, but I've no idea what to make of it.'

'Go on, try me.'

'When we spoke to Peters yesterday, he told us he'd kept trying his wife's mobile, phoning her and sending texts, but got no response. He even talked to a neighbour, and asked after her at the village shop, but nobody had seen her since last weekend. Then he said the weirdest thing. He was about to report her as a MISPER, but before doing so, he tried her phone one more time. He said she answered and they had a five-minute conversation. During this, Bridget told him it was all over and that she was two months pregnant.'

'Hang on. Did you say this all happened during the afternoon following his return home?'

'Yes. But I don't see how that's possible, because by my reckoning Bridget Peters had been dead for at least sixteen hours by then.'

There was a long silence as Nash tried to come to terms with Clara's baffling report. Eventually, he came up with an idea which would eradicate Peters as a suspect. 'You said Peters is here waiting to give a statement, right?'

Clara nodded, wondering where Nash was going with this. 'Then why not get Viv to take a look at Peters' phone — with his permission, of course. If there was such a conversation, it would show up in the call log. It would be far longer duration than if it went straight to voicemail.'

'OK, but what if there *was* such a call? How do we explain that, and what should we do next?' Clara asked.

'I've no idea, except perhaps consulting a local spiritualist.'

* * *

It only took Viv a few minutes to search Peters' phone's log, and confirm there was a call that lasted four minutes and forty-three seconds. 'It was placed at four-fifteen on the afternoon following Peters' arrival home — the number belonged to Bridget Peters. He either spent a long time listening to the voicemail message, or he spoke to someone on that number,' he told them.

He also reported a host of abortive calls and frequent text messages. 'Every call but one lasted less than a minute, some only ten seconds or so. My guess is those went straight to voicemail. Most of the shorter ones were later on, so possibly Mr Peters had got fed up of leaving messages, and simply ended the call as soon as the recorded message started. There were earlier calls. I've checked, and some were to local hospitals, which confirm he was looking for her.'

Armed with the information culled by Pearce, Nash and Clara went into the interview room where Peters was waiting. They took him through the questions he'd answered previously, but this time for the benefit of the recording. Once he had repeated his previous answers, almost verbatim, Nash turned to the subject of the mystery phone call. Again, Peters' recollection of the conversation matched one he had given earlier. He then asked why the detectives were so interested in that call.

Nash didn't answer him directly, but instead asked, 'And you are absolutely certain it was Bridget that you were speaking to?'

'Of course I'm sure it was Bridget. I think I'd recognize my own wife's voice.'

'What was strange about the way she spoke to you? You inferred something of the sort to my colleagues yesterday.'

Peters hesitated, before saying, 'I was too upset at the time, what with her not answering sooner, and then telling me she was pregnant. But later, once I'd cooled off a bit, I did think she was behaving oddly. Every time I asked her something she waited for ages before she replied — and when she did speak, it was almost like she was reading off a script.'

That final word gave Nash an idea. He leaned forward as he asked, 'Could it have been a recording?'

Peters stared at the detectives, puzzled. 'I suppose so, but that's weird. Why do you ask? I fail to see why this is so important.'

Clara wasn't sure whether Nash would be prepared to reveal what they knew.

He was, and his reply stunned Peters. 'We believe it is highly important, because we know beyond a shadow of doubt that at the time your conversation took place, your wife was already dead.'

It was a long time before the full implication of Nash's words struck home. Even then, Peters was barely able to grasp what he'd been told, so Nash explained further. 'That means the evidence we have obtained proves conclusively that you could not have killed your wife. The phone call merely clouds the issue, but our priority, from here on in, is to discover who was responsible. The next question I'm going to ask might prove painful, but we know that Bridget was pregnant and that you were not the father. Do you have any idea who she was seeing, or who might be responsible?'

'Absolutely not. I was away for long periods, and I had no knowledge of how she spent her time while I was at sea. I definitely wasn't aware that she was in a relationship.'

'Could it have been the result of a casual encounter — a one-night fling, perhaps?'

'I very much doubt it. Bridget wasn't the sort to indulge in anything of that nature.' Peters smiled sadly. 'Although I tried to get her into bed a few times during the early stages of our relationship, it was only after we became engaged that we began sleeping together.'

'You said you had no idea how she passed her time while you were away, but presumably she had a job. Where did she work?'

'Actually, she'd resigned from her job. I only found out when I rang her employer, and was told she quit six weeks or so back. She worked as an accounts clerk for Walmsley's, the chartered accountants in Helmsdale. I was surprised she packed it in, though, because she enjoyed her job.'

'You have been extremely helpful, Mr Peters, and it leads me to another request I have to make. Normally, in order to search someone's house we would require a warrant, but would you give your consent to us doing so without going through that rigmarole? We might well draw a complete blank, but there is always the outside chance that we might find a clue as to who murdered Bridget.'

There was no hesitation before Peters replied, 'By all means. If it helps catch the bastard who killed her, go ahead.'

CHAPTER FOURTEEN

Nash organized a forensic team to join them at Warren Peters' house. On the drive over, he explained his request to Peters. 'You did tell us there seemed to be nothing out of the ordinary in or outside the house, but these guys are experts, and they could find something that ordinary folks, such as you and I, might miss. There's also the possibility of them discovering evidence that isn't visible to the naked eye, such as finger-prints. I'm not suggesting that anything positive will emerge, but we would be neglecting our duty if we didn't try.'

Peters listened as Nash continued, 'In the meantime, I want you to concentrate on the house as you found it when you returned. In particular, I want you to try and remember anything that was out of place, or something that you found that shouldn't have been there. Alternatively, and possibly even more important, try and think of anything you might have expected to see, but was missing. It might be the small-est, seemingly unimportant thing, but it might prove crucial.'

Although Peters concentrated on the question, it wasn't until the vehicle, he mentally dubbed as the search party, pulled up outside the house that he came up with an idea. 'Bridget's diary,' he said abruptly, breaking the silence and startling Nash and Mironova.

'Sorry, what about it?'

'Bridget kept a diary. It was nothing dramatic, no great piece of literature, just a record of her day-to-day life. She usually had it on the dressing table in her bedroom. Although we hadn't been sharing a bedroom for a long time, there was the odd occasion when I . . . er . . .' he fumbled for a polite way of expressing what he had to say in front of a lady, 'when I was granted visiting rights. I teased her about the diary once, asking if she was recording my performance.'

'What caused your relationship to break down?' Nash asked him.

'It didn't break down as such, we merely drifted apart. I suppose I'm as much to blame for that as Bridget. She thrived on company, and enjoyed the social side of life, whereas I was more content being on my own. It must have been very lonely for her, stuck out here while I was away. The village is more of a dormitory these days, so there's not much to get involved with locally. I can understand her need to seek consolation elsewhere, and I'd accept my share of the blame if that happened. Although I wouldn't have been happy giving a home to another man's bastard.'

'Would you have considered asking her to abort the child, or seeking a divorce?' Clara asked.

'Neither of those would ever be an option. Bridget and her family were Catholics. Although her parents are long dead, and she has no siblings, she would never have agreed to a divorce, and likewise, an abortion would have been regarded as murder.'

By this time, the forensic team was ready to begin work, so Peters handed over the house keys and, in response to their leader's question, told him, 'No, there are no alarms on either of the doors, or intruder alarms in the rooms. That sort of precaution has never been necessary round here.'

The officers discovered nothing out of the ordinary inside the house, or the garage, but when they moved on to inspect the exterior of the property it was a different matter. Noting the weed-free, well-cultivated borders, and the immaculately cut lawn, Nash, who knew from personal experience how time-consuming the work was, asked Peters, 'Do you employ a gardener?'

'No, Bridget does all the work — did all the work. I was hugely surprised when she showed so much interest, but she really enjoyed it. Bridget was like that — she never conformed to people's expectations of her. I'd say gardening was the love of her life — that, and Bruno of course. Sadly, I wasn't on that list.'

'Sorry, who's Bruno?'

'Bruno was Bridget's dog. She got him as a puppy a good many years back. Unfortunately, he died a few months ago. When I spoke to her after it happened, she was inconsolable. I don't know if I could have comforted her, even if I'd been at home. But I certainly couldn't do much when I was over a thousand miles away.'

'What breed was Bruno?' Mironova's question amused Nash, but it was only when Peters answered that he realized why.

'A Boxer. That's why she called him Bruno.'

Fortunately for the detectives, one of the forensic team was a keen amateur botanist. As he approached the greenhouse, he noticed something on the ground that made him stop in his tracks, and order his colleague to do likewise. He bent over, peering at something in the soft earth alongside the path. As he straightened up, he said, 'Would you bring the sleuths here? I want them to take a look at what I've just found.'

The botanist indicated the item that had caught his attention. 'This is part of a bracken leaf,' he explained to the detectives. 'At a guess, I'd say it was stuck to the sole of someone's shoe or boot, and came loose just here.'

'Why is that important?' Nash asked.

'Because it doesn't belong in this garden. This area is too well tended, and there aren't any here. It's found principally in woodland. What is more significant is that I noticed several of these close to where Bridget Peters' body was found.

That leads me to wonder if this was brought here on the killer's shoe.'

'Why would the murderer want to come here?' This time, it was Mironova who got the question in first.

'Maybe the answer will be in there.' Nash indicated the nearby greenhouse. 'Have you guys looked inside yet?'

'No,' the team leader replied. 'We were all set to, but then David Attenborough here stopped us.'

Their search of the interior of the greenhouse looked like drawing a blank. Watching from outside, Nash noticed the tomatoes and courgettes, ripe and ready to harvest, along the benches on each side of the building's interior. Their presence underlined the accuracy of Peters' comment about his wife's horticultural prowess. As they were about to retreat, having discovered nothing of interest, one of the officers moved a stack of empty plant pots under the bench nearest the door. As he did so, he heard something rattle inside the second pot down. He peered inside, pulled the object out, and realized it had absolutely nothing whatsoever to do with gardening.

He held the mobile phone up for the others to see. They stared at the gaudily decorated case, and Peters told them, 'That's Bridget's mobile. I'd recognize that cover anywhere.'

* * *

Although the forensic team finished their work without any further surprises, in view of what they had found, Nash suggested that he and Mironova should take another look inside the house.

'Can I help?' Peters asked.

Although Nash recognized the man's need to become involved, he explained that it was not possible. 'The search has to be conducted by officers, whose impartiality cannot be called into question at a later date.'

'You're talking about some smart-arse defence lawyer again, aren't you?'

Nash agreed, and Peters accepted this. To alleviate the man's obvious disappointment, Nash asked, 'I don't suppose by any chance you make a half-decent cup of coffee, do you?'

'I can certainly do that. How do you take it?'

Having stated their preferences, Nash and Mironova began their inspection. Nash asked Clara to concentrate on the first storey of the building, while he searched the ground floor.

Although not involved directly, Peters watched Nash's activity with interest, noting the extreme thoroughness shown by the detective, even to the extent of examining the contents of the chest freezer in the utility room. After a short coffee break, they resumed work. It was half an hour later, when Peters was about to ask if they wanted a refill, that Clara emerged from Bridget's bedroom and called for Nash.

When he reached the foot of the stairs, he saw Clara brandishing a slim volume in her gloved hand. 'Is that—?'

'The diary? It certainly is. I found it hidden under a couple of scarves inside a shoe box at the back of her wardrobe.'

'I think we should take it back to the station, and hand it over to the boffins. When they've finished with it, then we can look through the entries.'

Nash scribbled out a receipt to Peters for the diary and the mobile phone. 'Legally speaking, you're the owner of these items, so we need to ensure everything is done by the book,' he explained.

Privately, Clara asked Nash why the diary interested him so much. 'Mr Peters told us that when he saw Bridget's diary, the entries were mundane, run-of-the-mill stuff, nothing to get excited about.'

'That may have been so, previously. But if there was nothing controversial inside that book, why go to such extreme lengths to hide it?'

* * *

That evening, when Clara entered the apartment she shared with her fiancé, she was surprised to see the table set for dinner, with candles glowing in the centre. One of her favourite pieces of music was playing softly on the music centre, and a bottle of red wine was open on the sideboard, the empty glasses awaiting their contents. An appetising aroma wafted through from the kitchen. As she was taking all this in, David appeared in the archway between the rooms, a welcoming smile on his face.

'OK,' Clara said, with a gesture to the table, 'what's this about? What have you done wrong? Don't tell me you've broken one of my favourite ornaments.'

'I haven't done anything wrong, at least, I hope not,' David protested. 'Let me explain.'

Still smiling at David's explanation, Clara greeted Nash the next morning then said, 'You'll never guess, Mike. . . When I got home last night, David had a big surprise waiting for me.'

Nash hid a smile as he replied, 'Are you sure I want to hear this?'

'That's not what I meant, and you know it.' She shook her head, tutted, and continued, 'He'd prepared a lovely meal for us, and it was all to celebrate the new job he's got. I knew he had something in mind, but when he said he'd rejoined the army, I was angry at first. That was until he explained he isn't to be a frontline soldier. His new posting is local, but he'll travel to other parts of Britain acting as a liaison officer, helping men who have returned from war zones. They could be suffering from either physical or mental problems, such as PTSD. David will help co-ordinate their return to civilian life or, alternatively, assist them through the rehabilitation process. The inspiration for this came from helping Lance Corporal Fulton after he was attacked.'

'That's great news, Clara. Please tell him I think it's a brilliant idea.'

'Er, that's not all.'

'No?'

'No, now he's sure he's going to be UK-based, he, er, said it's time we got married.' She bit her bottom lip. 'I'm sorry, Mike, I didn't want to steal your thunder, but David and I have been together such a long time.'

Nash jumped to his feet. 'Clara, that's wonderful news. I'm delighted for you both. When do you think it will be?' he asked, as he hugged his smiling sergeant.

'Soon, apparently.' She laughed. 'David is treating it like a military exercise, and has already been making enquiries at the Registrar's Office. He said he's sourced a reception, and knows where we're going on honeymoon — for Christmas.'

At the office door, Steve Meadows appeared, clutching a small package. 'Oh, sorry, am I interrupting?'

'Certainly not. We're just celebrating the fact that Clara is at last going to marry her soldier.'

'Congratulations, Clara.' He smiled at her, then added, 'This has just arrived.' Seeing their wary expressions, he explained, 'Don't worry, it's only the diary and phone you asked Forensics to examine. They said to tell you they found nothing by way of fingerprints or DNA, other than the victim's. There was nothing of significance on the phone, but they thought you'd be interested in one or two of the more recent entries in the diary.'

He handed it to Nash and wandered away, smiling at both Clara's news, and the alarm he'd caused.

Nash extracted the book, and began examining the entries covering the past few months. Bridget's distress over the declining health of her beloved pet was obvious from the moment she first took Bruno to the vet's. That anguish had increased sharply, when the diagnosis revealed that the dog's ailment was so serious the only option was to have him put down.

The entries for the week following this terrible news centred purely on her decision to proceed with the euthanasia of Bruno, plus the selection of a burial site in Layton Woods, close to his home. The place where Bruno had loved to walk, giving him chance to indulge in fruitless pursuits of rabbits, squirrels and pheasants.

Nash read the next entry aloud, the sadness reflecting in his sombre tone of voice. "'*Tomorrow I will lose my best friend, my constant and loyal companion. I will take him to his favourite place, and lay him to rest there. The task is daunting enough, both physically and emotionally, but fortunately a friend has volunteered to help by carrying Bruno to the site, and also to dig the grave for me.*"

Nash's mood turned to anger as he read the next entry. "*'I was heartbroken when I lost sight of Bruno when the earth covered his noble head, and sleek-coated body. My friend comforted me, and then suddenly everything went wrong. I had asked for nothing more than a little solace, an easing of my grief, but he must have thought I wanted more, and he was too strong for me to fight off. As soon as I could free myself I came home and spent hours in the shower, trying in vain to wash away my shame.*'"

Nash looked at Clara, and her expression mirrored his anger. 'That sounds like rape to me. Taking advantage of this poor woman at such a time is totally despicable.'

Later diary entries covered her discovery that she was pregnant, and the need to confront the man who had assaulted her. Once again, Bridget had referred to him only as "her friend", causing Clara to wonder why that was, and to comment, 'With friends like that, who needs enemies?'

Nash thought for a second, and then said, 'That's why the diary was hidden. Perhaps Bridget was afraid if Warren found it and discovered the man's identity, he might go seeking vengeance.'

They sat for a while, pondering their next course of action, until Nash suggested, 'Perhaps we should find the dog's grave and exhume the pet.'

Clara looked at him, her surprise apparent. 'What would that achieve?'

'We need a sample of Bruno's hair. If the man carried the dog to the grave site, there is a good chance of transfer onto his clothing, and DNA testing would establish if those hairs belong to Bruno.'

'I take it you're assuming that the man who raped Bridget is the same person who murdered her?'

'I think that's a fairly obvious conclusion to draw, don't you? Finding him might be a nightmare, though,' Nash said, as he took out his phone to speak to Forensics.

Clara went through to the general office to update Viv and Lisa, and to tell them about the wedding. As the call connected, Nash closed his office door to block the squeals of delight from Lisa at Clara's news.

The forensic team leader couldn't understand why Nash wanted them to return to Layton Woods and seemed aggrieved that the detective implied they had missed something. Even when Nash explained what he wanted them to do, the officer resisted, saying that he could not see what that might achieve, and would merely be a waste of time and resources. 'You said you want us to exhume a body that you believe is close to where Bridget Peters was found, correct?' The man sounded horrified by the idea. 'How many people do you think have been buried there?'

Nash smiled as he corrected him. 'It isn't a person, it's a dog. Bridget Peters' dog, to be precise.' He continued by explaining his reason for the request, adding, 'I know it might seem like a long shot, but sometimes outsiders *do* win races.'

'OK, if we're not needed elsewhere, we'll go there this afternoon, it should only need two of us. At least the rain's stopped.'

* * *

It was a while before they located the grave. The site was sheltered on one side by a line of trees that marked the edge of the forest. A tiny, crudely constructed wooden cross marked the spot, the name *Bruno* inscribed in shaky lettering on the cross member.

The forensic officers began to loosen the soil, a task made easier following the recent rain, and they were soon able to uncover the remains of the animal. As one of them was preparing to remove a sample of the dog's hair, his colleague restrained him, one gloved hand on the man's arm as he pointed with the other. 'What do you think that is in the top corner?'

Together, they peered at the object lying alongside the dog's collar and lead. The metal surface glinted in the weak sunshine. At first, they thought it might part of the collar, but the size and shape seemed all wrong. The first officer reached in with his trowel and carefully lifted the item clear. He stared at it for a second before rubbing some of the loose soil from the surface. Glancing across to where the detectives were standing, he called out, 'Inspector Nash, I think you ought to see this.'

Nash and Mironova looked at the item on the trowel. 'That looks like a cigarette lighter,' Clara commented.

Nash picked it up, turned it over, and rubbed with his gloved hands at the base of the small oblong metal container. 'You're dead right, Clara, but it isn't any old cigarette lighter. This one was manufactured by Dunhill, and their products are highly expensive. I believe some of the older ones are considered collector's items.'

He handed it back to the officer. 'I want that back the minute you've tested it. For all we know, you might just have unearthed the clue that helps us trap Bridget Peters' murderer.' He looked at their team leader, who was standing nearby, and added, 'I told you it wasn't a fruitless exercise.'

* * *

Late that afternoon, Steve Meadows brought them another package which he handed to Nash. 'I suppose this one could cause an explosion,' he said with a smile. 'It's that cigarette lighter you found in the dog's grave. There's an email report to follow.'

Nash and Mironova examined the Dunhill. 'This lighter has been well used,' Nash commented. 'You can tell by the wear and tear. And I reckon it's been dropped at some point, judging by that big dent on the edge of the cap.'

As he turned it over, Clara pointed to the base. 'There's a serial number on it. Do you think that might help us trace the owner?'

'I've no idea. I reckon the best way to find out would be by asking an expert. There isn't a tobacconist in Helmsdale any longer, but there is one in Netherdale. I've to go through there tomorrow, so I'll call at the shop.'

'Oh, you're off to the big city, are you? Any particular reason, or is it simply work avoidance?'

'The chief and I have a meeting with the officers from West Yorkshire, East Yorkshire, and Teesside who are heading up this region's section of the County Lines operation. I'm hoping this will be the last one I'm involved in, because it's taking up more than enough of my time. I ought to be concentrating my efforts on the murders.'

Nash was about to add that he hoped there wouldn't be any further killings, but remembered Sod's Law and decided against voicing that thought.

CHAPTER FIFTEEN

The tobacconist was an elderly man, who, Nash guessed, would have retired a good while ago, had he not been self-employed. Luckily, although his physical powers might have diminished with age, there was nothing wrong with his mental faculties. He only needed one swift glance to identify the lighter Nash was holding.

'That's a Dunhill Rollagas Signature — you don't see many of those about. They made them in gold or silver plate. The one you've got is the gold version, and that's worth around five hundred and fifty quid these days.'

'Is it possible to identify either the owner, or the retailer who sold it, via the serial number on the base?'

'I suppose if you were really lucky you might be able to trace the retailer, but I can't be sure. As for tracing the owner, I wouldn't hold your breath. That would only be possible if you could find the shop, and if they still kept a record of the transaction.' He paused before expanding on the last comment, 'To put what you're asking in perspective, I think it was around 1986 or 1987 that Dunhill started putting serial numbers on their lighters. As these are sold worldwide, I reckon it would be a bit like looking for a needle in a haystack.'

'Are they still widely available?'

'Not really. They're an expensive item to stock. And with all the anti-smoking malarkey, and those do-good campaigners warning of the evils of tobacco, the demand for lighters is much lower than it used to be. Having said that, I did sell a second-hand one recently.' The old man smiled. 'Made a nice boost to my takings.'

Nash left the shop bearing a copy of the sales receipt from that transaction. He was now confident that having discovered the identity of the person who had bought the lighter, he also knew who had murdered Bridget Peters. Proving it, however, was likely to prove far from easy.

On his return to Helmsdale, after the meeting at HQ, Nash glanced round the CID suite. 'Where's Lisa?' he asked.

'She's gone to Netherdale. Some young lad's been caught pilfering food off one of the market stalls. Unfortunately for the thief, the stallholder took photos of him on his mobile, and one of the uniform guys recognized the youth. Lisa's gone to confront the parents and give the lad a good talking-to. The stuff he nicked was only worth around a fiver, so the greengrocer isn't too bothered about pressing charges. He just wants the lad teaching a lesson. It was a toss-up who went to deal with it, and Lisa called wrong.'

'OK, Clara, will you and Viv come into my office? I've some work for you — for all of us in fact.'

'Before we start, Mike, I've had a look through the forensic report on Bruno's grave. They think they'll be able to get the dog's DNA, for any potential match. They also managed to retrieve a fingerprint from the lighter. It's only a partial, and it's fairly smudged, so they don't think they'll be able to get a hundred per cent likeness, if we get a suspect.'

'That's not going to prove very useful,' Nash responded. He looked at Pearce. 'Viv, I want you to work your magic on the computer and find out everything you can about this man.' He handed Pearce a sheet of paper.

Glancing over his shoulder, Clara frowned. 'That name rings a bell. Where have I heard it before?'

'Warren Peters. He told us his wife worked for a firm of chartered accountants called Walmsley's.' Nash gestured to the receipt Pearce was holding. 'I'm willing to bet that the man who bought this lighter, and paid for it with a credit card in the name of G. Walmsley, is her former employer, or a close relative of his. I'm also willing to bet he is the man who raped, and later murdered, Bridget Peters. The fact that he bought a used Dunhill lighter identical to the one we found in Bruno's grave, suggests to me that he needed to replace one he'd lost before someone started asking awkward questions. Only now,' — Nash smiled, grimly — 'we're going to be the ones asking awkward questions.'

Fifteen minutes later, Pearce reported back. 'You were spot on, Mike. This Geoffrey Walmsley' — he indicated the receipt — 'is a chartered accountant. He and his wife live at Gorton Park.'

Clara drew a sharp intake of breath. 'Gorton Park, that's the damned great mansion you can just see through the trees along the road to Gorton village.'

'Is that the one with the huge lake in front of it?'

'That's the one, Mike. There must be more money in cooking the books than I ever imagined.'

'I'm not sure that's the case, Clara,' Viv told her. 'I had a word with Tom Pratt. The disadvantage of Jack retiring is we've one less source of local knowledge — besides missing the gossip and scandal. Anyway, Tom told me a fair bit about Walmsley, or to be precise, Walmsley's wife. Caroline Walmsley owns the land on which Helmsdale Golf Club is situated, hence Tom knowing so much about her.'

'I knew I should have taken up golf,' Nash muttered.

'Anyway, Tom reckons all the money comes from Caroline's family. Before she married, she was one of the Hendersons. They own three big quarries, and a large amount of the aggregate dug out of them formed the hard core under the M1 and M62 motorways. According to local gossip, Caroline is more interested in anything with four legs, a tail and runs quickly, than in anything else.' Pearce grinned as he added, 'Opinion on Geoffrey is divided. Tom reckons that half the local people have Walmsley down as a waster — the other half think he's just a loser.'

Having learned this background information, Nash suggested that he and Clara should visit Geoffrey Walmsley, and question him about Bridget Peters' murder. 'What's more,' he added, 'I think we should do so immediately.'

Clara glanced at the wall clock and pointed out that the offices would be closed by this time. 'Accountants don't keep the same weird hours that we do.'

'That's OK, Clara,' Nash responded with a wicked smile, 'if you don't mind slumming it? I thought we should visit Walmsley at Gorton Park. That way, if his wife is in residence, we might get more information from him there, than talking to him in his office where he would feel more comfortable.'

On arrival at Gorton Park, Clara half-expected them to be greeted by a butler. However, there was no response when they rang the doorbell, although they could hear the deep, mellow chimes resonating within the building and, in the distance, the deep tones of a barking dog.

They were about to depart, when an angry voice behind them said, 'Who are you, and what are you doing on my property?'

The detectives turned around to see a woman Clara guessed might be about her own age, although her thin, angular frame, and bony, almost skeletal features and leathery tan made her appear older. She was wearing cord trousers, a waxed shooting jacket with a cartridge belt around her waist, and was carrying a shotgun over one arm. The sense of relief Clara felt on seeing that the gun was open, the empty barrels visible, was only minimal.

Nash produced his warrant card. 'I'm Detective Inspector Nash and this is my colleague, Detective Sergeant Mironova. We were hoping to have a word with Mr Geoffrey Walmsley.'

'He's away on business,' the woman snapped. 'What's this all about? Not another speeding ticket, surely?'

'Hardly.' Nash didn't hide his sarcasm. 'We don't deal with trivial matters. I assume you must be Mrs Walmsley. Do you always greet visitors with a .12 bore?'

'Not usually. We have a vermin problem — they need dealing with. I've called a halt because the light is fading. Now, why do you want to see my husband?'

'We're investigating the murder of Bridget Peters. Mrs Peters worked for your husband's firm until recently, and we need to ask Mr Walmsley about some evidence we discovered at the crime scene.'

'In that case, you'd better come inside. If you wait in the hall, I'll put this away.'

While they were waiting, a black Labrador entered the hallway and loped towards them. The dog sniffed at Nash's trousers and then circled him, tail wagging. Without thinking, Nash bent down and stroked the dog.

'Sorry, I have to keep her inside. She's in season.' Mrs Walmsley eyed Nash for a moment and asked, 'Do I take it you're a dog owner? She doesn't usually respond well to strangers.'

'You could put it down to my natural charm — or the fact I also have a black Lab.'

Caroline ushered them into the drawing room, and invited them to sit down. Much to Clara's surprise, Nash's interview technique was far different to any she'd seen him use before, and certainly not what she expected when he was speaking to a suspect's wife. He began by asking where Walmsley had gone, and how long he would be away.

'He's in Birmingham all week at a seminar. Something to do with his work, or so he claims. What's this evidence you want to ask him about?'

Nash pulled the clear plastic evidence bag from his pocket, and held it up. Caroline stared at it for a moment. 'That's a Dunhill, isn't it? Geoffrey has one like it. I bought it for him.'

'When was that?'

Caroline thought for only a second before replying, 'It was ten years ago. I'm not keen on him smoking, but it was all I could think of as an anniversary present. Much good it did me.'

Nash caught the note of bitterness in the woman's voice, but didn't appear to react, merely asking, 'If you bought a lighter identical to this one for him ten years ago, can you explain why he bought another one less than a months ago?'

Shock caused Caroline to remain silent for a moment. Then she said, 'All I can think of is the careless sod lost it.' It was only when she finished speaking that the implication behind Nash's question dawned on her. 'Can I see that lighter?' she demanded.

'You can, but please don't remove it from the bag, because the evidence must not be contaminated.'

She looked at the lighter as closely as the plastic would allow, turning it over several times, before handing it back to Nash. Clara noticed that Caroline's hands trembled, and her face was white with shock. There was a world of sadness in her voice as she told them, 'That's the lighter I bought him. There can be no mistaking it.'

'How come you're so certain?'

'You see that dent on the cap? He dropped the bloody thing only a couple of days after I gave him it. Not only did he damage the lighter, but when it dropped, the force of the fall broke one of the tiles on the conservatory floor. It cost me a small fortune to replace the broken tile. It's an Italian ceramic, with a very distinctive pattern,' she added.

'I assume you must have seen reports of the woman's murder either on the TV, or in the papers. Did your husband mention that Mrs Peters used to work for him?'

'No, he never said a word, even though we saw it on the local news.'

'Don't you think that's rather strange? Mrs Peters had worked for your husband for several years.'

'I don't think it's odd — I think it's bloody suspicious!' Caroline pointed to the evidence Nash was still holding. 'I assume from what you said earlier, that the lighter was found close to the body?'

'It was, but there's more, much more, I'm afraid. I wouldn't normally reveal facts such as these, but I think, in this instance, it's justified.'

As Nash outlined their suspicions, Clara watched Caroline carefully. The woman's expression changed from mild distaste, to revulsion, and a look that could only be described as outright hatred for her husband.

When they left the mansion an hour later, Clara was weighed down by the numerous evidence bags she was carrying. As they exited the front door, Nash asked Caroline when she expected her husband back. 'Friday afternoon, but I don't want him here.'

'Don't worry. We'll be waiting for him. He won't even reach your front door.'

'You'd better be. Because the way I feel at the moment, I'll be waiting with the shotgun — and next time, it *will* be loaded.'

* * *

On their return journey, Clara asked, 'What did you make of Caroline Walmsley?'

'At first glance, I thought we'd found Shergar.'

Clara laughed at his reference to the famous missing racehorse.

Nash continued, 'What I noticed almost immediately was that she seemed to have little, or no affection, or even respect, for her husband That was patently obvious by the fact she made no attempt to defend him.'

'Was that why you confided in her? I was astonished when you revealed as much as you did about what we suspect he's done.'

'Yes, because within minutes of talking to Caroline Walmsley, I recognized her type. Rigidly moral, and wouldn't be party to any misdemeanour, and too proud to reveal the content of our conversation to anyone. The way she spoke about him was also a big clue. I'd say there's very little love lost between them.'

'She certainly looked absolutely furious when you outlined the case against him.'

'She'd be angry for several reasons. For a start, there's the disgrace of being associated with someone who is likely to be convicted of murder. Then, there's the blow to her own self-esteem, being unable to control him as she would want. Finally, there's sympathy, for the victim and the bereaved husband. When I told her about Warren Peters' return home after a long absence serving Queen and country, she was very distressed. Once she knew the facts, she was more than happy to provide the contents in those evidence bags. If we're lucky, Forensics might get something from the footwear that will tie Walmsley to the crime scene. His clothing might provide traces of dog hair we can identify as belonging to Bruno. Above all, the sample we obtained from Walmsley's hairbrush, might give us a DNA match to the foetus Bridget Peters was carrying. We need to get the boffins working on these items ASAP, so we'll have the results by the time Walmsley returns from Birmingham.'

* * *

It was three days later when the reports came in on the samples they had provided. Having read through the paperwork, Nash told the team, 'I'd say this evidence is fairly conclusive, albeit mainly circumstantial.'

Lisa, who had been concentrating her efforts on the other murders, asked what the various pieces of information signified.

'First, we have the entry in Bridget Peters' diary which tells us exactly when, and where, the assault that resulted in her pregnancy occurred. That account tallies with the rare, and expensive, Dunhill lighter that must have been dropped as the suspect was burying the dog. Incidentally—' Nash held up a sheet of paper — 'I received this in the post today. It's a receipt Caroline Walmsley obtained when she bought her husband an identical lighter. I'm delighted to say that the receipt has the serial number of the lighter on it, and even happier to report that it tallies with the one Forensics found.'

Nash paused before turning to the scientific evidence. 'DNA testing proves that Walmsley was the father of the foetus, and dog hairs on a pair of his walking boots are a match to Bruno, Bridget Peters' dog. The key element to this last piece of evidence is that the hairs were embedded in soil matching that from the crime scene. Also present on the sole of one of the shoes was bracken, known to grow near where Bridget Peters' body was found.'

'How do you account for that weird phone call you mentioned, the one Warren Peters told you about?' Lisa asked.

'Having read the diary, and reviewed the statements Bridget supposedly made during that call, I believe they originated from a message she might have left on Walmsley's phone. By editing that message, he was able to construct replies that would suggest she was still alive after Warren returned from sea, thus making him the prime suspect. Once Peters began phoning her mobile, Walmsley knew he was home, and he could activate his plan. I believe he hid Bridget's mobile in the greenhouse to add more evidence against Warren. My guess is he believed the body would remain undiscovered for far longer, thus blurring the time of death. He obviously didn't reckon on either the change in weather conditions, or the gamekeeper's diligence.'

* * *

Geoffrey Walmsley yawned. It had been a tiring week, both at the seminar, and socially. Not all his activities had been linked to the business event. He'd taken the opportunity during his separation from his wife to become acquainted with a couple of young ladies. Admittedly, Geoffrey had to pay for the intimate services they provided, but the enjoyment had justified the cost. Unfortunately, the sums he'd paid could not be shown on his expense account, but you can't have everything.

One of the girls had demonstrated early on that she preferred their liaison to involve rough physical contact — which suited him just fine. He'd enjoyed the encounter with her so much that he'd visited a couple of times, and even retained her contact number for future reference. All he had to do was to find some excuse to revisit Birmingham.

As he turned off the main road, on the final leg of his journey home, Geoffrey noticed a police van on the lane leading to Gorton village. The vehicle was stationary, parked in the area reserved by the local authority for dumping gravel and salt to treat the roads. That suggested the occupants were either taking a scheduled break, or skiving. The idea that their presence might be in any way connected to him never crossed his mind.

Had Geoffrey been able to hear the message relayed by one of the officers, after his Audi had passed them, he would have been more than a little alarmed.

'Suspect's vehicle has just driven down Gorton Lane, now turning into Gorton Park.'

'OK, follow him in. Let's welcome him home.'

A few seconds later, the police van pulled out into the lane.

Walmsley was surprised to see a car parked on the drive. He assumed it must be a friend of Caroline's — most of the people she knew drove Range Rovers. He was not surprised that Caroline wasn't at the door to greet him. Their relationship had not been warm enough for that sort of affection for a long time. He got out of the Audi, and walked towards the boot, intent on removing his luggage, when he looked up, distracted by the sound of car tyres on the gravel approach to the house.

It was only when he saw the brightly coloured panels of the vehicle that he began to feel a twinge of alarm. Had they come to question him about Bridget Peters? He quelled his misgivings. Even if they did want to talk to him about her death, there was no way they could possibly link him to her murder.

The door of the house opened, and Walmsley's heart sank as he recognized the man from photos he'd seen several times in the *Netherdale Gazette*. His dismay increased as he recalled the many instances of this detective's success. He fought to remain calm, silently repeating the mantra, 'They have no evidence, no evidence, no evidence.'

Fear turned to shock when Nash addressed him by name, arrested him, and proceeded to recite the formal caution. The first hint of the extent of their knowledge was indicated by the charge of rape as well as murder.

Walmsley attempted to bluster his way out of trouble. 'That's all nonsense. There's no way you can pin that on me. Ask my wife. She'll back me up.' He looked round, wondering why Caroline hadn't appeared by now.

'We already have done,' Nash replied. 'She's at Helmsdale police station giving a written statement as we speak.'

'In that case, ask her where I was. She'll tell you I was at home with her when that unfortunate young woman was killed.'

It was only when he saw Nash's smile that Walmsley realized his mistake, but it was too late to retract that statement now.

'That's extremely interesting,' Nash turned to his colleague. 'Take note of that statement would you, sergeant? He has been cautioned.' Nash signalled the two patrol officers forward. 'Take him away,' he ordered.

Clara watched with amusement as Walmsley, protesting loudly, was bundled unceremoniously into the back of the police van, and driven away. She looked at Nash. 'He's clever, isn't he?'

'Yes, he is. For him to state so categorically that he was at home with his wife at the time of the murder, you mean? Especially when those details haven't been released to the press.'

* * *

When Clara later reflected on their return to Helmsdale, she reckoned the scene could not have been stage-managed better by a Hollywood director. As the officers led their suspect inside to book him in, Andrews and Pearce emerged from the nearest interview room, with Caroline Walmsley following close on their heels.

'Caroline,' Walmsley exclaimed, 'this is all a dreadful mistake. I promise you, we'll soon have it cleared up.'

Caroline looked directly at her husband, or more accurately, straight through him. Without speaking a word, or giving the slightest sign that she acknowledged his presence, she turned and walked from the building, her stride almost a quick march, as if eager to distance herself from something distasteful.

It was the encounter with his wife, Clara realized, that destroyed the last element of Walmsley's bravado. When the arrested man's solicitor had been presented with the evidence against him, his advice suggested the ensuing interrogation should be little more than a formality.

Even so, following a 'no comment' interview, the team, knew the watertight evidence would secure a measure of justice for Bridget Peters, and for her bereaved husband.

They gathered in the CID suite where there was an upbeat mood, the reaction being a natural one. Although he was pleased with the outcome, Nash warned his colleagues against complacency. 'Remember, we still have two unsolved murders, with no clue as to the perpetrator or motive. I think it would be better to put euphoria on hold, until we've made some progress with them.'

CHAPTER SIXTEEN

The next couple of days following Walmsley's arrest had been spent preparing their case against him to the satisfaction of the Crown Prosecution Service. The rest of their time was spent conducting re-interviews and cross-referencing every scrap of information about the other murders, although there wasn't much.

Nash and Clara were discussing the satisfactory outcome of their presentation to CPS as they walked into Helmsdale station, to be greeted by Steve Meadows, who asked to have a word with them.

'What's the problem, Steve?'

'Netherdale control got a phone call yesterday evening from a guy who lives in San Francisco. He wanted them to check on his sister who lives in Bishopton. Apparently, she calls him once a month without fail, but he hasn't heard from her recently. The last time they spoke was about six weeks ago. He said everything seemed fine then, and she sounded really happy. The woman's name is Jenny Granger. She's twenty-eight years old, single, and, as far as her brother is aware, isn't in a relationship. He's tried both her landline and mobile, leaving messages, and sending texts, but has had no response. So he decided to report her as a MISPER.

'Control sent a couple of uniforms round, and they got no response. It's a Victorian semi, the curtains and blinds were drawn, so they spoke to the elderly woman who lives next door. She told them she'd been putting Ms Granger's milk delivery in her own fridge, as she assumed she was still away and had forgotten to cancel the milkman. Fortunately, the neighbour had a spare key for emergencies, which, as it was a welfare check, saved them using the red key. They found no sign of Ms Granger. Everything seemed to be in order, nothing suspicious, the fridge had been emptied of perishables, so they reported back, secured the house and left. Netherdale passed the case onto me this morning, for some weird reason they believe Bishopton is more in our parish than theirs.'

'I have two questions for you,' Nash responded. 'Firstly, why did the neighbour assume Ms Granger was away? I think you used the words "still away", which implies the neighbour had been told that she was going somewhere. The second question is, why are you involving us? It seems more of a job for uniform?'

'The officers said it was over a week ago that Ms Granger's brother had told the neighbour they'd been called urgently to visit their sick mother in the Isle of Wight. He was going to collect some of his sister's things, intending to follow her. Our guys asked if the brother had phoned to tell her all this, and the neighbour said he was at the house and had a key.'

'Hang on, Steve. I thought you said that her brother lives in San Francisco. Did I get that wrong, or does she have more than one brother?'

Meadows' face was sombre as he replied, 'No, Mike, you weren't wrong. Once I'd heard that, I got a bit suspicious, so I did some checking. Jenny Granger has only one brother, who was headhunted several years back by one of the technology giants, and now works in Silicon Valley.' He took a deep breath before adding, 'And that's not all. I also discovered Jenny Granger's parents both passed away several years ago.'

He saw their startled expressions and continued, 'That's only part of the reason I want you to handle this, Mike.' Meadows gestured to the MISPER form he was holding. 'The other is something else her brother mentioned, when he was speaking to Control last night.'

Meadows watched as the detectives scanned the sheet of paper, and saw the look of surprise on their faces as they read one of the entries regarding her employer. 'That's a weird coincidence,' Nash muttered.

'You don't believe in coincidences,' Clara pointed out.

'No, I don't, and judging by his reaction, neither does Steve.' Nash gestured to the entry. 'Have you followed up on this, via a phone call, or a visit from one of your officers?'

'No, I thought it better to leave anything like that to you super-sleuths.'

As he and Clara were going upstairs, Nash said in a loud voice, 'He's getting more like Jack Binns every day.'

When Andrews and Pearce arrived, Nash briefed them. 'Viv, I'd like you and Lisa to go through to Bishopton. Inspect Ms Granger's house and see if there's anything our uniform guys missed — the neighbour has a key. By the sound of what Steve told us, it seemed they were pretty thorough, but two more pairs of eyes can't do any harm. Also, ask the neighbour to describe this so-called brother.'

Once the detective constables had left, Nash told Clara, 'I'd like you to phone Ms Granger's employers. I find it very strange that nobody from Helm Logistics has reported her missing, especially in view of the fact that Andrew Derrick also worked there — and we all know what happened to him.'

'But are you sure this isn't actually a coincidence?' Clara asked.

Nash sighed as he headed for the door.

Clara wasn't beaten. 'And what will you be doing while the rest of us are busy?'

Nash looked shocked by her question. 'You don't think the coffee machine refills itself, do you?'

On his return, Clara gave him the gist of her conversation with Jenny Granger's employers. 'I spoke to the receptionist. Ms Granger is employed as something described as a systems analyst. Viv might know what that is — I haven't a clue — but it sounds like a proper sort of job. Anyway, the woman said they'd received a phone call from Ms Granger's brother, who told her much the same story as the neighbour mentioned to our uniform lads. Only he went into a bit more detail. He said something along the lines of, "Jenny's had to fly down to the Isle of Wight as a matter of urgency, because our mother has had a stroke, and things are looking pretty bad". I thought that was about it, but then the receptionist said, "And, of course, I knew it was Jenny's brother by his American accent".'

'When did this happen, or didn't you ask?'

Clara glared at him, but then saw the slight twitch of a smile at the corner of his mouth. 'Of course I asked! We're not all as careless as you,' she retorted. 'It was eleven days ago. She checked the timesheets to confirm it, as it was the same morning Jenny failed to turn up for work.'

'This is getting to sound very bad, given the similarity between Ms Granger's disappearance, and what happened to Andrew Derrick. If the connection *is* Helm Logistics, I don't see where Cheesy Wilson fits into the picture. I think as soon as Viv and Lisa return, we ought to get our hi-tech wizard busy, to find out all he can about this company. Then I think we should pay them a visit.'

'That's an awful lot of thinking, Mike. Are you sure you're OK?'

He shook his head and went through to his office to answer the phone. As soon as he heard Lisa's voice, he knew she and Viv had found something.

'Everything looked normal until we entered the bedroom. There were no signs of a struggle, and without the level of previous knowledge we had, the uniform guys wouldn't have given it a second thought, but as soon as we saw Ms Granger's clothing strewn across the bed, it reminded us of Wilson and Derrick's houses when we searched them.'

'OK, Lisa, I think we should order a forensic team to give the place the once-over. I'll order them to go there now, and instruct them to take photos. In the meantime, we'll ask the media to put out a MISPER about Ms Granger. In order to back that up, we could do with a recent photo. Take a look round and see if you can find one we can borrow.'

Nash paused, and thought for a second before adding, 'In fact, if you do, see if there are any that look recent and have someone else in the picture. Although nobody's mentioned a boyfriend, or any kind of relationship, I find it odd that she's apparently without close friends.'

Another thought crossed his mind. 'I don't suppose there's a laptop, a tablet, or any kind of computer in the apartment, is there? That could be extremely useful. We could let Viv loose on it.'

'There isn't, Mike, I mentioned the fact to Viv. I thought it curious that a woman of her age would be without one. But Viv suggested she's probably sick of the sight of them by the time she's finished staring at them all day at work.'

'OK, when Forensics have arrived, come back here.'

Nash had an idea, and spoke to the officer in Netherdale control room who had taken the call from Jenny Granger's brother. The outcome of their conversation troubled him so much that Clara asked what was wrong.

'When you spoke to that receptionist, she said Granger spoke with an American accent, right?'

'Yes, she said that was how she knew it was Ms Granger's brother, because Jenny was forever going on about him. Why do you ask?'

'Because Granger was born and brought up around here. Spent most of his life here, until he went to work in Silicon Valley, and that was only a few years back. I thought it strange he'd acquired an American accent so quickly, so I spoke to our man who took the call. He said the person who called from San Francisco had an accent that was pure Netherdale, with an occasional US twang.'

Nash thought for a second and then said, 'Get Lisa or Viv on the phone, and ask them to make sure they question the neighbour about the so-called brother's accent.'

On their return, Lisa reported on their visit, while Viv began researching Helm Logistics. The information they had gleaned tallied with much that Nash and Mironova had discovered — and seemed to confirm their worst fears about the missing woman's safety.

'It worked out well having to wait for the boffins to arrive,' Lisa told them. 'We had a cuppa with the old lady, and asked her for a description of the man she'd spoken to. But she couldn't give us a description, because she only saw him from the side. It was a cold day, and he was muffled up under the hood of his jacket, and a scarf round his face. She thought she saw fair hair, but couldn't be sure. He said he was in a hurry, and called across to her as he unlocked the door, and went in. She knew he was Ms Granger's brother, because Jenny had spoken about him working in America, and that explained his accent.'

Lisa looked up and saw Nash and Mironova exchange glances. 'Is that important?'

'It is, because it confirms what the receptionist at Helm Logistics told Clara. They also had a phone call from someone with an American accent. However, Netherdale control confirmed their caller's accent is more North Yorkshire, than Western America.' He watched as the meaning dawned, then asked, 'Did you manage to get hold of a photo of Ms Granger?'

'We did, and as there were a good few to choose from, we checked with the neighbour as to which provided the best likeness. However, we didn't find any that had someone else in the picture, apart from older ones. Ms Granger's companion in those photos looks very much like her, so we assume it to be her brother. They both have dark hair, not fair.'

'OK, send the photo to Tom Pratt. He's going to see the press officer to organize a press release, even as we speak.

With a bit of luck, we'll be in time to get it on the local news bulletins this evening, and into tomorrow morning's papers. While you're doing that, I'm going to blow the budget for the next few years by phoning San Francisco. I'm sorry to say it will probably mean that for the foreseeable future you and Viv will have to attend crime scenes on a push bike. If it needs both of you, I suppose we could stretch to a tandem, but only if we can rent one.'

'Hang on, Mike. Will he be at work?'

'Good thinking, but they're eight hours behind us. I have his home number.'

Jenny's brother told Nash his Christian name was Stewart. Nash's silence after hearing the name made Granger chuckle. 'Yes, just like the actor,' he told Nash. 'My mother was a great movie fan — so I've had to put up with a lot of ribbing about it.' But he quickly offered any help that he could provide.

Nash began by asking about his sister's involvement with men.

'No,' he replied, 'Jenny was never that bothered about boys. She had one or two short-term boyfriends when she was in her late teens, but they weren't what you'd class as great romances. There was a more meaningful relationship with a guy she met at York University, but it fizzled out. The last I heard, he'd married, and was living and working in Canada.'

There was a short pause, before Granger continued, 'More recently, I got the feeling she might have begun another relationship, but she was very cagy about her personal life, so I can't be certain. Jenny and I are pretty close, more so since Mum and Dad passed away, but she wouldn't share something as intimate as her love life with me, unless she needed my help or support.'

Nash thanked Granger, and told him they were pulling out all the stops to locate his sister, even enlisting media assistance, and would report back as soon as they had any news.

He ended the conversation, aware that what he had offered was only cold comfort. Granger's concern wouldn't be lessened until he knew Jenny was safe and well, something

146

Nash certainly couldn't promise. Withholding the precise details of what their investigation had revealed so far was an easy decision to make, because Granger's anxiety would have gone into hyper-drive, had he learned what they suspected.

It didn't take long for Pearce to report what he'd been able to discover from his research. 'Helm Logistics is a fairly successful company, operating in telecommunications and similar media. It was founded twelve years ago by a husband-and-wife team, Neil and Vanessa Blackburn. They owe its prosperity to the spread of hi-tech equipment, and the need for coverage, particularly in rural areas, such as ours. Although they're by no stretch of the imagination market leaders, I guess their progress will have some of the bigger companies looking nervously over their shoulders. I think they've seen a gap in the market, and have done pretty well at plugging it.'

Viv glanced down at the print-off he'd made before continuing, 'Neil Blackburn, the managing director, is the technician and driving force, but it's Vanessa's money that has enabled them to achieve what they have. His wife is the sole shareholder, with one hundred per cent equity. I had a word with Tom Pratt, and he told me that Vanessa Blackburn is a member of the Fletcher family, and she owns Bishopton Priory, that large estate on the outskirts of the village.

'I was curious enough to look the place up, and the history of the Priory is extremely interesting. The house that is there now is not entirely the original building. That, together with the nearby monastery that gave the place its name, was destroyed by soldiers of King Henry VIII during his persecution of the Catholics. The family rebuilt the dwelling, but weren't able to enjoy it for long. In the early part of the nineteenth century an outbreak of diphtheria wiped them out. There was nobody to inherit, so it was put up for sale, which is when the Fletcher family purchased it. Apparently, one of the interesting features of the house is the rumoured existence of a priest's hole, although nobody has ever found it.'

'What's a priest's hole?' Lisa asked.

Nash shook his head in mock disgust. 'Didn't they teach history at your school, Lisa? Priest's holes were secret spaces, usually within the fabric of an existing building belonging to a Catholic family. Their purpose was to conceal visiting priests. Many of them travelled the country, holding masses, taking confessions, and even conducting christenings and wedding ceremonies, using the Catholic Liturgy, which had been outlawed following Henry VIII's schism with Rome. The persecution of those following the Catholic religion continued during the reign of Henry's daughter, Elizabeth I. The priests were in constant danger. If they were captured, they would probably have been — and often were — executed.'

'One thing you have to admire about Mike is his extensive knowledge of history,' Clara remarked, adding with a sweet smile. 'That's probably because he's lived through far more of it than the rest of us.'

Although they weren't to know it, Nash's knowledge of history would later provide the solution to an aspect of the case they were investigating — and in so doing, set them what was likely to be an insoluble mystery.

'Let's go back to the original point, Viv, now that Clara's run out of insults to throw at me. What about Vanessa Blackburn and her antecedents?'

'The Fletcher family made their fortune initially from shipbuilding during the nineteenth and early twentieth century, but after the Second World War they diversified into property, and that's where their continued prosperity comes from. Rumour has it their annual rent roll is well into seven figures, coming mainly from agricultural land, plus several large industrial estates, and a lot of town centre commercial properties. Although this is partly guesswork, Tom reckons Fletcher Estates owns about half the shops and office buildings, in Netherdale, Helmsdale, and Bishopton, as well as many more in other towns.'

Having assimilated all the information the team had acquired that day, Nash and Clara agreed their only immediate course of action would be to visit Helm Logistics, and attempt to discover more about Jenny Granger and her role in the company. Plus trying to establish what the connection was between her and her murdered fellow employee, Andrew Derrick.

'I'm certain this is the key to the whole mystery,' Nash told Clara, 'but how on earth these two are linked to a low life such as Cheesy Wilson is still way beyond me. Nevertheless, I'm absolutely certain there is a link. It's all very frustrating.'

* * *

Next morning, at Helm Logistics, having interviewed Neil Blackburn, Clara commented they had learned very few facts that they didn't already know.

Nash agreed, but both detectives were of one mind about the man they had just spoken to.

'I don't know what you thought, Mike, but it seemed to me that Neil Blackburn is scared stiff of something, or somebody. Viv and Lisa said the same. It might simply be nervousness at being visited by the police, but I got the impression it was something totally different.'

'I thought so too, Clara, but there's more to it than simply fear, I reckon. I'd say Blackburn is hiding something. I'm fairly sure that it's to do with Jenny Granger. But I noticed he looked more than a little bit shifty when we talked about his mechanic's murder.'

'What was it that made you think he's hiding something to do with Jenny Granger?'

'It wasn't anything he said, more his reaction to our mentioning her name, and when we talked about her. It wouldn't surprise me if there was something going on between them, because he struck me as that sort of bloke. You've seen the photos. Jenny Granger is a very good-looking young woman, and I reckon somebody like Blackburn would be unable to resist the temptation, given the opportunity. And let's face it, working together in a small suite of offices, such as theirs, would provide plenty of chances to develop a relationship.'

'Is this pure supposition, or have you something concrete to back up that theory? Admittedly, it isn't by any means the wildest you've ever had, but there are lots of contenders for that award. Still, it would be nice to have something definite to work with.'

Nash grinned at Clara's unflattering description of his thought process, but told her, 'All I was going on, was the way Blackburn eyed you, and the fact he spent most of the time we were in his office staring at your legs. That gave me a strong clue, and I don't think it would take much encouragement for him to stray from the straight and narrow.'

'Ah well, they do say that it takes one to know one,' Clara retaliated.

CHAPTER SEVENTEEN

Ollie and Ted had been pals even before they attended Bishopton Primary School together. Their friendship began at playgroup, and was strengthened by the fact that they lived only a few doors from each other. In a small, close-knit community like Bishopton, such bonds as theirs are likely to last a long time, unless something traumatic causes a split. Even then, there is a chance that anything as shocking as what happened to them will bring them closer together, rather than driving them apart.

The boys shared similar interests. At the tender age of eight, they were far too young to have discovered the attraction of girls, so their hobbies were primarily focused around sport and adventure. The latter part was fuelled by the natural penchant of young boys for the macabre, having not yet absorbed the sadder aspects associated with life — and death.

It was in pursuit of this predilection that Ollie suggested an unusual way for them to pass the free time after reporting home from school. A game of hide-and-seek might have been classed as mundane by many of their contemporaries, but Ollie was certain that his idea for the site in which to play it would definitely take it to another level of enjoyment.

Their minds were so in tune that as soon as Ollie put forward the proposition, Ted accepted it, eagerly. Both boys knew they weren't allowed to play in the churchyard, but who would see them? They would be hiding behind the gravestones. Ignoring the obvious means of entry, via the lychgate at the edge of the verge, the boys scrambled over the low stone wall, into what was to become their playground.

Once they had scaled the obstacle, Ollie said, 'My dad says it was a waste of money putting this wall up. He said the people who are inside can't get out, and the people who are outside don't want to get in.' Ted giggled at the joke, but soon, their game took all their attention.

The idea had been Ollie's, so he naturally claimed the honour of being the first to find a place of concealment. It took quite a while for Ted to find him, a task made more difficult by Ollie's bending of the rules, by moving stealthily from behind one headstone to another whenever Ted approached.

Eventually, Ted found him, and their roles were reversed. Ollie had only spent a couple of minutes searching when he spotted his friend. This puzzled him, because Ted didn't seem to be making any attempt to hide. Instead of crouching behind one of the gravestones, or even the shelter offered by the several large yew trees, Ted was standing motionless in plain sight, near the lychgate, staring fixedly at the ground in front of him.

Ollie crept slowly forward to find out what Ted had found so fascinating. It wasn't until he was alongside his friend that Ollie also stopped, gazing at the naked corpse lying on the grave.

'Is she asleep?' Ted whispered.

Ollie, the braver of the two, decided the lady was sleeping, and should be woken up before she caught a chill from the cool autumn breeze. He headed for the trees, where he selected a fallen branch, and returned to his friend's side. He poked the shoulder of the woman, gently at first. Getting no response, he tried again, before stating knowingly, 'I think she's dead!'

Ted's eyes opened wide. 'Dead?'

'Yeah, her face is a funny colour.' He prodded his friend in the arm. 'Don't look. It's rude to stare. Gran said so.'

They both turned away, but Ted looked over his shoulder at the scene, thinking. Then, with his eyes wide, turned to face Ollie, and whispered, 'What if she's a zombie?'

Terrified by the idea, they turned in unison and ran, scrambling over the wall, racing home, screaming for their mothers, their voices shrill with increasing fear at the horror they had just witnessed.

The boys' fathers had now arrived home from work, and together they walked to the cemetery, convinced their sons' imaginations had run wild. It didn't take them long to find the body, and even less time to contact the police.

* * *

Clara was duty officer, and responded to the call from the patrolmen requesting assistance. She phoned Lisa, and they met at the cemetery gate. They had taken a look at the scene, and now accompanied the fathers to the boys' homes. On the way, they heard about the boys' hysterical homecoming, and how the mothers were trying to calm them.

They were first introduced to Ollie, who was seated on the sofa alongside his mother, staring wide-eyed at the detectives as they entered the house. After his father assured him that there were definitely no zombies in the cemetery, only a lady who wasn't well, the man looked at Clara with an apologetic expression. 'I don't want him upset any further.'

Clara nodded her understanding, as Ollie had now calmed down a little. His father, hiding his own distress, explained to him, 'This nice lady is from the police. She's a detective, and wants to talk to you. OK, Son? Mum and I are both here.'

Clara smiled at the child, and decided to try and gain his confidence. She wished Nash was here. He, at least, had more experience with boys. She crouched down to the boy's level, and said, 'Hello, Ollie. My name's Clara. Are you feeling better now?'

He nodded.

'That's good, because I wondered if you would tell me what happened when you were in the churchyard?'

He looked at his mother who smiled and said, 'It's OK, Ollie, tell her what you did. You're not in any trouble.'

He began hesitantly, 'We're not supposed to go in there. Dad says it's not a playground.' He glanced at his father. 'But we were playing hide-and-seek. It's really good, 'cos there's lots of hiding places.'

'Well I don't mind about that, and I won't tell anybody. So what happened?'

'It was Ted's turn to hide, and when I looked for him he wasn't.'

'Wasn't what?' Clara asked.

'Hiding.'

'Right, I see. What was he doing?'

'Staring.'

'Staring?'

'Yes, at the lady.' Ollie was beginning to think this woman wasn't very smart.

'Oh, I understand. So what did you do?'

'I poked her with a stick.'

Clara was finding this difficult and looked at the mother for assistance. Lisa was trying to stifle a smile.

'Oliver, tell the lady exactly why you did that,' his mother said firmly.

Using his full name meant possible trouble, and Ollie wasn't going to risk that. 'We thought she was asleep, and wanted to wake her up before she caught cold. It's rude to look at people with no clothes on, and you can't touch them. Then I poked her with the stick to wake her up. Then I told Ted I thought she was dead. Then Ted said she might be a zombie. Then we ran home.'

Clara thanked the boy, assuring him he had done exactly the right thing, before she and Lisa went to speak to Ted. He was still in tears, clinging to his mother, but managed to give a similar account of events — while at the same time ensuring everyone knew that it had been Ollie's idea, and not his, to play in the churchyard.

* * *

Alondra was standing at the Aga in the large farmhouse kitchen, on the point of serving their evening meal. Mike was seated in one of the carver chairs at the end of the kitchen table, when his mobile rang. She giggled slightly at the comical expression on Mike's face as he glanced at the caller ID. When she heard his reply to what he'd been told, she adjusted the oven settings. Better to serve up a well-cooked meal than a dried-out, burnt one.

'Yes, Clara, what's the problem?'

Nash listened for a second and then said, 'OK, I'll be right there. Give Viv a shout, will you? I want all hands on deck for this one. I take it you've spoken to Mexican Pete? Sadly, I think we can all guess who the victim is.'

When Nash reached Bishopton, he listened as Clara told him, 'The young lads came into the cemetery to play a game of hide-and-seek, would you believe? They'd only been here a few minutes when they found the body. They were too scared to do anything but run home to their parents.'

'Did you ask if they'd seen anybody in the graveyard?' Nash realized what he'd just said when he saw Clara wince, and corrected his question, 'I meant, did you ask if they'd seen anyone else hanging around?'

'They were too upset to answer in-depth questions, Mike, particularly ones like that.'

Lisa nodded agreement to Clara's statement, and added, 'To be fair, the parents weren't in a much better state, particularly the fathers. It was their unenviable task to come and verify the boys hadn't made the whole ghastly thing up.'

'See if you can arrange for them to come to the station. We need a statement from the boys and their fathers.'

'Shall we start knocking on doors?' Lisa asked.

Nash agreed. 'Yes, you and Viv make a start. Clara and I can wait for the professor.'

While they waited, Clara wandered away from the grave, ducking under the incident tape the officers had wrapped around four adjacent headstones. That showed ingenuity, but also a modicum of disrespect, she thought. However, the occupants wouldn't be raising any objections.

She continued her stroll, idly inspecting the epitaphs on the resting places she passed. Along the line of more recent interments, one of the inscriptions caught her eye. She read the name of the deceased and sighed. The sorrow the wording brought was a cruel reminder of the terrible waste of a young life, and much more besides.

Unaware that she was being watched, Clara remained still for several minutes, her memory going back to a far happier time for the young woman lying within that grave. Nash watched his deputy for a while, and noted the sombre expression on her face.

Eventually, he walked across and asked, 'Something wrong, Clara?'

'I met this young woman once, a long time ago. Her name was Amanda Headley back then. She and her boyfriend witnessed a bar fight in a club where he was appearing on stage. I remember thinking at the time what a lovely couple they were, and so right for one another. That obviously remained so, judging by her married name.'

'You said he was on stage. What was he, a singer?'

'No, he was a magician. Sleight of hand, that sort of thing. According to the club secretary I spoke to, he was a bit of a second-rater, called him hopeless.'

'Was she ill? Thirty-three seems very young to die.'

'No, she was the victim of a hit-and-run. As I recall, she was out jogging, and got hit by a car.'

Clara glanced away, hearing the sound of approaching vehicles. Nash strolled a few paces to his right, and called out, 'What did you say that lady's maiden name was?'

'Headley, why do you ask?'

Nash signalled for her to join him. 'Because I reckon the hit-and-run driver might have got two victims with that incident, although this one was by proxy.'

The position of the grave suggested that the deceased had been interred at a later date than the accident victim. A swift calculation from her date of birth suggested that Susan Headley was sixty-seven or sixty-eight years old. The inscription on the headstone listed Susan Headley's only child as Amanda.

They walked back to meet up with their colleagues, neither of them aware that Nash's arithmetic, concerning the number of deaths resulting from the hit-and-run, was slightly adrift. He returned to the subject they'd been discussing. 'I remember the hit-and-run incident, but don't recall any of the details. You obviously followed the case more closely than I did. Were they able to identify the make of car?'

'I suppose I took more of an interest because I'd met her. But no, despite checking with motor dealers and repair shops, they drew a blank. Sadly, the accident happened somewhere around here, and there were no witnesses.'

Clara wasn't to know that her statement, like Nash's arithmetic, was also inaccurate.

* * *

The pathologist's ill humour at being dragged away from home in the evening was apparent the moment he stepped from his car. 'I wish you'd train your killers better, Nash. Try and get them to show some consideration by working less anti-social hours. Nine-to-five murderers would benefit all of us. I feel sure you'll agree, having been dragged away from your beautiful *señorita*.'

Nash entered into the spirit of Ramirez' game by responding, 'We actually found the body this morning, Professor. But we thought it better not to inform you until now, certain that you'd have nothing better to do.'

Ramirez sniffed disdainfully. 'Believe me, Nash, I wouldn't put it past you.'

When the forensic team had set up arc lights, his examination of the body didn't take long. Neither did his report. As he signalled for his assistants to remove the corpse, he told Nash, 'The young woman appears to have suffered the same fate as the previous two victims. So you now have a serial killer on your hands who has some form of water fetish. Post-mortem at eight o'clock tomorrow. That's morning, not evening,' he added, sarcastically.

'Thank you, Professor. I'll try to fit it into my crowded schedule. One thing I can tell you is the victim's name. Obviously, we'll require formal identification, but her appearance matches the description of a woman by the name of Jenny Granger. Reported missing two days ago, in what we discovered to be highly suspicious circumstances.'

Ramirez muttered something in Spanish that might have been 'thank you', but Nash rather doubted it. He considered asking Alondra for a translation, but decided against that idea.

As Nash and Clara were conducting a preliminary inspection of the graveyard they were joined by Viv, and a short while later, by Lisa Andrews.

'The householders I spoke to couldn't tell me anything,' Viv told them. Lisa confirmed much the same.

'We've had a quick look round here,' Nash indicated the crime scene, 'but there doesn't seem anything significant to get excited about. I suggest we get a couple of Steve's minions to take care of the site overnight, and we'll organize a search of the area in the morning.'

'Is that what's called working the graveyard shift?' Pearce asked.

Nash waited until the chorus of groans died away, and then told them, 'I'll be in late tomorrow. I've to attend the post-mortem. From there, I'll drop in at HQ and bring the chief constable up to speed on this development.'

'What about letting the victim's brother know the bad news?' Lisa asked.

'We can't do that at this stage. It would be different if he was living nearby, but I'd rather get formal identification first. Think how dreadful it would be to drag him all the way from the west coast of America, suffering the distress the news would bring. Only to find the dead woman is a complete stranger.'

As Nash was driving home, he had an idea prompted by their recent conversation. He pressed the short code for Clara on his mobile, and grinned when he heard her long-suffering, 'What now, Mike?'

'I had a thought about the identification of the corpse. I reckon we should ask Neil Blackburn to view the body, and verify it is Jenny Granger.'

'Why him? Usually that's a task for the next of kin. I know that isn't practical in this instance, but surely, some-body like the lady next door would be more appropriate?'

'True, but we've already discounted dragging the brother all the way from San Francisco. And I think the neighbour will be scared enough when she discovers Jenny Granger has been the victim of foul play.'

'Is that your only reason for suggesting we use Blackburn?'

'No, it isn't. You're getting to know me too well. I think if my reasoning is accurate, and he *was* having an affair with Jenny Granger, the sight of her body on the mortuary slab might upset him enough to give us some useful information. Even if he doesn't spill the beans, it'll be interesting to gauge his reaction.'

There was a pause before Nash added, 'I think what's equally important is that when we ask Blackburn to attend the morgue, we do so in person, rather than over the phone. If we can deliver the shock news, face to face, that might pro-voke a response. You can't gauge facial expressions, or body language, in a phone call. Not unless you're using Skype, or whatever the kids play with these days.'

* * *

Nash wasn't sure whether it was the early hour, the fact that the pathologist was on home turf, or simply the nature of the task he was performing, but something had quelled the professor's propensity for sarcasm. The post-mortem results were much as Nash expected. The cause of death, the fibres in her airways, and the prolonged positioning within a body of water, were all identical to those revealed by the previous two autopsies.

As Mironova replied when Nash phoned her, 'So we're no further forward in identifying either the killer, or their motive.'

'Thanks for cheering me up, Clara. It's true, though. All I can think of, to try and get forward, is to force the issue, by putting pressure on someone who was acquainted with at least two of the three victims. If anyone knows why Jenny Granger and Andrew Derrick were killed, it will be Neil Blackburn. If we can discover that reason, it might provide us with the link to Cheesy Wilson.'

'By "putting pressure on" Blackburn, I assume you mean by getting him to identify the body?'

'I do, and I think the sooner we put it to him, the better. Once I've called at HQ, I'll head straight back, pick you up, and we can go to Helm Logistics.'

CHAPTER EIGHTEEN

The receptionist at Helm Logistics looked both puzzled and slightly anxious, when she saw the two detectives walk in. The swiftness of their return obviously surprised her. 'Mr Blackburn has someone with him at the moment,' she told them. 'But he shouldn't be long. He's interviewing candidates for the service manager's job, the one that Andrew Derrick had.'

Clara managed to refrain from voicing the thought that Blackburn might soon have a lot more interviews to conduct, once he knew that Jenny Granger was dead. They only had to wait five minutes before he appeared in reception, ushering out a young man.

Blackburn turned towards them, and Clara noticed his expression change when he recognized the visitors. There was a world of trouble in his face, that was certain, but along with it, something Clara recognized instantly — fear. In addition to natural concern over the fate of a member of his staff, Blackburn's reaction suggested he was afraid. That, in turn, meant he knew he was in some form of danger.

'What is it now?' he demanded, trying to bluff it out.

'We'd like a word — in private, if you don't mind,' Nash told him.

Blackburn led them through to his office. 'Well?'

The bravado wasn't even a good act, Clara thought, watching Blackburn closely as Nash told him the reason for their visit, which she suspected he'd already guessed.

'I'm afraid we have some bad news. A body has been found, and the description is an extremely close match to Ms Granger, your employee, who has been missing for some while. Before we can proceed, we are duty bound to obtain formal identification of the body. Unfortunately, that poses a big problem. Under normal circumstances, we would ask the next of kin to perform that sad task, but Ms Granger's only living relative is her brother, who lives in San Francisco. Given that you knew the young woman well, we hoped that you would carry out the identification for us?'

Blackburn looked appalled by the suggestion. Before he had chance to say anything, Nash continued, 'I take it you have no objection to doing this? In fact, I'd say it will be better this way, rather than the distress it would cause to someone who was close to Ms Granger. We can go now, and get you back here before close of business.'

Later, reflecting on the meeting, Clara realized how astutely Nash had phrased his request. By giving Blackburn chance to refuse, Nash was inviting him to admit that his relationship with the dead woman was far more than that of a boss and an employee. In the circumstances, Blackburn was left with no alternative but to comply.

Clara excused herself, and went outside to ring the mortuary and inform them of their intention. Blackburn got his jacket, and, accompanied by Nash, climbed into the Range Rover. He remained in complete silence for the journey.

When they arrived, Ramirez was absent. His assistant had the body resting on the examination table, draped from head to toe in a large, drably coloured, olive green sheet. Nash led Blackburn, whose slow walk underlined his reluctance to be there, and guided him to a position alongside the victim's head. Clara took her place directly opposite Blackburn, from where she could gauge his reaction.

Nash waited for a moment, before signalling to the attendant, who gently pulled back the sheet, exposing the head and neck. Clara watched closely, and saw the colour drain from Blackburn's face. He reached forward, and gripped the corner of the table to steady himself, his knuckles white with pressure. Had it not been for that support, Clara felt certain, he would have collapsed.

'Well?' Nash asked. 'Is that your — employee? Is that Jenny Granger?'

Clara noted the almost imperceptible pause before the word "employee" and so, judging by his reaction, did Blackburn. His head came up abruptly, and she knew he was wondering if Nash was implying something totally different. And if so, what might the extent of his knowledge be?

He breathed in and out deeply, several times, before managing to croak, 'Yes, that's her. That's Jenny.'

After another long, searching look at the woman, Blackburn turned away and asked Nash, 'How did she die? Was she . . . ?' He seemed unable to complete the question, the implications too horrible for him. Both detectives were now convinced Jenny Granger had been his mistress.

'We wouldn't usually divulge such information at such an early stage of our investigation. But I can tell you that the post-mortem indicates the cause of death was identical to that of two previous murder victims. One of them is a local man named Charles Wilson, and the other is your former employee Andrew Derrick. We're trying to establish a connection between all three of them. Obviously, Helm Logistics is the link between Mr Derrick and Ms Granger, but we haven't been able to tie Mr Wilson into the equation. We wondered if you might perhaps be able to provide us with the missing piece of the jigsaw.'

Blackburn shook his head, seemingly either unable, or unwilling, to speak. Clara felt sure the reason for his silence was that he *did* know the link — and it terrified him.

Having returned Blackburn to his office, a journey that was conducted again in absolute silence, the detectives continued to Helmsdale station. As Nash drove, he asked Clara what she had made of Blackburn's facial expressions and body language.

'I think your assessment was spot on, Mike. There's no doubt in my mind that Blackburn and Jenny Granger were lovers. What's more, I'm convinced he does know the connection between all three victims, even if he won't admit it. And the reason he won't say anything is because he's scared out of his wits.'

'I trust your judgement, Clara, which is why I wanted you to observe Blackburn. Unfortunately, the knowledge doesn't get us much further forward. You get yourself off home. In the meantime, I've got to brace myself for one of the most unpleasant tasks in my job.'

'What's that?'

'I have to phone Jenny's brother in San Francisco, and tell him his sister has been murdered.'

'I certainly don't envy you that.'

* * *

When Nash arrived home, not only did Alondra know at once that he had suffered a harrowing day, but it seemed that Teal, their young Labrador, also sensed it. As Nash explained the distressing nature of the transatlantic phone call, the dog sat alongside him, her body leaning against his leg, her head on his knee, as she stared up at her master. The canine therapy did the trick, and Nash brightened up as he listened to Alondra describing the different events of her day.

'I have to say it's lovely to have a companion when I'm out in the wilds painting landscapes, but it doesn't do much for my concentration, or productivity, when I keep having to break off to throw a ball for someone to retrieve.'

Nash laughed as he told the dog, 'I think we can guess who she's referring to, Teal.'

The Labrador wagged her tail, her face reflecting her innocence.

Alondra continued, 'But I wouldn't think of going anywhere without her, if it can be avoided. That reminds me, Mike, I have to go through to Manchester the day after tomorrow. The gallery that held my earlier exhibition want another three paintings, to replace ones they've sold. Will you be able to look after trouble here?' She pointed to the dog.

'That won't be a problem.' Nash remembered the conversation he'd had with Clara prior to her leaving the office, and added, 'In fact, I might be able to put her to good use.'

Alondra laughed. 'Don't tell me you're going to train her up as a police dog?'

'Certainly not, she's far more valuable here, taking care of us. Anyway, I don't think she's right for the job, unless there's a sudden mass outbreak of food theft. Then she'd come in handy sniffing out the stolen goods. No, it's something rather different I have in mind.'

* * *

Neil Blackburn knew he was in danger. He knew Jenny Granger's death was linked to the previous two. He knew why they had died. What he didn't know was the identity of the killer. Other, equally disturbing thoughts went along with that acknowledgement. Had he given himself away in front of those two detectives? Were they aware, as one of them had implied, that he and Jenny had been lovers? Even if that were so, they could hardly have guessed the whole truth.

If that brought Blackburn any consolation, it was only cold comfort.

He had hoped the truth would remain buried. Those who knew were few enough. The number had lessened, first with Andrew Derrick's death and then with Wilson's. Now Jenny was gone, he was the only one left alive who knew the full facts. Or was he? Could one of the victims have been indiscreet, revealed the secret? Or had somebody discovered the facts another way?

Blackburn dismissed both these ideas as too fanciful for words. There was no way it was possible. Despite his denials, a scintilla of doubt remained, one that haunted his thoughts through every waking moment, and interrupted his sleep with increasing frequency.

His home, Bishopton Priory, was in darkness when he arrived, but this was hardly surprising, Vanessa had been away for almost two months now. Blackburn drove through the gates, kept open permanently for easy access, and along the drive to the converted stable block. There, he operated the remote control to raise the up-and-over garage door, drove his BMW in, and parked between Vanessa's Mercedes and the other vehicle, shrouded by a protective sheet.

He then walked across the approach towards the front door, his footsteps crunching on the gravel path. It would seem strange being alone in the Priory tonight, he thought. It certainly wasn't because he missed Vanessa's company; they had drifted apart too long ago for that to trouble him. If things had been normal, he would occupy his time using the range cooker to experiment with various culinary delights, one of his favourite hobbies, or try his luck at an online casino he frequented occasionally.

Tonight, however, was far from normal. To be fair, normality had gone even before he knew that Jenny was dead. The news of her murder merely served to confirm the fear that had gripped him since her disappearance — or possibly before that, when he'd been told of the other slayings.

He opened the front door, and pressed the numerical code on the keypad to deactivate the alarm system. Despite the outside temperature being mild, the house seemed colder, reflecting the state of his marriage. Or could there be another, more sinister reason for the place being so chilly?

Blackburn gave himself a mental shake — far-fetched imaginings such as this would not do. He must try and occupy his time, and the kitchen would be the best place to do that. However, he would have to change into more suitable attire. The sartorial requirements of a successful company's CEO, were hardly the correct clothing to wear when working as a chef.

Having reached the first floor, he turned right, across the Minstrel's Gallery. He opened his bedroom door, took one pace inside, then stopped. His whole being flooded with terror. He was unable to move, transfixed by fear, as the hooded figure approached. Two seconds later the intruder watched, impassively, as Blackburn collapsed to the floor unconscious.

* * *

Nash walked with Teal into the station, where the dog stopped to greet Sergeant Meadows, wagging her tail furiously as he stroked her head. 'Morning, Steve,' Nash said. 'We've got visitors today, both four-legged and two-legged. The young boys who found the bodies at the cemetery are coming in with their fathers to make statements. Give me a ring when they arrive, will you?' He released Teal's lead and she set off upstairs, heading straight for Nash's office, to her dog bed in the corner.

Clara entered the room, patted Teal, and asked Nash how he wanted to conduct the interviews with the children.

'Bring them all up here. I've got an idea that might help.'

Clara was puzzled, but did as she was asked, escorting them to the prearranged seats in a semi-circle. Nash told the boys they could call him Mike, reminded them they had already met Lisa and Clara, and introduced them to Viv.

The boys were obviously afraid, but when they had settled, Nash went to his office and returned with Teal on her lead. He told the boys, 'This is a very special police dog, called Inspector Teal. She wants to know what happened in the churchyard, and it needs to be written down. But she can't write.' He shrugged his shoulders, and waited until the boys had stopped giggling. 'So someone has to do it for her.' The boys sat, wide-eyed, and nodded.

'Ollie, can you start? Tell Inspector Teal exactly what happened, and Clara will write down what you say. Is that

OK?' He took Teal to sit in front of Ollie, where she sat patiently, looking directly at him, while he stroked her ears as he gave his account of events.

When this was done, Nash repeated the process with Ted, as Lisa took his statement. The fathers signed them on behalf of their sons, as Nash said to the boys, 'Thank you both very much. Now Viv and I are going to go downstairs with your dads. But I'd like you to stay here with Clara and Lisa. One thing Inspector Teal likes when she's been working is a snack. So if I give you some dog biscuits, would you look after her, please?'

The boys scrambled from the chairs onto the floor, as Nash produced dog biscuits for Teal, and also two bags of toffees. Warning them not to give the sweets to Inspector Teal, he left and went downstairs.

When they had all the statements, and the boys had left, Clara spoke to Nash, who was looking rather pleased with himself at the outcome. 'There's only one thing to say.'

'What's that, Clara?'

'You're getting soft.'

CHAPTER NINETEEN

Vanessa Blackburn had been shopping. After passing the morning visiting a number of boutiques in the centre of Athens, she decided that as a reward for her labours, she would treat herself to a light lunch in one of the delightful alfresco restaurants in the Plaka, the old heart of the city.

Athens represented the final leg of her journey, something she regarded as a sort of latter-day Grand Tour. She had been pondering the idea of taking an extended vacation for a long time, and this had seemed to be the ideal opportunity to be away. The time spent on her travels might serve to act as a cleansing and healing operation from the hurt she had suffered. The disillusion had been growing for long enough, until a single event shattered what remained of her regard for those close to her.

Whether the break would prove effective, and whether the future would hold any happiness, was something only time would tell. Time was supposedly a great healer, but no matter how much Vanessa hoped it might prove equal to the task, she had little expectation of its succeeding.

She had begun her vacation in the Portuguese capital, Lisbon, and from there a short journey across the border, had taken her to Madrid. Remaining in the Spanish section of the Iberian Peninsula, she had visited the Catalan capital, Barcelona, before moving on to Paris. Swapping France for Italy, she had then gone to Rome, and after suffering the delights of that city, she had ventured to the final, most distant destination of her travels, the Greek capital Athens.

Once Vanessa had taken her seat in the *kafenion*, she ordered a gyro pita and was awaiting its arrival when one of the mobiles she was carrying bleeped, signalling an incoming text. She didn't react to it immediately, the tone being less familiar than on her other device. Three ladies at the adjoining table also made the same mistake, all reaching for their handbags, before realizing their error.

When she read the message, Vanessa smiled grimly. The wording might have been meaningless to anyone else, but Vanessa knew exactly what had occurred for the sender to deliver this particular piece of information. Furthermore, she knew exactly what she must do next. She would act according to the precise instructions given shortly after she embarked on her trip, 'Wait until you get a text that reads "all set for the grand finale", then do as follows . . .'

Now she had a few days left before returning to England, her decision must be how to spend that time, and how to celebrate.

Having received her cue, her first step was to book a return flight, the journey to be undertaken no earlier than seven days following receipt of that text. Only when she had visited a travel agency, and ensured they remembered the eccentric Englishwoman who had made the reservation, insisting on a flight to Manchester on one of three specific days, could she then move onto the next, equally necessary, carefully choreographed steps.

Aware she still had plenty of time to kill, Vanessa decided to defer making the travel arrangements until the following day. After lunch she would return to her hotel, take a siesta, and later dine out at the nearby restaurant, hoping that the handsome young waiter would be on duty.

Next morning, having made a suitably unforgettable impression at a travel agency, by knocking over a plastic display stand, scattering brochures across the tiled floor in the process, Vanessa emerged and headed to her favourite *kafenion*. As she drank her coffee, she extracted her other mobile from her handbag and began composing a text.

The wording was brief, to the point of curtness, with none of the affection that might have been expected given her relationship with the recipient. The message read simply, "Coming home", then quoted the flight number, date and time of arrival at Manchester, followed by the instructions, "meet me there".

Having sent this and finished her coffee, she decided to spend the rest of the morning doing a little more shopping. A couple of days earlier she had seen a particularly attractive pendant, with matching bracelet and earrings. Perhaps she should buy them, have them gift-wrapped, and pretend they were a gift from the handsome young waiter she had flirted with the previous evening.

After what had become her customary siesta, Vanessa showered and prepared to go for her meal. Before leaving her hotel room, she composed and sent a follow-up text, which read, "Did you get my message? Acknowledge". She left her mobile on the dressing table, well aware that she would not require it again that evening.

Twenty-four hours later, as Vanessa prepared to go to her favourite dining spot, she phoned a mobile number in the UK. As she expected, the call went straight to voicemail. Having left a curt, angry message that expressed her displeasure at being ignored, Vanessa switched her phone off. She placed the device on the bedside table, and then spent several minutes ensuring her appearance was satisfactory before leaving her room.

She felt a tiny thrill of excitement as she strolled towards the restaurant. She had been hugely disappointed the previous night when the handsome young waiter had not been on duty. Her regret enhanced for a moment when his replacement explained that Costas was at home, as his wife was in labour.

'That is the problem with being married,' the stand-in told her. 'Costas is very impulsive. I, on the other hand, am not shackled by the bonds of either parenthood, or matrimony.' He had bowed then, and told her, 'My name is Andreas. I am Costas' older brother, and you are the most beautiful customer I have had the honour to serve for many a day. I hope I can fulfil your needs, by providing you with what you desire most.'

At first, Vanessa had thought the slightly odd phraseology might have been down to Andreas' unfamiliarity with the English language. The next day, she had second thoughts, wondering if Andreas might have implied something far different than the food she'd been about to order. Perhaps this evening she would find out, but maybe better not to dwell on such possibilities. Athens, at that time of year, was still hot enough without getting over-excited.

Next morning, Vanessa used her mobile again, this time contacting a landline to leave a message on the answer machine. Aware that it was Sunday, she knew better than to try and contact the recipient's work. As for the rest of the day, Andreas had told her it was his day off, and volunteered to show her some of the parts of the ancient city, not usually seen by tourists. That had sounded promising, and it spurred Vanessa on to hope that Andreas might have more in mind, than the planned activity he had mentioned.

On Monday morning, Vanessa opted to have breakfast served on the balcony of her room, sharing the simple meal of yoghurt and honey, toast and orange juice with her companion, before returning to the bedroom. Minutes later, the chambermaid passed the room door, and noticed the sign on the door, *min enochleíte, Do Not Disturb*. Hearing the squeals of rapture from within, the woman smiled, knowing exactly why the occupants wanted to be left in peace.

It was almost lunchtime before Vanessa turned her attention back to the task she had been set. She began by repeating the process of attempting to make contact via text, phone, and email. Then, shortly before 1.45 p.m., which she knew equated to 11.45 a.m. in England, she made another call. Seconds later, she was speaking to the receptionist at Helm Logistics.

The information she received was sufficient to confirm that all was still going to plan. In reply to her enquiry, the receptionist told her, 'When I arrived this morning, there was a note from Mr B on my desk. He said he'd been called away, urgently, and wouldn't be back until Thursday. Have you tried his mobile?'

'I've left him a message. No doubt he'll reply when he's ready.' Vanessa ended the call and smiled. That was good news. The final piece of the jigsaw was almost in place. With her flight due to leave on Friday, she could relax until her next instruction had to be carried out. What's more, after the enjoyment of the previous night, Vanessa knew exactly how to pass the time, providing Andreas wasn't working.

On Thursday morning Vanessa phoned Helm Logistics. The receptionist had just arrived and barely reached her desk when Vanessa demanded to be put through to her husband, explaining she was still waiting for him to confirm that he would collect her from the airport.

'I'm afraid Mr Blackburn still hasn't returned. Nobody here has seen, or spoken to, him all week. Have you tried your home number?'

'Of course I've tried it, time after time! Plus his mobile. And I've sent him texts and emails. I don't understand what the hell's going on. Didn't he give anyone a clue as to where he was going?'

'No, not a word, Mrs Blackburn. To be honest we're starting to get a bit worried, especially after what happened to Jenny.'

'Jenny? You mean Jenny Granger? Why, what's happened to her?'

'I'm sorry to have to tell you, but Jenny's dead.' The receptionist lowered her voice to a whisper, as she added, 'The police think she was murdered, just like Andrew Derrick.'

'Andrew Derrick, the mechanic?'

'Yes, Mrs Blackburn. I thought you would know.'

'How would I know? Oh my goodness, this is terrible.' Vanessa paused for dramatic effect. 'OK, I'll make my own way home from Manchester, but in the meantime I'm going to speak to the police about Neil. We need someone to take action of some sort. However, if by any chance Neil should happen to turn up, tell him I want a word with him as a matter of urgency.' For effect, she added, 'And he'd better have a damned good explanation for the angry silence, otherwise there's going to be trouble.'

The receptionist winced, knowing the ferocity of Vanessa when she was on the rampage. She certainly wouldn't want to be in Blackburn's shoes when Vanessa caught up with him. The receptionist promised to contact her should her husband reappear.

Having ended the call, Vanessa made another one, this time to the control room at Netherdale police headquarters. This conversation lasted far longer. She had only just ended it when there was a knock on her hotel room door. She switched her mobile off, opened the door to allow Andreas to enter, and replaced the *Do Not Disturb* sign on the outer handle. Andreas had taken the day off, although he would have to work that evening. This was the last chance they would have to be together, and Vanessa was determined to make the most of it.

They had agreed that when the day was over they should go their separate ways. 'Better to retain the magic of what we had during our brief time together, rather than risk spoiling it,' he'd told her. It sounded right, and both of them believed it — almost.

* * *

Steve Meadows sighed when he saw the heading to the email — another day, another welfare check. He pressed the print button on his computer. He waited until the machine spewed out the single sheet of paper sent from Netherdale, and picked it out of the tray, glancing idly at the contents. He'd only scanned the first couple of lines when he stopped reading, muttered, 'Bloody hell,' under his breath, and dashed towards the stairs in his haste to reach CID.

The quartet of detectives was making their reports when the uniform sergeant entered at a gallop. Ignoring the opportunity for sarcasm this presented, Meadows told them, 'We've just received another MISPER report. Netherdale sent officers to carry out a welfare check in response to a phone call from Athens, of all places.'

He paused, as much to draw breath as for dramatic effect, and then added, 'The caller was Mrs Vanessa Blackburn. She's been trying to contact her husband, Neil, for over a week, because she's flying home tomorrow, and wanted him to collect her from Manchester airport. She spoke to the receptionist at Helm Logistics this morning, who said he hasn't been in the office all week, and when the receptionist told her about Jenny Granger, she began to get really concerned.

'Our guys went to the house, Bishopton Priory, and found the place all locked up. They used the big red key — on the back door, not the big oak front one,' he stammered, in response to their look of unease. 'That triggered the alarm system, but the house was empty, with no sign of Blackburn. They could see three vehicles in the garage, but that's all they could make out. They can't leave the house until the place is secure again, so they're waiting on site for instructions.'

By the time Meadows had finished speaking, all four detectives were on their feet, with Nash heading to his office to collect his car keys. 'Thanks, Steve. We'll take it from here. Clara, you're with me. Viv and Lisa, follow us.' He strode quickly towards the exit, snatching the report out of Meadows' hand as he passed.

CHAPTER TWENTY

In the country lane approaching Bishopton, Clara noticed a large bunch of flowers placed against the buckled upright posts of the signpost marking the town's border. The bouquet was obviously fresh, none of the petals having wilted, or been damaged by the recent heavy rain. That, Clara thought, must be the place where the jogger had been killed by the hit-and-run driver. Although she felt renewed sadness at this reminder of the tragedy, she put it to the back of her mind as they attempted to come to grips with the potential problem awaiting them at Bishopton Priory.

When they passed under the wrought-iron archway at the entrance to the drive, they could hear the burglar alarm sounding. Their view of the Priory was obscured by the twin row of poplar trees lining the drive. What they could see quite clearly were the two vans parked on the gravel sweep in front of the building. One obviously belonged to their uniform colleagues, but the purpose of the other vehicle puzzled them until they halted alongside it. The name and logo on the van read Dale Contract Cleaning. Their presence raised several questions in Nash's mind, which he would make his first priority.

Having been introduced to the leader of the four-member cleaning crew, speaking loudly over the noise, he asked, 'Is this a regular visit?'

'That's right, we come every Thursday,' the woman replied. 'It's such a big building we do half of it on each visit.'

'Is it normal for nobody to be at home when you turn up?' Nash shook his head, and screwed up his face at the vibrant tones echoing round them.

'Yes and no. I mean it doesn't happen often, but we know Mrs B is away. She told us about it before she left, so we weren't surprised. Do you want me to turn that off?' She gestured to the building.

'Sorry, I can't allow you to go in. Would you mind giving my colleague the door key and the number sequence for the keypad? Don't worry, she's quite trustworthy.'

Clara grabbed some overshoes, and headed for the door, moments later everything went quiet.

'That's better.' Nash smiled. 'When Mrs Blackburn's absent, does her husband let you in?'

The cleaner's disdainful sniff spoke volumes about the woman's low opinion of Blackburn. 'No, we only see him once in a blue moon, thankfully. Mrs B gave us a key and the numbers for the alarm system a long time ago. If there's no one in, we've to sign a book on leaving, to confirm the alarm has been set.' Then she added, by way of explanation, 'There was a bit of trouble a few years back. One of our team forgot to reset it before they left. He no longer works for us.'

'OK, I think you're going to have to skip your job for the time being. We'll need to check the house over. Can you pass the details of the former employee to Helmsdale station?' Nash saw the look of disbelief on the woman's face. 'Purely to rule him out,' he added.

After the cleaners had gone, Clara demanded, 'What do you mean, *quite* trustworthy?'

Nash grinned. 'I just wanted to be sure you were listening.'

'I certainly was, and I don't think Mrs Mop has a very high opinion of Neil Blackburn.'

'Yes, I got the same impression, which leads me to wonder why.' He called to Viv. 'Look for the security company name on the alarm box, will you, and ask control to phone them. Tell them it was us that set it off. Otherwise, we'll have them turning up as well.' He looked round. 'Right, let's have a word with our guys, and get kitted out.' Nash looked at the building and suggested, 'I think we'd be best splitting the search into two teams, otherwise we'll be here for weeks.'

'What about getting the workmen in for the door?'

'That's something our uniform colleagues can deal with. Give them Jimmy Johnson's number and ask them to call him first. He should be able to recommend a reliable carpenter to fix the back door.'

'That's an unusually bright idea — for you.'

Nash grinned at Clara's retaliation to his jibe.

The task of searching the property took a long time, despite the division of labour. It was beginning to seem like a wasted effort until Nash, with Lisa Andrews alongside him, entered one of the bedrooms. Lisa stared in dismay at the shirt, tie, suit jacket and trousers, underpants, socks, and even a pair of leather shoes, strewn haphazardly across the bed. The discarded clothing bore marked similarity to what they had discovered in the homes of previous victims. 'Go find Clara and Viv,' Nash told her. 'We need everyone here. In a mausoleum of this size, your best bet would be to shout or whistle for them.'

By the time the others arrived, Nash had completed his inspection of the wardrobe and chest of drawers on one wall of the room, and reported, 'This is obviously Neil Blackburn's room. There's only men's clothing in here.' He gestured to the wardrobe. 'That suggests he and his wife were no longer sleeping together. Would one of you find out which room Mrs Blackburn occupies when she's in residence, and check the wardrobes in the lady's chamber.'

'I'll do it,' Lisa volunteered.

'Do you think we need to search the rest of the house after finding this?' Clara pointed to the clothing.

'We'd better do, Clara. Actually, you and I can tackle that job along with Lisa, after she's finished inspecting lingerie.' He turned to Pearce. 'Viv, while we're doing that, would you go outside and take a look in the garage? That's probably the old stable block. See what vehicles are inside.' As Pearce was about to depart, Nash added, 'And if you need to contact us, the fastest way would probably be to phone.'

'You're in a very flippant mood all of a sudden, Mike. Why might that be?'

'It's called distraction therapy, Clara, because I'm trying to wrestle with two great anomalies about this crime scene.'

'Would you like to share them with your loyal assistant?'

'I don't see why not, going on the principle that two heads are better than one. When our colleagues arrived, they had to use the door enforcer to gain entry, and that triggered the alarm system.'

'Yes, I get that. So what?'

'When we found Blackburn's clothing on the bed exactly like the previous instances, we automatically assumed he'd been abducted, agreed?'

'Yes,' Clara replied cautiously, still wondering where this was leading.

'Now, you could argue that perhaps Blackburn set the scene, and is responsible for all this. We know he was nervous about something when we spoke to him. Alternatively, he let the abductor into the house, unaware of the danger he was in. Or the intruder could already have been inside, waiting to pounce.'

'I still don't get the point.'

'Whether the abductor was inside, or not, when Blackburn arrived home, isn't that important. What *is* extremely important is, how did the kidnapper, if there is one, manage to reset the alarm after he'd abducted Blackburn, if that's what happened?'

'That's not possible, surely?'

'Not unless—'

'Somebody supplied him with the sequence of numbers on the keypad,' Clara added.

'And a door key.'

'Yes, that sounds feasible, but for one thing.'

'What?'

'If this is the work of the same person, that implies they had keys to all the victims' properties. Somehow, I don't think that's the case.'

Nash shrugged. 'No doubt we'll find out, eventually.'

They were searching the cellars, which seemed to be almost exclusively devoted to storage of the largest collection of wine bottles Clara had ever seen, when Lisa called down for them to join her.

They hurried upstairs, and as they were dusting cobwebs from their clothing, Lisa said, 'Viv's hit a bit of a snag. He can't gain entry to the garages. He says they've got up-and-over doors, operated by remote control. There ought to be one that opens the doors from outside. But he hasn't the remotest idea where to look for it.'

Clara groaned, despairingly. 'Don't you start with the bad puns, Lisa. We've enough problems with His Lordship here.'

Nash apparently ignored the insult. 'I suggest we separate, and look through the back rooms on the ground floor again, because that must be where the control is kept. Anywhere else would be too remote.'

He smiled at Clara, who sighed at him, shaking her head.

Five minutes later, having located the control on a shelf in the cloaks cupboard near the rear entrance, they gathered outside, as Pearce used it to open the garage doors. They stared at the vehicles with increasing awe. Two of the cars were obviously new, or recent, models. The top-of-the-range Mercedes and BMW gleamed in the sunlight. But it was the third car that, once Viv and Lisa had removed the dust sheets covering the bodywork, commanded their attention and respect.

Nash looked at the shape of the vehicle. 'That's a pre-war model. It probably hit the road for the first time in the early nineteen thirties. It's a Rolls Royce Phantom 2 Cabriolet, and I guess it's worth the thick end of a quarter of a million quid. Check it over carefully, and then replace the cover. Whatever you do,' he stressed, 'don't scratch the paintwork.'

As they were covering the bonnet with one of the dust sheets, Pearce was unable to resist the temptation to stroke the figurine that was the Rolls Royce figurehead. Nash, who was watching, told him, 'It's called the Spirit of Ecstasy, Viv. That small chunk of metal is probably worth more than your monthly salary.'

They were about to leave the outbuilding, when Nash saw something on the floor to the rear. He bent over it, puzzling as to what it was, and how it got there. 'What do you reckon this might be?'

They all peered at the small flakes of something metallic. 'They look rather like paint,' Clara suggested. 'But I haven't a clue where they might have come from — there are no scratches on the cars in here.'

'I think it would be a good idea to ask our forensic guys to give the garage the once-over, when they've finished in the house — and, in the process, be sure to mention this little item. I'm not sure whether they'll find anything significant or useful, judging by the state of the previous victims' houses. But who knows? We might get lucky.'

'You're definitely treating this as an abduction, then?' Clara asked.

'I can't see any other explanation, can you?'

'I'm not sure.'

'Why not try us with it?' Nash said, with a hint of a smile.

'It goes back to your comments about the alarm being reset. What if Blackburn *is* behind all this, and *has* staged his abduction to give the appearance of him being a victim.'

Viv, who had not been party to their earlier conversation said, 'Blimey, Clara, there's no stopping you when you get a wild idea. That one's probably more outrageous than any of Mike's — and that's saying something.'

* * *

Once the forensic team had begun inspection of the property, the detectives returned to Helmsdale, with the exception of Viv Pearce, who remained on site to liaise with the officers. Shortly before they departed, Jimmy Johnson arrived, along with a carpenter to rectify the damage caused by the forced entry.

Clara continued with the theory she'd mooted earlier, telling Nash and Lisa, 'I can't shake off the feeling that this abduction isn't real. I know the evidence points to it, and the "crime scene" appears to be identical to what we found with the murder victims, but I wonder if it's been staged that way simply for our benefit.'

'What would the purpose be in doing that?' Lisa asked.

'If Blackburn has something to hide, a disappearance we treat as a kidnapping would lead to us discounting him as a potential culprit.'

'It's an interesting line of thought, Nash agreed. 'But there are one or two potential flaws that should be taken into account. The biggest of those is, in order to set the stage as precisely as this, Blackburn would have to know what the others looked like — and that would give him away as the killer. That might be the case, but by leaving the house as he did would be tantamount to signing a confession.'

'I didn't think of that,' Clara admitted.

'There is some mileage in your theory, though,' Nash continued, 'because if the real killer abducted him, he might have hoped to deceive us into believing Blackburn to be the guilty party. However, on a more practical level, how would Blackburn have left the Priory unless someone took him? Both his and his wife's cars are in the garage along with that old banger. I can't see him legging it on Shanks' Pony with all that expensive vehicular transport available. One of you should ring round the local taxi firms; ask if they've had a call to the address in the last week.'

He thought for a moment. 'There is one possible way to discount Blackburn as a serial killer, and that entails trying to establish if he has an alibi for the times the murders were committed. If we can prove he was elsewhere when Derrick, Wilson, and Ms Granger were killed, that would disprove the theory once and for all.'

'It's going to be difficult to find out where he was, if we can't ask him.'

'There is a way that might work. Lisa, go to Helm Logistics and check with the receptionist and other members of staff. If one of them can provide us with information as to his movements, then we'd be home and dry.'

* * *

Lisa's report, on her return from Helm Logistics, did nothing to disprove Clara's theory. 'I spoke to every member of staff who was available. That includes the ones who are office-based, and several of the sales force. None of them could provide details of Blackburn's whereabouts at around the probable time of each murder. The receptionist even allowed me into Blackburn's office to examine his diary. Although there were copious entries for almost every working day over the past three months, significantly, on the dates you gave me, many of the pages were blank.'

'That actually tends to strengthen the theory, rather than drive holes in it,' Nash agreed. 'As we can't rule Blackburn out as a suspect, I think we ought to pay more attention to him, rather than writing him off as a potential victim.' He smiled ruefully, then added, 'That's one more suspect than we had this morning.'

The only other significant piece of information to come from what was proving to be a highly frustrating day, was the report Viv Pearce gave on his return from Bishopton Priory. 'Forensics checked the house and outbuildings, and didn't find anything you could class as suspicious. I asked them to take those flakes of paint away for analysis, and although they thought it was a waste of time, they agreed. They believe it might be metallic automotive paint, but as they're grey in colour, I reckon they could have come from almost half the vehicles in Britain.'

'It's certainly true, there's a lot of metallic grey cars about. What makes them so popular?' Clara wondered.

'Probably the fact that they don't show the dirt as much as other colours.'

Although they smiled at Nash's flippant comment, the detectives knew they were little nearer finding the killer or motive for the murders than previously.

* * *

When the plane had taken off from Athens, and the journey to England was under way, Vanessa relaxed, and contemplated the four-hour flight ahead. Normally she would have occupied her time with Sudoku puzzles and crosswords, but she felt too tired to concentrate on these. She smiled slightly as she acknowledged the reason for her weariness.

Before leaving the Greek capital to take a taxi to Venizelos Airport, Vanessa had said farewell to Andreas. Once she was alone in the privacy of her hotel room, she had removed the SIM card from one of her mobile phones, cutting the card into minute pieces. She had then taken a stroll through the narrow streets, dropping the shredded card into a litter bin, and the mobile into another, thereby disposing of any connection to events that had happened in the UK during her absence.

As the aircraft climbed to its cruising altitude, Vanessa's thoughts returned to the events of the previous week. Much of her time had been spent in a series of passionate encounters with a man who was little more than a stranger — one, moreover, from a different land, with a markedly different culture. That hadn't concerned her one iota. Neither had the fact that she had broken her marriage vows time, after time, after time.

She had been surprised by her willingness to indulge in such behaviour, which was far from typical, and had never happened before. What also shocked her was the level of enjoyment she had derived from their activity. She wondered, briefly, if it was the freedom from any form of commitment that had caused such delight, or the knowledge that Andreas was completely different to the man she had married. Then she acknowledged it was neither of these, but something far more physical that had caused her so much pleasure.

As for the transgression of her marital commitment, Vanessa couldn't care one jot about that. The words she had issued on her wedding day no longer held any meaning for her. It had become patently obvious, from the early days of their marriage, that her husband had only been after her money, and was more fascinated by the size of her bank balance than that of her breasts. Love hadn't died, she acknowledged, because it had never existed in the first place.

There was one other aspect to her supposed infidelity that Vanessa dwelt on. For all she knew, by the time she had taken Andreas to her bed, she might have already become a widow. If that thought disturbed her, it certainly wasn't apparent from the smile on her face.

The smile was generated by thinking of Andreas. He had no idea if she was married or single, affluent or poor. His sole interest was in taking her to bed, and making love to her as often, and in as many ways, as he could. If only she'd married a man like Andreas, someone who worshipped her body, rather than her wealth. Or possibly, someone who would be as dedicated to their partner as the man she had met a few months ago. That man had demonstrated a love that was stronger than life itself, and was prepared to demonstrate his devotion in the most extreme way.

Vanessa had deliberately kept her financial circumstances from Andreas, playing the part instead of someone of average means, not wishing to spoil things between them. As it transpired, Andreas hadn't been in the slightest bothered whether she was a princess, or a pauper.

As she pondered the affair, Vanessa had a stray thought. Neither she nor Andreas had taken precautions prior to making love. What if she was carrying an additional souvenir home from Athens, by way of becoming pregnant? Although in earlier times, that would have worried her, Vanessa's new-found freedom relieved her from such anxieties. If such a thing *did* happen, the only problem might be entering the father's name on the birth certificate. She felt reasonably certain that "Andreas the waiter" had never appeared on one of those forms before. The idea made Vanessa giggle, causing the woman on her left to glance at her, wondering what she found amusing.

As the aircraft approached British airspace, Vanessa came to a decision. It was prompted both by what she felt certain awaited her at home, and also by Andreas' final comment before they parted. 'I know when we first made love we agreed to walk away when it was over, but I no longer wish that to happen, because I have never been with a woman who can arouse me the way you do, or who I want to remain with. My only hope is that you might feel something of the same. If you decide to return to Athens, I will be here for you.'

Vanessa made her decision as the plane began its final approach to Manchester airport. She *would* return to Athens, and she *would* continue her relationship with Andreas and see where it took them. She had no idea whether their affair would become permanent. If it was not to be, it was too enjoyable to miss.

The thought of returning to him was beginning to excite her, but first there were matters to deal with in England. As the jet's wheels touched the tarmac, Vanessa remembered that many Greek women wore black, and wondered if it would suit her, because she felt confident that before long, she would qualify for that colour.

* * *

Nash was mildly surprised that Vanessa Blackburn had failed to contact them immediately on her return from abroad. Having reported her husband missing, he thought it odd that she had failed to follow up by asking what progress they had made in tracing him.

Her lack of interest was intentional, as she had her instructions. Besides which, she had other priorities now.

On leaving the terminal, instead of returning home, Vanessa booked into a hotel near the airport, and remained there overnight. Her time was spent binge-watching serials on her hotel room TV, and daydreaming about Andreas. During that time, her mobile remained permanently switched off. The reason, as she would later explain, was that she had left the charger in her hotel in Athens. What she would *not* tell them was that this had been a deliberate action. Nor would she elaborate on her reason for remaining away from home for an extra day, other than by saying she needed time to make arrangements for transport.

With no means of contacting the missing man's wife, Nash's only recourse was to ask Steve Meadows for a patrol car to maintain a drive-by, and to check the entrance gates to Bishopton Priory. Having been told by one of the patrol officers the gate were normally left open, Viv had closed them at the end of the forensic investigation. If they were seen to be open, it was assumed someone would be in residence. When the report came in that the gates were now open, Nash told Mironova, 'OK, Clara, we're going slumming again.'

CHAPTER TWENTY-ONE

Vanessa Blackburn was a strikingly handsome woman, Clara thought. In addition to her good looks, she appeared suntanned, fit and well, and not the least bit worried about her absent spouse. Even the news that her husband had possibly been abducted failed to concern her. When Nash went on to inform Vanessa that the circumstances surrounding his disappearance bore marked similarities to those of three murder victims, it was almost, Clara thought, as if Vanessa was being told about something that had happened to a complete stranger.

When Nash continued, by describing how the officers responding to her call had been obliged to use force to enter the house, and told her what they had found, Vanessa's only comment was, 'Oh dear, I hope they didn't do any lasting damage. The oak front door is over two hundred years old.'

Nash told her it was the back door. Then, assuming that with her prolonged absence from England, Vanessa would not be aware of what had occurred locally, he went on to explain who the murder victims were.

Clara was surprised by Vanessa's reaction. When Andrew Derrick's name was mentioned, the look on Vanessa's face was of disinterest. This changed when Nash told her about Cheesy Wilson. Her expression changed to one of distaste, almost as if she had trodden in something extremely unpleasant. Although this was mildly intriguing, it demonstrated only that Vanessa knew of both men, and didn't approve of one of them.

Things changed dramatically when Nash turned to the subject of Jenny Granger's murder. Whereas previously, Vanessa had seemed detached, her attitude impersonal, there was no mistaking the look of hatred at the mention of Ms Granger's name. Was that evidence that Vanessa knew, or suspected, Blackburn was in a relationship with the dead woman? If so, it would prove Nash's theory to be correct.

Clara waited for Nash to continue, perhaps changing the subject to her husband's disappearance, but instead, he continued to talk about Jenny Granger.

'I understand that Ms Granger worked for Helm Logistics as a systems analyst, whatever that is?' He smiled apologetically. 'I'm a bit of a technophobe, so I'm not certain what that title entails. Can you explain what her role in the company was? Preferably in layman's terms.'

'I'm afraid not, Inspector Nash. Although I own the company, I wasn't involved in the day-to-day running of it. If I had been, perhaps things might have turned out different — or maybe not, knowing the people involved.'

It was only then that Nash asked the question Clara had been expecting.

'You don't seem too upset, or concerned, about your husband's disappearance, or the danger he might be in. Why is that? Could it be that you know, or suspect, that his relationship with Ms Granger was a more intimate one, rather than simply work colleagues?'

'That certainly wouldn't surprise me.'

Clara noticed that whereas previously Vanessa had been manifestly straightforward, she was now choosing her words with extreme care, while clasping her hands in her lap.

'In fact, there is very little about him that would surprise me. I've long since ceased to worry about his misdeeds. They say you pay for your mistakes, and I have certainly done that.'

* * *

'What did you make of all that?' Clara asked, once they were back in the Range Rover.

'I think Mrs Blackburn told us exactly what she wanted us to know — absolutely nothing of value. I believe she's an extremely accomplished liar. She is not only fully aware of the affair her husband was conducting with Jenny Granger, but also knows the motive for all three murders, plus her husband's disappearance. She possibly knows the identity of the killer, but getting blood out of a stone would be far simpler than getting her to reveal a single word that she doesn't want us to hear.'

'Is that it?'

'Far from it. I also believe that she isn't the slightest bit bothered about the fact that three people have been murdered. Or that her husband might soon be added to that list. That in turn, raises a very interesting question.'

'What's that?'

'If Vanessa was so disinterested in the fate of her husband, why did she phone, text and email him for a week or so, and then call us from Athens to report him missing? Why not wait until she returned home, if she didn't care one way or the other?'

'And the answer?'

'Two possibilities spring to mind. One, is that she was establishing, beyond doubt, that she had an alibi for the time of his disappearance. The other, is that she was following a carefully constructed script. In fact, she could well have been doing both.' Nash grinned as he got out of the car. 'I'd be interested to see what her reaction would be, if we were to ask if there was anyone in Athens who could corroborate her alibi.'

'Why do you say that?'

'The look on her face when she mentioned her stay there. It was the only time during our conversation that she looked content. I've seen that expression before, and I don't think she spent her time simply looking round the Parthenon.'

'If you're suggesting what I think, then I certainly wouldn't argue with an expert,' she said, as they headed for CID, where Pearce was waiting with news.

'Forensics has emailed the result of their work at Bishopton Priory,' he told them. 'But everything was negative, apart from those paint flecks you found, Mike.' He glanced down at the sheet of paper he was holding. 'It is automotive paint, but the amount we recovered was too small to tie it to a specific manufacturer, or model, with any degree of certainty. However, they did comment that Blackburn's BMW would qualify as a contender.'

'That might be so, Viv, but we didn't see any dents or scratches on his car,' Clara pointed out.

'That doesn't mean anything. He could have had it re-sprayed, if he'd been in a shunt.'

'Agreed, but I hardly think it's relevant to our investigation, do you?' she added.

'Whether it's important or not, I think we ought to look a lot more closely into Mr Neil Blackburn's life, especially given his wife's low opinion of him.' Nash said.

'How do you intend to go about it?' Viv asked.

'I think I know just where to start. In fact, I'm a bit annoyed with myself that I didn't think of it before. Clara, will you brief the others on our interview with Vanessa Blackburn, while I go and sort out a search warrant for Helm Logistics? If we're lucky, we can go today.'

* * *

It seemed for long enough that their search would once again prove to be a fruitless waste of time. Nash assured the assembled office staff that they were not looking for evidence of criminal activity by company employees.

'However,' he pointed out, 'two of your colleagues have been murdered. And now your managing director has vanished, in highly suspicious circumstances. We need to try and discover the connection between these incidents, in the hope that we can prevent something untoward happening to Mr Blackburn. With that in mind, if any of you know anything you think might prove beneficial, please don't hesitate to inform me, or one of my colleagues. Should you have any misgivings about doing so, rest assured that anything you tell us will be kept in the strictest confidence.'

'That was a fine speech,' Clara told him, as the employees dispersed. 'I actually believed parts of it.'

Nash had an idea. He turned to the receptionist for the information.

'The workshop?' she asked, clearly baffled by his request. 'We don't have a workshop. All the equipment we supply is brought in ready-assembled.'

'Sorry, you misunderstood me. I was referring to the place where Mr Derrick worked.'

'Oh, I see. The garage is on the ground floor of the adjacent building. We use the upper storey as warehouse space.' She handed Nash the keys.

'OK, Viv, I want you and Lisa to go over every inch of Blackburn's office with a fine-tooth comb. Look for the tiniest detail — anything that seems odd, or out of place. Clara and I will look round the garage. We'll join you when we've done.'

Seeing the receptionist's anxious expression, he told her, 'Don't worry, I promise we'll be out of your hair before the business is due to close for the day.'

As he unlocked the workshop door, Nash said, 'While we're in the building, it might be an idea to check the upper level. Will you do that while I deal with the area where Derrick operated?'

When Clara returned to the ground floor, she found Nash standing at the far end of the workshop. She frowned, puzzled by what he was holding. 'There doesn't seem to be anything of interest upstairs, Mike.'

He didn't reply for a moment, so Clara waited, as he was obviously deep in thought. Eventually, he turned towards her. 'OK, it was a bit of a long shot.'

'What are you doing with that?'

'I found this under the bench here, and it's given me an idea.'

Clara groaned. 'Not another one. I've told you before about getting ideas — you know it's bad for you. Are you keeping it to yourself, or would you like to share it with your glamorous assistant?'

'This is, or rather, was, the bumper off a motor vehicle. At a guess, I'd say it's the front bumper. I also found these,' he gestured to the objects on the workbench.

Clara looked at the two items. One was a spray can of paint, the other, a sheet of slightly crumpled paper. 'What's so significant about those?'

'If you examine the paint can, you can tell it's been used. There's a dribble of paint down the side. I could be wrong, but I thought it looked very similar in colour to those flecks of paint we found in the garage at Bishopton Priory. What we need to do next, is to ask the receptionist, or whoever handles such things, to dig out the registration documents for all the company vehicles.' He studied the label on the tin. 'We're looking for one where the colour is listed as *Sophisto Grey Xirallic*.'

'OK, I'll go and ask the question. What will you do while I'm gone? Not more thinking, I hope?'

Nash smiled. 'No, I'm going to follow up on the second piece of potential evidence I found.' He waved the paper in the air.

'What's so special about that?'

'It's a cash sales receipt from a scrapyard. Fortunately, it not only has the scrapyard phone number on it, it also has the receipt number.'

'I still don't understand why you think it's important.'

'I wondered why Helm Logistics' fleet vehicle foreman found it necessary to buy something from a scrapyard. And why he went all the way to Sheffield in order to do so. I reckon that's a round trip of close to two hundred miles.'

When Clara returned, she had news. Her research tallied with what Nash had discovered. 'There's only one vehicle in the company fleet with that colour.'

'Let me guess, the vehicle is Neil Blackburn's BMW.'

'How did you know?'

'Because I spoke to the scrap dealer, and got him to check the sales receipt. Although it doesn't say as much on this form, there's a code number on the dealer's copy that tallies with their stock record. This receipt is for the purchase of a BMW front bumper. Bumpers made nowadays are plastic, which means they can't be straightened, or repaired with filler and a quick re-spray. If the damage is more than a trivial scratch, they need to be replaced. I think we need to impound Blackburn's Beamer, and get our forensic guys working on it.'

'You obviously believe this to be important, but I can't see why. OK, so he had an accident. What if he just shunted another car?'

'If that was the case, why go to all that trouble to conceal the prang? Why not take it to the BMW main dealer? Get their workshop to fit a new bumper, and do a re-spray.'

'OK, I get that, but what do you think examining it will tell us?'

'I've no idea. It might not give us anything, but I think it's worth a shot.'

Nash was about to phone Forensics when DC Pearce appeared. 'There's something next door I think you should see.'

They secured the evidence from the workshop, and followed Pearce. From the outer office, they could see Lisa Andrews staring at the wall — or the ceiling, Clara wasn't sure which. 'What is she looking at?' she asked.

Pearce drew to a halt. 'When you go in, don't say a word. There's something hidden in the centre of one of the flowers in the pattern on the wallpaper. I can't be one hundred per cent certain without risking damaging the paper, but I believe it's a lens. If I'm right, it could have a sound recorder, and anything you say would be known to the person who installed it.'

'A lens, as in a camera?' Clara said in disbelief.

'Yes, I think it's part of a very minute surveillance system. Some of the most recent sophisticated models are no bigger than a shirt button.'

'Why would Blackburn have a device like that installed in his office?'

'You're assuming he was the one who had it fitted, Clara,' Nash responded. 'But what if someone else had the device put there? Someone, for example, who was suspicious about Blackburn's behaviour, or misbehaviour, and wanted to gather evidence of wrongdoing?'

'You're thinking of Mrs Blackburn?'

'She would seem to be the obvious choice, given the way she feels about her husband. What we should do is check the places where Blackburn might have come into contact with Jenny Granger — see if we can find any similar equipment.'

The task of examining the remainder of the premises in equally microscopic detail, threatened Nash's promise they would be finished by the end of office hours. They managed it, with minutes to spare, by which time, they had discovered two more devices. One of these was in Jenny Granger's office, the other in the company's boardroom. Significantly, from Nash's point of view, no such equipment was found in the areas Andrew Derrick was likely to frequent.

'I reckon our suspicions are shared by someone else who believed that Blackburn and Ms Granger were having an affair, and possibly using the boardroom as a bedroom,' Nash told the team.

'Where do we take it from here?'

'Good question, Lisa. First, we need to obtain a warrant to seize Blackburn's BMW, and in the process, I want to ask Mrs Blackburn some questions. One of which she probably won't be prepared to answer.'

* * *

They watched the BMW being winched onto the back of a low loader, and Nash raised the issues resulting from the search of Helm Logistics with Vanessa Blackburn. She had prompted the first of these, by asking why they were taking such a close interest in her husband's car.

'It's all to do with something we found in the company's workshop,' Nash told her, deliberately omitting details. 'Has the BMW been off the road recently, can you recall? I believe it might have required some bodywork repairs.'

Vanessa thought about the question for a moment. Clara, holding her usual watching brief, wondered if she was pretending to think it over, while in reality choosing her reply carefully.

'Yes, it was in dock a while back. Neil said he'd hit a deer while driving back from a business meeting in Scotland.' She attempted a joke. 'Why, has there been a complaint by the RSPCA?'

Nash ignored the flippancy, and asked, 'Can you explain why Mr Blackburn didn't take the car to a BMW main dealer to have the repairs carried out?'

'I don't really know. Possibly it's because there is, or rather was, a trained fitter at his works.'

'That doesn't explain why the replacement front bumper was purchased from a scrap merchant in Sheffield, rather than a bona fide BMW agent. If the accident was as innocuous as you suggest, there would have been no need for such secrecy, surely?'

'That's a question only my husband can answer. So you'll have to wait and ask him, if, and when, he turns up.'

Nash changed the subject abruptly, hoping to catch Vanessa by surprise. 'Why did you place spy cameras with microphones in his office, plus Ms Granger's, and the company boardroom?'

There was a long pause before Vanessa asked, 'What spy cameras?'

'The ones we discovered when we searched the premises. The location of the surveillance equipment, suggests someone wanted to establish the exact nature of the relationship between your husband and Ms Granger. The person most likely to want to know that fact is you, Mrs Blackburn. Did you think they were having an affair?'

'That sounds almost like an accusation, Mr Nash. I'm not happy to answer any further questions until I've sought legal advice.'

'As you wish,' Nash said. 'We'll speak again later.'

Once they were out of the building, Clara said, 'She was lying about the damage to the Beamer.'

'She was lying all through the interview. Not only did she know the real cause of the car damage, and why it had to be kept from public knowledge, but she also suspects that her husband has already become another murder victim — either that, or he's going to be one.'

'What led you to think that?' Clara looked surprised.

'She said, "You'll have to ask him *if and when* he turns up" which suggests she's convinced he won't return alive. And, unless I'm very much mistaken, she also knew about the surveillance equipment, and what those devices revealed.'

'It would be interesting to view that footage.'

Nash grinned. 'Not getting enough excitement at home, Clara?'

'I didn't mean that,' she retorted angrily. 'I was referring to the potential motive for the murders.'

As they drove away from Bishopton Priory, with the low loader following at a more sedate speed, their progress was observed by two spectators with special interest in their actions. One of them, Vanessa Blackburn, wondered what the police examination of the car would reveal. The other, watching from a nearby vantage point, was mildly irritated by the police activity, because the removal of the vehicle was likely to prove an inconvenience to his careful planning. Perhaps it was time for a re-think.

The second observer pondered the development for a while, but then realized that by employing his specialist skills, he could achieve the same result, and even provide an amusing side effect that would add to the enjoyment.

CHAPTER TWENTY-TWO

Nash and his colleagues spent the next few days in a kind of limbo, punctuated by a series of reports from the team examining the BMW. The first of these came less than twenty-four hours after they seized the vehicle. Nash listened with interest to his informant, then wandered into the main office to brief the others. 'I've just had word from the boffins. They've been concentrating on the vehicle interior to begin with, and guess what they found?'

'A dead deer in the boot?' Viv joked.

'No, Viv,' Nash shook his head. 'They found several stains on the upholstery, which they've identified as semen and vaginal fluid. That suggests our theory that Blackburn was having it off with Jenny Granger, was correct. Although we will have to wait for the DNA analysis to confirm who he was copulating with. However, that isn't all. We're not the only ones who will know the truth. Our guys also found another surveillance device, concealed in the car dashboard. What we can't be sure of, is whether these discoveries are relevant to the murders and Blackburn's disappearance. Or, whether it's simply his wife checking on his infidelity.'

Two days later, they got another update, and this one promised to be far more informative. Lisa Andrews had arrived at work before her colleagues, and told them of the call she had received minutes earlier. 'The boffins put the BMW over an inspection pit, and removed the front bumper. Somewhere underneath, on the front part of the chassis, they discovered specks of dried blood.'

'That might bear out the story Blackburn told his wife, about hitting a deer,' Viv said.

'Unfortunately, you're wrong, Viv. The preliminary tests show the blood isn't cervine.'

'Isn't what?' Clara asked.

'Belonging to a deer,' Lisa explained. 'The species is homo sapiens. The blood is human.'

'So that's why Blackburn was so anxious to cover up the damage to the BMW. He was obviously involved in an accident,' Nash suggested. 'What we don't know is where or when it happened, and to whom.'

'We might have a clue as to the identity of the person involved before long,' Lisa told him. 'The forensic guys reckon there's sufficient blood to get a DNA match.'

* * *

The third report from the scientists came the following Monday As he read the email, Nash realized that the contents were dynamite. When the other team members arrived, he signalled them into his office. 'Viv,' he began, 'I want you to print off an RTA report, please. It concerns a fatal hit-and-run incident. The victim's name is Mrs Amanda Clark.'

Clara gasped with astonishment. 'Is this . . . ?'

Nash nodded — his expression grim. 'DNA test results are back, and they reveal the blood taken from the underside of Blackburn's BMW, is that of Amanda Clark. I think we might just have obtained the motive for the murders of Derrick and Granger — and, most likely by now, that of Blackburn.'

'We still don't know where Cheesy Wilson fits into the equation, though,' Clara pointed out.

'That's not a priority. What we need to concentrate on is finding the person, or persons, close to Amanda Clark, who might feel strongly enough to take revenge for her death.' He paused for a moment. 'What we also need is to work out how they got their information. I can't for one minute think they were able to stroll into Helm Logistics, fit three surveillance cameras, and walk out again, without someone knowing what they'd been doing. Fitting a spy camera into Blackburn's car would have been just as difficult, unless . . .'

'Unless what?'

'Unless the person, or persons, concerned, got assistance from within — from someone who held a strong enough grudge against Blackburn to cooperate with Nemesis.'

'Who?'

'Nemesis, the Greek goddess of retribution.'

The report printed off by Pearce brought them little satisfaction. Details of the hit-and-run were horrendous enough, but the results of the post-mortem brought even more distress.

Clara summed up their feelings after reading the first page of the document. 'The autopsy suggests that if Amanda Clark had received medical treatment within a reasonable amount of time after sustaining those injuries, she would certainly have survived. In other words, it was a life wasted because of Blackburn's selfish need to avoid punishment. And possibly, to avoid discovery of his affair.'

'Lives, not life,' Nash corrected her, having turned to the second page of the report. 'Amanda Clark was pregnant when the accident happened. The baby would almost certainly have survived, too, had Amanda been given treatment in time.'

Other aspects of the case were equally distressing, as Clara recalled, notably the death of Amanda's mother shortly afterwards. She reminded Nash of the graves they'd seen when they were called to the Jenny Granger dump site.

'Yes,' he agreed, 'and now we're aware of the full facts we need to speak to Amanda's husband. It grieves me to say it, but I think James Clark has just become the prime suspect for three murders — probably four, by now.'

* * *

Talking to James Clark was easier said than done. When Nash and Clara went to the Bishopton address listed on the file, they found the house deserted. Priory Close was a small crescent of only twelve semi-detached houses, numbered sequentially. Number 12, the end of the row, had an estate agent's FOR SALE board in the front garden. 'Do you think Clark's done a runner?' Clara asked, on seeing the notice and taking into account the unkempt lawn and weed-filled flower beds.

'I very much doubt it,' Nash told her. 'I think his work isn't done yet, so he'll be more determined to finish it than to think about escaping justice. I reckon he's gone into hiding, because he doesn't want us to frustrate him from dealing with his prime target.'

'If Clark gave the estate agent instructions on the sale, he must surely have supplied them with contact details. That should make him easy to track down.'

'Good idea, Clara. You deal with it when we get back.'

Although Nash was now confident James Clark was the man they were seeking, he had a growing sense of unease that the task of finding, and detaining, him, might not be as simple as Clara had suggested. He had never considered himself to have the gift of prophecy until he thought about this later.

Back in Helmsdale, Clara contacted the local branch of Nixon's, the nationwide estate agency chain. While she was doing this, Nash instructed Viv to contact the passport office, and the DVLA. 'We need a recent photo of Clark. Although the ones they hold will hardly be ideal, they'll be better than nothing. Lisa, if you've nothing better to do, will you give Viv a hand?'

Nash had barely finished speaking when Clara came to him with some disturbing news. 'I spoke to the manager of

Nixon's Netherdale office, and he said they have no record of that house, or anyone named Clark, on their books. In fact, he told me they currently have no properties either for sale, or to let, in Bishopton. I asked him if it might be through another branch.' Clara smiled. 'His comment was something on the lines of, "not if the manager of that branch wants to keep his job". Apparently, they have clearly defined branch territories, and a very strict policy forbidding anyone from encroaching on another office's turf.'

'Then why would Clark put a sign up if his house wasn't on the market?'

Their enquiries at both the Passport Office and the DVLA proved equally fruitless, as Viv and Lisa reported the following day. 'The nearest person geographically who holds a passport in the name of James Clark is a nine-year-old boy,' Viv told them. 'The closest match in terms of age lives in Leeds, and works as a butcher.'

'I had a similar lack of success with the DVLA,' Lisa reported. 'They have the Leeds man that Viv mentioned, plus a sixty-five-year-old who lives in Teesside, a twenty-three-year-old in Halifax and a couple of guys across the border in Lancashire. But nothing in our neck of the woods.' She paused and asked, 'Are you sure about the name — and the address, come to that? I mean, could it be spelled with an E at the end, for example?'

'The name has to be correct to match that of the hit-and-run victim,' Nash pointed out, 'but as for the address, I'm no longer sure. It might be an idea to check with the local authority.'

'That was another bright theory that didn't hold up in practice,' Lisa reported, soon afterwards. The council told me there is currently no one registered to vote, or listed in the garden waste recycling scheme. Previously it was a Mr James and Mrs Amanda Clark, so it seems as if we're back to square one — again. We can't even put a BOLO out for him, because we've no photo. And we can't wait for him to turn up at a house it seems he no longer lives in. So where do we go from here, Mike?' She was getting frustrated.

'I haven't got a clue.'

Lisa then asked, 'Are we certain we're after the right man? It's almost as if we're chasing a ghost, or someone who never existed?'

'We're fairly sure he exists. The report on file into his wife's death gives his name, same in the newspaper reports,' Nash told her. 'It says in the report that he was away in America on business at the time. . .' He stopped suddenly as an idea came to him. 'I wonder what that business was. Clara, you met him, didn't you? When he was much younger, admittedly, but at least you could give us some idea what he looked like, back in the day. Tell us what you can remember about the mysterious James Clark?'

She took a moment to think. 'I can't tell you much,' she said, eventually. 'As I recall, he was about six feet tall, maybe a touch more.'

'What about his facial features, distinguishing marks — like a wart on the end of his nose, a dimple in his cheeks, or double chins? Hair colour, anything?'

'The one thing I definitely can't tell you, Mike, is what his face was like. When I interviewed him, and Amanda, he had just finished his act. Part of his stage persona was to appear masked and hooded with a cape, such as magicians were fond of wearing. I never got to see his face. He might have had blue eyes, but I can't even be sure of that.'

* * *

Driving home that evening, Nash reflected on what had been another wasted, frustrating day. He would have liked to make more progress. The team had been so wrapped up in the murders that he had missed a weekend visit to Daniel.

He was trying to work out when the next visit could be, when a thought occurred to him. 'Of course,' he exclaimed.

The one avenue they hadn't thought to explore was James Clark's childhood, his upbringing, parentage, and education. It might just pay dividends for them to discover where he had gone to school, and from there possibly trace his antecedents, living relatives, or close friends. The educational subjects that Clark excelled in might also give some clue as to what business he was in. One so important, that it had taken him across the Atlantic, thousands of miles away, when his wife had been killed.

One idea followed another. Next morning, prompted this time by Lisa Andrews' comment "someone who never existed", Nash mentally kicked himself for not having thought of it earlier. The records of James Clark's birth and marriage would be held at the Registrar's Office and would therefore be readily available.

Nash allocated duties to each of them. 'Lisa, will you contact the Registrar's Office please, and see if you can determine some facts about Clark? His parents' names would be a start. From there, we might be able to discover if he had any siblings or cousins.'

He turned to Pearce. 'Viv, I want you to phone round the local secondary schools, check if they had a pupil by the name of James Clark, somewhere around fifteen or so years ago.'

Nash then asked Clara, 'I don't know if it's asking too much, but can you recall the details of the incident that resulted in you interviewing Clark and his girlfriend? If we had the name of one of the brawlers, we might be able to get the file up. See if there's anything in it that you might have forgotten — it could prove useful. I think you said it was in a pub, or a club, wasn't it? Even the name of the establishment might be handy.'

'No, it wouldn't, because the club closed down several years ago, and the building is now a convenience store belonging to Good Buys supermarkets. As for the brawl, I believe it was settled out of court, so I guess the paperwork got shredded way back.'

She'd only just finished when Pearce entered Nash's office, his pace only marginally short of a gallop.

'Bishopton Grammar,' he announced excitedly. 'I got lucky with my first try. I spoke to the headmaster — he remembers James Clark very well. He also remembers Amanda Headley, who became Clark's wife. He even told me they were sweethearts back then. After that, he said something really curious, but I didn't get chance to follow up on it. He said, "What happened to Amanda must have been heartbreaking for James. As if he hadn't already suffered enough tragedy in his life".'

'What did he mean by that?'

Viv shrugged. 'Unfortunately, that was as far as we got. I was about to ask, but he told me he had to go — physics lesson.'

'Well, don't just stand there! Get round to the school at lunchtime and see what he knows.'

CHAPTER TWENTY-THREE

The headmaster, who Viv guessed to be in his mid-fifties, greeted him, and ushered him into his study. 'You said earlier that this was about James Clark. Can I ask why you're asking?'

'His name came up in part of an ongoing enquiry.'

'Oh, I see. So how can I help?'

'Basically, I need anything you can tell me about him. Apart from the fact that he attended this school, and that his wife died in tragic circumstances, we know absolutely nothing about him.'

'Yes, that was a terrible accident. I only read about it after I returned from holiday in Italy, otherwise I would have attended Amanda's funeral. Poor James must have been absolutely devastated, especially with what happened to him before. The last thing he needed was another tragedy.'

'I'm sorry, but you're going to have to explain. You said something earlier like that. Was there another incident in Clark's past?'

'You didn't know about that? I'm afraid that's an elementary error on my part. Something all teachers should be wary of is assuming knowledge that other people don't have. Please, sit down and I'll explain. The details are more than a little heartrending.'

Viv took out his incident book and pen, listening as the headmaster continued, 'James was born in Manchester, and they moved here when he was quite young, after his father got a new job. As far as I can recall, James was about seven years old, maybe eight, but no more than that, when the accident happened. They were going back to Manchester on a pre-Christmas shopping expedition. The weather was bad, and there was a pile-up on the M62 motorway. James' mother and father were killed instantly. James was trapped in the back seat, and it took firemen to cut him free. He survived, but it was touch-and-go for quite a while, I believe. Sadly, in addition to the anguish his parents' death must have caused him, James had to live with a permanent reminder of the tragedy. The injuries he suffered healed well enough, but he was left with an unsightly scar that ran from his forehead to his chin, so every time he looked in a mirror, it must have brought back dreadful memories.'

'How did you learn all this? Did James tell you?'

'Absolutely not. James was a quiet, withdrawn, almost shy little lad — far too introverted to reveal something so personal. It was Susan Headley, Amanda's mother, who told me about James' background before he came to school here as an eleven-year-old. She knew how cruel children can be, and wanted to ensure he was protected from bullying because of the disfigurement.'

'How did she know so much about him?'

'Susan Headley's late husband had worked with James' father, and the families became close friends. After the Clarks were killed, Susan adopted the boy.' The teacher smiled and added, 'However, I don't think even she could have guessed how things would develop between James and her daughter.'

'Do you have a photograph of James? I appreciate that it would be years out of date, but if you have a clear enough image, we have technology that can age it fairly accurately.'

The teacher's reply both surprised and saddened him. 'I'm afraid we have no photos of James. He wouldn't allow the photographer to include him, even in the school group photos. In the circumstances, it would have been cruel to insist on him taking part.'

He smiled at a memory. 'I bumped into James and Amanda in Helmsdale a couple of years ago. I remember teasing them because they were walking hand-in-hand. I told them some things never change, because they used to hold hands when they thought nobody was watching, even when they were in year five.'

'Did you know that Amanda's mother died soon after her daughter was killed?'

'Oh no, I wasn't aware of that. How awful. She was such a nice, kind, gentle lady. Coming on top of everything else, that must have been dreadful for James. He thought the world of her.'

'There is one more thing, and then I'll be on my way, I've taken up enough of your valuable time already. Do you have any idea what trade or profession James entered after leaving school?'

'Not in the slightest. Although if I had to hazard a guess, I would say he could have gone into electrical or mechanical engineering. James was forever tinkering, dismantling machinery, and electrical equipment, finding out how they worked and re-assembling them. He was exceedingly good at it. He loved the science classes.' The headmaster smiled. 'He might even have put his conjuring skills to use, but I think the disfigurement might have put a block on him appearing in public. Then again, if he'd not been an honest, upright citizen, I guess he would have led your people a merry dance.'

'What do you mean by that?'

'I told you he was good with anything mechanical, but there was one particular skill that made him outstanding. I don't think there has been a lock manufactured that he couldn't open, and I've got practical experience of that.' He explained, 'I live on the other side of town, and I almost always cycle in to school. On a teacher's salary, it's far cheaper than a car, and more environmentally friendly. One morning I arrived and realized I'd left my office keys at home. It had come on to rain heavily, and I wasn't fancying the ride back in a downpour. James came by just as I was trying to make my mind up to brave the elements. He must have sensed there was a problem, because he asked what was wrong.

'I explained, and he told me not to worry. He produced one of those multi-tool implements from his backpack, and a couple of minutes later, he'd opened my study door. I thanked him and told him that was fine, but I also needed some papers from my desk. He promptly unlocked it for me. The whole process took less than five minutes. When I asked how he'd managed it, he just laughed and said, "magic". Like I said, fortunately he wasn't of a criminal mind, because I don't think even banks would be a problem for him.'

Viv thanked the headmaster for his time, and headed back to the station where he told the others what he had heard. 'If he is responsible for the murders, then we know how he got through all the locked doors.'

'I agree,' Clara said. 'But what a terrible, tragic life James has had. If he discovered who was responsible for Amanda's death, it's hardly surprising he decided to seek revenge. To be honest, I can't bring myself to blame him.'

'I take your point, Clara. There comes a time when upholding the law brings us into direct conflict with natural justice and our own sympathies. However, we have a sworn duty to perform, and our personal feelings mustn't be allowed to intrude on that.'

Clara nodded and added, 'I suppose it's understandable that he appeared on stage masked, if only to hide the disfigurement. It would be seen as part of the act by the audience.'

'That's an interesting thought, and it gives us another avenue to pursue.'

'I don't follow you?'

'If he *did* continue working as a magician, he would need an agent to secure bookings for him. If we contact theatrical agents, we might find one with James Clark on their books. They'd need his address and bank details in order to pay him for his appearances.'

'He might have given it all up, though. Do you remember the description that club secretary gave me of his act? He called Clark a second-rate magician,' Clara reminded him. 'By the sound of that, he might have packed it in.'

'Maybe, maybe not. If you think about it, Clark was only in the early stages of his career then. What would he be, twenty to twenty-five years old at the most? I remember reading in an article somewhere that Les Dawson was working the club circuit for years, getting nowhere, but then he changed his routine, and ended up as one of Britain's finest comedians. It's worth a try.'

Nash asked them to begin ringing round. 'I still think it's a long shot, but let's face it, we've very little else to go on.'

The task was likely to be a prolonged one, and before they had completed it, the team was faced with another perplexing mystery.

* * *

When Nash reached the station the following morning, Steve Meadows was waiting in the doorway. His urgent hand signal told Nash something was amiss. He hurried across the car park and asked what was wrong.

'I've had the head of Forensics at Netherdale on the phone three times, jumping up and down. He's desperate to speak to you, and he said your mobile goes straight to voicemail.'

Nash grinned, a trifle sheepishly. 'I wasn't on call. I . . . er . . . switched it off last night so we . . . er . . . . I didn't get disturbed. Did he give you any clue as to what the panic's about?'

'No, just that it was vital he spoke to you ASAP.'

'OK, I'll ring him from my office. He's probably lost his fingerprint brush, or something equally silly.'

Clara's car pulled into the car park. She accompanied Nash upstairs as he told her about the forensic man's panic. 'Let's find out what's gone wrong.'

Clara heard Nash's greeting, before he listened for a moment and then said, 'It's done what?' After a pause he said,

'Yes, that's what I thought you said. How on earth did that happen? Was someone careless enough to forget to lock up?'

Clara saw Nash wince, and then hold the receiver away from his ear. She guessed, from the agitated squawking sound issuing from the earpiece, that the person on the line was rather upset. 'OK, we'll come over and see for ourselves.'

Nash replaced the handset, his expression one of bewilderment. 'They've only gone and lost the Beamer!'

'They've done what?'

Nash grinned at Clara's incredulity. 'When they'd finished their examination of Blackburn's BMW, they parked it in the compound outside the workshop, and locked it up — or so they claim. When they arrived this morning, the compound was securely locked, but the BMW had vanished.'

'How did that happen?'

'I have no idea. And by the sound of it, neither do they. I asked if someone had accidentally left the compound unlocked, and he wasn't at all happy by the allegation, as you probably heard.'

'Yes,' Clara nodded. 'It was rather obvious. It's curious that the thieves should choose Blackburn's car, though. Admittedly, it's a high-end, very expensive lump of metal, but it wouldn't have been easy to remove from that compound, even for professional car thieves. It could be pure coincidence that they chose that particular car, but as you don't believe in coincidence, we'll have to come up with an alternative theory.'

'Let's go and examine the crime scene. That might give us some inspiration, and if we utter some soothing words to the boffins, it might prevent their chief from having an apoplectic fit. We'll brief Steve Meadows, and he can update Viv and Lisa when they arrive.'

* * *

At Netherdale headquarters, the forensic chief looked harassed. This was probably because he was being subjected to an in-depth grilling by the chief constable. She turned to the detectives as they approached and asked, 'What's your take on this, Mike?'

'I'm not sure yet. In fact, I'm not sure about anything surrounding current events. The mystery of the missing Beamer is just the latest baffling aspect of the case. We believe we know the who, and the why — but we've no idea of the how, or the where.'

'What exactly does that mean?'

'We're fairly certain James Clark committed the murders — that's the *who*. We believe he is taking revenge on the people involved in the death of his wife — that's the *why*. We're not sure *how* he killed them, and we certainly don't know the *where*, as in the murder site. Added to that, all our efforts to trace him so far have run into a brick wall, and we don't have a bulldozer to hand. We've no idea what he looks like, or what he does for a living. He's the closest thing to a phantom you could imagine. As I see it, although it goes against the grain, all we can do is to await developments, and hope we get some clues, as and when that happens.'

'By developments, I hope you don't mean another murder?'

'I'm afraid that's exactly what I do mean, ma'am. Neil Blackburn, the head of Helm Logistics, who we're certain was driving the BMW when it hit and killed Amanda Clark, has gone missing. His disappearance bears marked similarity to that of the other murder victims. Another fact that has me puzzled is how Clark discovered who was responsible for his wife's death — and the subsequent cover-up.'

'I wonder what's so significant about the car? Can we trace the BMW? Won't it have one of those location finders installed?'

The forensic chief interrupted. 'That's a good thought, ma'am, but unfortunately, the vehicle's GPS tracker had been disabled. That was the first thing we tried. What we can't work out, is not only how this man got in and out of the compound, but how he also managed to open the BMW door, get in, start the engine, and lock up after himself.'

Nash smiled at the chief constable before telling the scientific officer, 'The answer is obvious. The man who entered the compound is a skilled magician, with lock-picking skills. He got into the BMW, started it, and drove away by the old-fashioned method. He used the ignition key. Blackburn's ignition key, to be exact.'

Their lack of success continued when, back at the station, Viv and Lisa reported a total failure to find a theatrical agent who had represented a stage performer by the name of James Clark. Thinking back to her encounter with the magician, Clara had a moment of inspiration. She instructed the DCs, 'Try those agents again and this time instead of asking for a named performer, ask about one who always wore a mask onstage. Clark might not have appeared under his own name, because he was reputed to be very shy.'

Clara turned in time to see Nash staring at her. He held the pose for so long that Clara wondered if she'd offended him. 'Should I have run it past you first?'

'Not at all. It's just the fact that it was such a good idea that I was wondering if you were feeling OK.'

'Hah! You don't have a monopoly on good ideas, you know.'

Seeing Nash about to rise to the bait, Lisa cut in hurriedly, 'We'll get on with those phone calls.'

Later that afternoon, they reported what at first seemed like another dead end. 'There is no magician who appears masked,' Pearce told them, 'In fact, the only performer who did wear a mask on stage whenever he appeared was that famous escapologist, the one who recently announced his retirement. Magnus something or other, his name is.'

Nash hadn't appeared to be paying close attention, but as Pearce finished speaking, Nash's head jerked up, sharply. 'Of course,' he said.

Clara sensed the excitement in his voice.

'Magnus Evadere — it all makes sense now. Obviously, the victims couldn't emulate Harry Houdini. That's who we should be looking for.'

'Mike, Houdini's been dead almost a hundred years,' Clara told him.

'Sorry, I didn't mean we should look for Houdini.'

'Then would you mind explaining that statement, to those of us who don't have the same weird thought processes as you?'

'What I meant was, we should look for Magnus Evadere. I'm convinced it's the stage name of James Clark.'

'Is that how he worked abroad?' Clara asked. 'We were looking for a passport in the wrong name.'

'My guess is he changed his name by deed poll,' Nash replied.

'OK, so where does Houdini come into it?'

'You read the article about his retirement. Magnus Evadere was an escapologist. He always wore a mask on stage, which fits with Clark's wish to hide his disfigurement. It isn't a huge step from being a magician, to becoming an illusionist and escape artist. One of the best known tricks in the repertoire of top-class escapologists is the Harry Houdini Water Torture. That involves the escape artist being placed upside down in a tank, which is then filled with water. I believe Houdini was handcuffed, and had his ankles restrained, to make the trick appear more difficult. If Clark's victims were dunked repeatedly to obtain their confession, it would be a simple task to finish them off by inverting them in the water tank. Unless they could emulate Houdini, by getting free from their restraints, they would drown.'

'So all this time, while we've been searching for a mysterious figure we were beginning to doubt even existed, the man was right under our noses as one of the most famous stage performers the county has ever produced, right?'

'That's correct, Viv, and it shows what an excellent illusionist James, or Magnus, is.' Nash thought for a moment before adding, 'Whether Clark adopted the name because it appealed to his sense of humour, or because he didn't want people to associate the escapologist with the failed magician, I don't know. But one thing I *am* certain of — James Clark *is*

Magnus Evadere, and under either name, he has committed three, potentially, four murders.

'There is one other point I think we should bear in mind, and that is how every good stage performance ends. I think Blackburn is Clark's last victim. So he'll want the finale to be a spectacular ending — one that people will remember. I have absolutely no proof for any of this, but I'm prepared to bet I'm correct.'

'It's probably a good thing you're not a gambler,' Clara told him, 'because if you were, bookmakers would be going bankrupt, left, right and centre.'

CHAPTER TWENTY-FOUR

The phone calls, first to the *Netherdale Gazette*, followed by Helm Radio and the local TV station, were made in quick succession. All gave identical information, and the caller allowed no chance for questions before ending the one-sided conversations. Ever the meticulous planner, Magnus Evadere wanted to ensure that the first act of his finale would enable him to go out in a blaze of glory, with the scorching spotlight of media scrutiny on him.

He waited for sufficient time to elapse to ensure that reporters, photographers, and news crews were en route before placing his final call to Netherdale Police. 'I wish to report a fatal road accident,' he told the officer. 'It will happen in approximately two minutes' time. If you send patrol cars to control the crowd, and the press, and also an ambulance to ensure the victim is dead, I would be obliged. The crash scene is on the outskirts of Bishopton, on the Helmsdale road near the Black Fell turning.'

The officer was still wondering whether the call was a hoax, when the caller added, 'The person killed in the incident is the one you've been looking for, a loathsome creature by the name of Neil Blackburn. He will be in collision with a grey BMW, registration number as follows . . .'

Having recited the number, he ended the call, and placed the mobile on the passenger seat alongside him. After a few moments, he clipped his seat belt on, and started the ignition. He checked his target was watching him, before he moved the gear selector into drive. Ramming his foot down hard on the accelerator, he was pleasantly surprised by how quickly the BMW reached full speed. Without attempting to apply the brakes, he aimed the car at the helpless man.

* * *

Nash had just finished shaving when Alondra called from the foot of the staircase. 'Mike, your mobile's ringing. Shall I answer it?'

'Yes, please. I'll be down in a jiffy.'

When he reached the kitchen, Alondra told him, 'I've taken three calls, one from the chief constable, one from Sergeant Meadows, and one from Viv Pearce.'

'OK, I'll phone Steve Meadows first. That way I'll know what to expect when I speak to the others.'

He listened to Meadows, then turned to Alondra. 'I'll have to leave you to it. I must get to Bishopton.'

'What about your breakfast? You haven't even had a coffee.'

'I'll do without.' He grabbed his car keys and headed for the door. 'I'll contact the chief and Viv en route. There's going to be absolute mayhem — if there isn't already.'

His conversation with the chief constable was brief. 'Steve Meadows told me what's happened. The man pinned to the signpost is Blackburn, and he's been crushed by his own BMW. The driver has locked himself inside the car, and refuses to get out until paramedics arrive to confirm Blackburn is dead. That should be a formality by what our guys reported to Meadows. Apparently, the car has almost cut him in two.'

'Yes, but what you don't know, Mike — and that's the reason I called you — is that someone, and we must assume it was Clark, phoned the media beforehand. Then, and only then, he called control to report that the collision was about to happen. I've already had your old flame Becky Pollard from the *Gazette* on the phone. I've also taken calls from the station manager at Helm Radio, and the producer of the breakfast show on regional TV, all asking for a comment. I've directed them to the press officer, not that he knows any more that I do. All of them had sent reporters to the scene.'

'If they broadcast this on TV, it'll put people off their corn flakes. Don't worry. I'll deal with the paparazzi when I get there.'

Before he had chance to make his next call, his mobile rang. After a momentary sideways glance, he said, 'Viv, what's the panic?'

'Someone has posted photos, and a video of this, on social networks and YouTube. The video clip shows the car accelerating, and you can hear Blackburn screaming as it hits him. Then the car reverses and takes a second run at him. This time, there were no screams. The clip's gone viral.'

'Contact the companies and try and get it removed.'

'I'll try. Do you know about the sign?'

'Only that Blackburn was tied to one. Why?'

'The *"Bishopton Welcomes Careful Drivers"* wording has been covered over. It now reads *"This murderer escaped the law, but could not escape justice"*. Lisa's just arrived. She's helping uniforms keep the press back.'

* * *

When Nash reached the incident, he already knew pretty much what to expect, with one exception. Although he had been told that Clark had locked himself inside the BMW, nobody had mentioned he was wearing his full stage costume, complete with cape, hood, and mask. Once he had been assured by Nash that Blackburn was dead, adding that paramedics had checked both halves of his victim, Clark unlocked the car, climbed out, and did not offer any resistance when officers approached. While he was being handcuffed, Nash administered the caution.

When one of the officers attempted to remove the mask, Clark pulled to one side and said, 'Not here. Not in front of the cameras. Please, Inspector Nash.'

Nash nodded to the uniformed men. 'No, leave it on. Take him to Helmsdale.'

He waited until the patrol car had left, before sending Viv and Clara to inform Vanessa Blackburn that her husband had been found. He then faced the media, telling them that a statement would be issued in due course.

'There will probably be a press conference later. I know how much you enjoy those. Until then, you'll have to remain patient. I appreciate that won't be easy for you. If any of you have photographs, please be careful what you publish. At least show some respect for the victim's family. Now, will you all move back and allow us to do our jobs.' He turned and watched the Forensics team trying to erect a tent around the scene, as Professor Ramirez drew to a halt alongside him.

After a cursory examination, the pathologist told Nash, 'Post-mortem this evening — on both halves of the body!'

* * *

The interview with James Clark began shortly after lunch-time. After some debate, Nash opted to take Mironova into the room with him.

'I was pondering whether to ask Lisa,' he told Clara, as they walked downstairs from the CID suite, 'but she's dark-haired and bears a slight resemblance to Amanda Clark, so I decided I'll have to put up with you.'

Clara was about to protest until she noticed the smile. 'That'll be a pleasant change for both of us,' she retaliated. 'It's usually me that has to put up with you.'

All humour died when they started to interrogate Clark, now devoid of his costume and wearing a grey tracksuit. The prisoner apologized to Clara, 'I'm sorry if my appearance distresses you, but this is who I am.'

He then made it clear from the outset that he didn't require a solicitor, and would answer questions fully and frankly, but only those he was prepared to reply to.

'Was it necessary to kill Andrew Derrick simply because he repaired Blackburn's car?'

Clark's response to Nash's question surprised both detectives. 'That's by no means all that Derrick did wrong. He was a liar and a coward, and he deserved to die.'

Although Nash pressed him for an explanation all Clark would say is, 'All in good time. Everything will become clear if you have a little patience.'

'OK, then will you answer this? How does Cheesy Wilson fit into your scenario? How does a low life like that belong in your revenge crusade? We couldn't find even a hint of a connection between Wilson and Blackburn.'

Clark laughed. 'The link is there, all right. You'll have to wait and see. The time isn't right yet, because I have other things to do beforehand.'

When he reflected later, Nash realized he should have known Clark wasn't making idle promises with that remark. Hindsight may be the clearest vision, but it is of little value at times.

Eventually, having received similarly evasive replies, Nash put the direct question to Clark. 'Are you now confessing to the murders of Andrew Derrick, Charles Wilson, Jenny Granger, and Neil Blackburn?'

'I certainly killed all four of them, but I prefer to think of it as executions.'

'Is there any other crime you have committed that we haven't charged you with? If so, now would be a good opportunity to say.'

Clark thought for a moment and then leaned forward, his face grave. 'Yes. I believe there is.'

'And what might that be?'

'When I took the BMW from your compound, I didn't have the owner's consent. Not only that, but I don't hold a valid UK driving licence, or insurance.' He leaned back and folded his arms.

Having terminated the interview, Nash and Clara briefed the chief, Ruth Edwards, who had arrived and was waiting in the CID suite. 'Did Clark confess?' she asked, the moment they entered the room.

'He did indeed,' Nash told her. 'He confessed to all four drowning murders, plus another crime. Well, three actually.'

Clara turned away to hide her laughter, as Nash explained about the BMW, and Clark's lack of a driving licence and insurance.

'Oh, very funny,' Ruth said, crossly.

'That's exactly the point,' Nash told her. 'Clark didn't seem to be taking the interview seriously. It was almost as if he thought he could own up to the murders, and then walk out of here.'

'Perhaps everything he's been through has proved too much for him, and he's flipped his lid,' the chief said. 'Anyway, well done. It's nice to have the murders wrapped up. It'll do wonders for our statistics.' She paused and smiled slightly before adding, 'As a reward for your excellent detective work, you can accompany me to Netherdale. I am holding a little soiree with the ladies and gentlemen of the media. They are sure to have lots of questions, and I wouldn't want to be selfish and reply to them all myself.'

'In that case, I won't be long. I'm going to charge him and get Steve to remand him in custody. We'll need to organize a police van to take him to Netherdale, prior to transfer to Felling Prison.'

Just as he finished speaking, the wail of a siren assaulted their ears. The detectives ran down the stairs at breakneck speed to find Steve Meadows standing in reception looking confused. He stared at them, shaking his head in disbelief. 'He's gone!'

'Who's gone?' they chorused.

'Clark. Before he was taken back to his cell, he asked for a drink. When the attending officer took it back to the interview room — Clark was gone.'

'How the hell did he get out?'

'He must have had some implement concealed about his person, but I'm not sure what, or where. He didn't pass me.'

Viv Pearce set off at a run along the adjoining corridor to the ambulance bay, returning moment later. 'The link door's wide open. He's gone.'

Steve went to turn off the alarm as Doug Curran appeared, the master key swinging from his finger. 'Did you know someone's left your connecting door open? And what's with all the noise?'

'We've an escaped prisoner,' Nash informed him.

'Huh, well I can tell you what he's driving.'

The detectives looked puzzled.

'One of my team's had his car nicked.'

Having put out an alert, the chief and Nash set off to face the media, knowing they would have to shield their embarrassment.

When Nash drove home much later that evening, following the post-mortem on Blackburn, he was feeling down. He admitted to Alondra over a late dinner that he had little sympathy with the victims, but more for Clark.

'He seems to have been dogged by ill fortune throughout his life. As if the suffering in his early childhood wasn't bad enough, he lost his wife and unborn child in horrendous circumstances. Then he had to watch the woman who had adopted him, the woman he was close to, die of cancer, causing more heartbreak. And when, or should I say if, we catch him, he must face a prison sentence that will see him locked away until old age.'

* * *

Next morning, Nash was up and about early. He was conscious of the mountain of paperwork he would have to tackle.

Before that, he had promised Alondra he would take Teal for her pre-breakfast constitutional. It was a couple of minutes before 7 a.m. when he opened the front door of Smelt Mill Cottage. He stopped dead, staring at the neatly wrapped brown paper parcel on the doorstep. Mindful of the earlier bomb scare, he bent over it, and then stepped back, gasping in astonishment at the words on the label.

"To Detective Inspector Nash. Don't worry, this isn't a bomb either. The contents should provide you with some of the answers to the questions you asked me yesterday." The note was signed, *"Magnus Evadere".*

Nash was still wondering whether he dare pick up the parcel, when his mobile rang. It was the chief constable. 'I know it's early, but the media don't understand the word "press officer". I've had word from Control that they're waiting outside the station already. So I thought I should warn you.'

'That's kind of you, but I was about to phone you. I've just opened my front door and found a parcel on the doorstep, with a note, signed by Magnus Evadere.'

Before she would allow anyone to handle the package, and despite Nash's protests, the chief constable insisted the bomb squad should be called in.

Mike roused Alondra, muffled her up in her coat, and ushered her and Teal to the back garden, just in case.

'I already knew you lead an exciting life,' Alondra said. 'But do you have to bring your work home, or have it delivered during the night?'

Nash bore the teasing, glad that he now had Alondra to share his home, and his life. That, he thought, was in stark contrast to the fugitive who had delivered the mysterious object. After enduring too many cold, lonely nights wishing Alondra was here with him, a little gentle ribbing was a small price to pay for his contentment.

'Are you sure we're safe here?' She looked worried.

Mike slipped his arms around her and held her close.

'Of course you are. You've got Mike to protect you.' The reply came from Clara, who, having been made aware by the chief constable, had headed straight for Smelt Mill Cottage.

'We're OK, Clara. I'm just annoyed that we have to go through this performance before we can find out exactly what's going on.' Mike stamped his feet, shoving his hands deep into his pockets in an effort to keep warm.

Once the bomb squad declared the package to be innocuous, a forensic officer, instructed to come by the chief constable, swooped on it and announced he was taking it to Netherdale for testing.

'Sorry, not this time,' Nash said, as he donned a pair of gloves. 'We know who it's from, and need to see what's in there. Don't worry, we won't lose it.'

The officer laughed. 'I should hope not. We only lost a car — you've lost a car and a prisoner!'

CHAPTER TWENTY-FIVE

Back at the station, with little else to go on, Nash hoped the contents of the small cardboard box might give them some clue as to Clark's whereabouts. The first item he removed was a photograph, the caption on the reverse causing Clara to bite her lip in distress as Nash read it out. "*This is my final memory of my beautiful Amanda, taken when we got confirmation that she was carrying our child. Six weeks after I took this photo, Amanda and our child were slaughtered.*"

Knowing what had happened to Clark's wife, even looking at the photo was heartrending. There was no doubt that Amanda had been a singularly beautiful young woman, her beauty enhanced by the joyful expression on her face.

Nash put the photograph to one side, and concentrated on the sheet of paper Clark had enclosed. Further evidence of the illusionist's attention to detail came via the neatly tabulated index to the set of flash drives in the box. Nash read from the list, while Pearce plugged the corresponding device into his computer. 'Drive number one, Blackburn's office at Helm Logistics.'

The drive showed Blackburn and his mistress talking, planning to kill Vanessa, making her death appear accidental. This would leave Blackburn in control of Helm Logistics, and extremely wealthy, as Vanessa's only beneficiary. They also discussed the hit-and-run incident, their concern being to avoid the consequences, should investigators focus their attention on Blackburn and his car.

A later section of that flash drive explained Cheesy Wilson's involvement — and provided the motive for his murder. In the video clip, Wilson was seen showing Blackburn a series of photos, taken at the scene of the hit-and-run. The images of Blackburn and Granger emerging from the BMW, looking at Amanda's body, then climbing back into the car, and driving away, were shocking enough.

As Wilson placed these photos in front of Blackburn, Nash and the team realized that Wilson could also have summoned help for the injured woman. However, the crook was more concerned with collecting evidence that would enable him to demand money for his silence. The amount, £20,000 in untraceable notes, was never collected, because Wilson was murdered before the deadline.

'OK, so Wilson didn't survive to collect the blackmail money, but what about Andrew Derrick's involvement?' Clara asked.

'Perhaps the next drive will give us a clue.' Nash handed it to Pearce. 'This one is from the boardroom at Helm Logistics.'

The first part of the video contained a series of torrid, passionate, encounters between Blackburn and his mistress. Almost immediately, the scene changed. The conversation between Blackburn and Andrew Derrick revealed the mechanic's part in the conspiracy of silence, and the lengths he was prepared to go to, in order to further his own interest.

Having agreed to perform the restorative work on the BMW, and to do this in secret, was one thing. The mechanic then went on to suggest a possible way of avoiding embarrassing questions, regarding Blackburn's location at the time of the hit-and-run, and who his companion had been. 'If anyone asks, you could always tell them you were at my place. You could say I'd challenged you to a game of pool, and we were playing it at the time the accident happened. I'd be prepared to back you up, and also to keep quiet about you and Jenny. But only if you make sure I'm looked after. A few grand more on my salary might do the trick.'

Drive three, from the surveillance device within the BMW, provided further evidence of Blackburn's liaison with Jenny Granger, plus their reaction to the hit-and-run. In addition, it showed further discussions about the murder plot they were hatching to dispose of Vanessa.

Summarising the evidence, Nash told the team, 'This merely confirms what we already suspected and more, by giving us insight into the motive for Cheesy Wilson and Andrew Derrick's murders. But it leaves one outstanding mystery — or maybe two, come to think of it.'

Lisa was puzzled by Nash's remark. 'What mysteries are those? I thought those flash drives cleared everything up.'

'It does regarding the murders. Having heard and seen what was on those drives, I have very little sympathy for any of the victims. There are two unanswered questions, though. First, who planted those surveillance devices? It can't have been Clark, because some of the earlier scenes of Blackburn and Granger, examining each other's vital statistics, are dated well before the incident that killed Amanda. The most likely candidate for the role of snooper would be Vanessa Blackburn. If she *did* plant the bugs, then I think we have the answer to my other question, which is the identity of the person who passed the flash drives to Clark.'

'Are you going to bring her in for questioning?' Clara asked.

'On what grounds? All she's done, even if she admits doing it, is to pass some information to Clark. She cannot be held responsible for what Clark did as a consequence — so any half-decent defence counsel would argue.'

There were two further items in the box. The first was a set of house keys. 'I assume these must be for Clark's house in Bishopton,' Nash said. 'We'd better send someone to check the place over, although I doubt whether Clark would be stupid enough to go there, having given us the keys and escaped from detention. Lisa, pop downstairs and ask Steve to send a couple of his guys, will you?'

Lisa took the keys from him and asked, 'What's the address?'

'Number twelve, Priory Close,' Nash told her.

Lisa returned a few minutes later and Nash pulled out the final item. The envelope had his name on it, and after extracting a single sheet of paper, he began to read the letter aloud.

"Dear Inspector Nash,

My work is now complete. When I learned the shocking truth about Amanda's death, or as I class it, her murder, I also discovered the wickedness of those evil people who had slaughtered her, left her to die alone in agony, and then conspired with others to hide the truth of what they had done.

Once I knew all this, my one remaining purpose in life was to bring retribution on those who killed her, or sought to capitalise on her death for their own ends. So I left them naked, humiliated, and exposed for the world to see. As you will now be aware, my profession is that of an escapologist, and so I set them a challenge, one they were unable to rise to — literally.

Proof of this will be readily available via the house keys I have left for you. When you visit the scene, or, as I prefer to call it, the place of execution, you will find their confessions, which will bear out everything you have already seen, heard, or suspected.

As a professional entertainer, I could not resist the opportunity to stage a grand finale, and I apologize if my headline-seeking performance has caused either you, or your colleagues, any embarrassment. Finally, I wish to thank you

228

for the kindness and understanding you showed me during my brief detention. Your sympathy was in stark contrast to the unfeeling, self-centred attitude of those I punished.

I now intend to go to the place that remains dearest to me. It is the beautiful place where Amanda and I first made love. I can think of no better site for my curtain call. If you believe in such things, perhaps you can spare the time to pray that I will soon be reunited with Amanda, my one and only true love.

James Clark.'"

There was a long silence after Nash finished reading, the emotional impact of the letter having affected all the detectives. Eventually, Nash cleared his throat, and said, 'I find it intriguing that Clark remains an illusionist until the very end. He hints about his intention to commit suicide, but gives no indication of where, or how, he is going to do it. He also suggests we will find more evidence via that set of keys, but the way he phrases it seems to imply that our initial assumption that they are for his house might be way off target. We'll just have to wait and see, but for the meantime, I'm ready for a coffee.'

An hour later, Steve Meadows reported that the keys Clark had left in the package did not fit any of the doors to his house.

'If they're not for Clark's house, where are they for? And why did he leave them for us?' Clara asked. 'It's as if he's challenging us to some sort of guessing game.'

'Of course he is,' Nash told her. 'And at the moment he's winning the game, hands down. Think about it, Clara. James Clark or Magnus Evadere, call him what you like, is an illusionist. He said it himself — this is his curtain call, and we are his audience.'

'OK, so what's next on his agenda?'

'I haven't the foggiest idea, but I know what's next on ours. We need Vanessa Blackburn to visit the mortuary. She has to identify the body Clark rammed with the BMW as that of her husband. It's purely a formality, I know, but we have to stick to the rules. Will you call her and make the arrangements?'

Twenty minutes later, Clara reported back. 'Mrs Blackburn wants to get the identification over and done with. I've agreed that we'll meet her at Netherdale General later this afternoon, and show her to the mortuary.'

* * *

Nash and Mironova watched Vanessa's face, to gauge her reaction, as the mortuary attendant lifted the sheet from the corpse. She stared at it for a moment and then nodded. 'Yes, that's him. That's Neil Blackburn. Can I go now?' Her voice was as expressionless as her face. It was almost, Clara thought, as if Vanessa had been looking at a total stranger.

Vanessa turned and spoke to Nash, 'I've made arrangements with the funeral director to have the body collected once you've finished with it. Here are their details.' She rummaged in her bag, and handed Nash a card. 'They'll take it to the crematorium and deal with the remains.'

'I'm afraid that may be some time. The Coroner will have the final say on that, and you may be required to attend an inquest,' Nash pointed out.

'Whenever, just let me know. You have my number.' She shook her head in irritation. 'Now, if you'll excuse me, I have a flight to catch in the morning, and I haven't finished packing yet.'

'Where are you going?' Nash saw Vanessa's expression change to one of excited anticipation, which caused him to ask, 'Is it Athens, by any chance?'

Vanessa blushed as she told him, 'You're very astute, Mr Nash. Yes, it is Athens.'

'When will you return?'

'Who knows? A week, a month, a year. Maybe never.'

Clara was shocked. 'Does that mean you're going to miss your husband's funeral?'

Vanessa laughed aloud, causing the attendant to stare at her in astonishment. He'd never heard laughter in that room before.

'No, Sergeant Mironova, it means that I won't be attending the funeral. I certainly won't miss it — or him, not one iota.'

As they returned to Helmsdale, Clara commented on Vanessa's indifference to her husband's fate.

'You're only half right, Clara. But then you missed what she said to me outside the mortuary, when you were collecting the paperwork.'

'What did she say?'

'She said, "I suppose in normal circumstances someone in my position would be keen for you to apprehend the person responsible for the death — but that would be hypocritical of me." Added to her comments about the funeral, more or less confirms that it was Vanessa who had the surveillance devices fitted, and she was the person who passed the flash drives to Clark. However, as I said earlier, even if she did, we don't know that she's actually committed an offence. Even so, I don't think we'd stand a chance of proving it.'

'Why not?'

'Because, I believe that Vanessa Blackburn and James Clark have more in common than their hatred of her husband and Jenny Granger. I believe they are both far too careful to leave the slightest scrap of evidence, unless it is something they want us to discover.'

CHAPTER TWENTY-SIX

Two days later, Nash and Mironova arrived at Helmsdale simultaneously. When they entered the reception area, Steve Meadows greeted them and said, 'I've just taken a call from someone at Scarborough Borough Council. There's an abandoned vehicle in the car park at Runswick Bay.'

Nash remembered the tiny village from his childhood. It had been one of his parents' favourite haunts for a day out. Nash had spent many happy hours playing on the beach there. He failed to see why Meadows was telling them this, until the sergeant continued, 'There was a notice taped to the inside of the windscreen. The wording read, "*Please inform Detective Inspector Nash, Helmsdale CID.*" When they checked the vehicle out, they found the registered keeper is listed as Susan Headley, number one, Priory Close, Bishopton.'

'Priory Close, isn't that where James Clark lives — or lived?' Clara asked.

'That's right, Clara, his address was number twelve. Susan Headley was his mother-in-law. Come on, we've work to do.'

Upstairs in CID, Nash told Clara, 'Get Forensics to organize a low loader, and tell them they're getting a day at the seaside. I want Susan Headley's car brought back here, and gone over with a fine-tooth comb. And tell them not to lose this one. You can also instruct them to have a team ready to go to Bishopton. As soon as Viv and Lisa arrive, we're all off to Susan Headley's house, Clark's family home. That's what those keys are for. I should have twigged it long ago.'

Within an hour, the detectives had arrived at Priory Close. Susan Headley's property was directly opposite Clark's house. 'He's got some nerve, I'll give him that,' Lisa told Clara. 'All the time we were trying to find Clark, he was probably watching us from inside here.'

They dressed in protective clothing, before they approached the property. The front door opened easily.

Nash led the team inside. 'Now let's see what Clark has left for us.'

With Clara and Lisa taking the upper floor, Nash began searching the downstairs rooms, while Pearce went through to the kitchen, and beyond there to the utility room, and built-in garage. Nash had barely started looking round when Pearce reappeared, his expression one of excitement.

'What's up, Viv?'

'Come and look, Mike. Better get the girls, too.'

Having called for Clara and Lisa, Nash followed Pearce through to the garage, where an extension had been added. In the centre, set several feet down in a hole in the floor, was a large rectangular glass container. Nash guessed it would measure somewhere in the region of seven feet tall by three feet wide. It looked identical to the tank used in the past by Harry Houdini, and in more recent times by Magnus Evadere, to perform the escape trick. Above, fixed to the rafters was a hoist, complete with chains and manacles.

'This must be where he learned his craft,' Viv said.

Alongside the tank was a small picnic table, on which were an old-fashioned cassette recorder and four cassettes. With his gloved hand, Nash examined the tapes, which were all labelled. He read the wording to the others. 'Tape one is Andrew Derrick's confession, number two is Charles Wilson's, then Jenny Granger, and finally Neil Blackburn. Lisa, pop outside, see if Forensics have arrived yet. If so, ask them to start work in here while we examine the rest of the house.'

With the garage and utility room now out of bounds, Pearce joined Andrews on the upper storey, with Nash's instructions ringing in their ears. 'Don't forget to look for a hatch or something leading to the roof space or attic. Who knows? You might find something of interest up there.'

'I hope Viv's gentleman enough to go up if they do,' Clara told Nash. 'That trouser suit Lisa's wearing is brand new.'

'I'll continue with the living room and dining room, if you tackle the conservatory at the back. Part of it looks to have been converted into an office.'

Almost immediately, Nash saw something he recognized, and it saddened him. On the dresser was a framed photograph, half hidden by an ornamental vase. Was that deliberate, he wondered? The teenagers in the foreground were obviously younger versions of James and Amanda. Her looks hadn't changed much over the years, and Clark, who normally eschewed photos, had allowed this one, despite the vivid scar down the entire side of his face. The loving expression on the youngsters' faces suggested they were lovers, to Nash's mind. The background to the photo more or less confirmed it. 'Clara,' he called through to the conservatory, 'come and have a look at this.'

As she inspected the image, he told her, 'That photo was taken at Runswick Bay. I recognize the background. I think we should get the coastguard involved. I think that was the place where they became lovers, the place Clark said he was going to revisit before ending it all. Regrettably, I think their duty will only involve recovery of a body, because it will be far too late for a rescue.'

'You think Clark drowned himself?'

'I'm fairly sure of it. That photo, plus finding Susan Headley's car there, more or less confirms it.'

Clara returned to her search of the conservatory-cum-office, and Nash completed his inspection of the lounge. He'd just finished when Viv and Lisa returned, to be joined a few seconds later by Clara. Nash explained the significance of the photo, and asked if the others had anything to report. Clara and Lisa began to speak simultaneously, but Clara signalled for Lisa to continue.

'There was a letter in the bedroom that we think Susan Headley wrote to James shortly before her death. It's addressed, *Dear James*, and it's really sad.'

Nash took charge of the letter and was immersed in reading it when Clara said she'd found something in the office, but didn't know what to make of it.

'What is it?' he asked, his attention still focused on the letter.

'It's a scrap of paper that was stuck to the bottom of the waste bin. It appears to have been torn from an application form, or something like that. The only part I can make out is the name, but it meant nothing to me, certainly not in the context of the case we're investigating.'

'What was the name?'

Nash had reached the part of Susan's letter where she advised James, "*You must not allow this to ruin the rest of your life. You have achieved so much already it would be a shame to throw your hard work away. Don't let what has happened to us claim another victim.*"

He was so absorbed by the melancholy the letter invoked, that he almost missed the name when Clara said it. After a few seconds, he looked at her and asked, 'What did you say that name was?'

'Nicholas Owen. Why, does it mean something to you?'

Much to their surprise, Nash gasped in astonishment, and then, after a few seconds, began to chuckle.

'Would you like to share the joke with us?' Clara asked.

'No, I don't think so — not at the moment. I need to mull it over first.'

Having handed over the rest of the house to Forensics, the detectives returned to Helmsdale. They alerted the coast-guard, and reported to the chief constable their belief that Clark had carried out his threat to commit suicide, by drowning in the North Sea near Runswick Bay. Nash agreed with

Ruth Edwards' comment about the futility of it all, but as soon as the call was over, he called Clara into his office and told her to close the door.

Once he was assured that their conversation could not be overheard, he explained what the name Nicholas Owen meant to him. 'Let me emphasize that what I'm about to tell you is pure speculation, and therefore, I don't want it repeating. I just hope you don't talk in your sleep. I haven't a shred of evidence — or maybe with what you found, just one shred — to back up my wild idea. And we might never know whether I'm right or wrong. We've alerted the coastguard, and sooner or later, Clark's body might be found, which would prove conclusively that I'm wrong. Even if a body isn't found, Clark will eventually be declared dead under the 2013 Presumption of Death Act. That presumption is based on Clark walking into the sea and drowning. But your discovery of that name set me wondering if that was simply what we were intended to believe.'

'OK, but what's so special about that name? Nicholas Owen sounds a perfectly normal sort of name. I don't understand why it's got you so agitated.'

'I agree, it's probably quite common. But given the location you found that name, there is one particular Nicholas Owen who might be highly relevant. The man I'm referring to was born in the middle of the sixteenth century, into a devout Catholic family. His father was a carpenter, and Nicholas also followed that profession. He spent years travelling the country, using his skills to build hiding places for Catholic priests, such as the one at Bishopton Priory that Viv told us about. He saved many lives thanks to his ingenuity, and there is a strong belief that some of his priest's holes have never been found. Eventually, Nicholas was captured, tortured, and killed, but despite the agony he must have suffered, he never revealed anything to his captors.'

'Where did you learn all this?'

'We studied that period of history as part of our exam course, when I was at school.'

'Much as I appreciate the attempt to improve my education, I still don't see the relevance of this character from five hundred years ago to what might, or might not, have happened to James Clark.'

'That's because I haven't finished the history lesson yet. After his death, Nicholas Owen was canonised by the Catholic church, becoming one of a group known as the Forty English Martyrs.'

Nash paused, then added, 'Saint Nicholas Owen became the patron saint of illusionists and escapologists.'

Clara was astounded. 'Really?'

Nash nodded. 'OK, I accept that the most likely scenario is that Clark felt unable to continue living without Amanda. Having taken his revenge, there would have been nothing left for him. Alternatively, did he follow Susan Headley's instruction to him in her last letter, not to become another victim?

'Finding what appears to be the torn edge of an application form in the name of Nicholas Owen merely increases my doubts. Has Clark fooled us into believing he committed suicide? When, in fact, he's created a new persona in the name of Nicholas Owen? In doing so, he'd have complied with Susan Headley's plea, to put the past behind him.

'Alternatively, did he deliberately leave that scrap of paper in a place we'd be certain to find it, simply to mislead us?'

'I'm not too sure about the last part, Mike, because he'd have to gamble on some clever . . . er . . . person, like you, knowing something as arcane as the patron saint of illusionists. One thing I do know, the media frenzy that's building up will go into hyper-drive once they learn that Clark is believed to have committed suicide.'

As Clara was about to leave his office, Nash said, 'What we don't know, what we might never know, is *did* James Clark perish in the North Sea off Runswick Bay? *Or*, has Magnus Evadere performed the greatest illusion, and escape act, of his career?'

It was a question that would plague Nash for years, long after James Clark had been officially presumed dead.

THE END

ACKNOWLEDGEMENTS

Every time I finish a new book, I wait with bated breath for my readers' opinions. They are the ones who tell me it makes sense, or not, as the case may be. As always, I have to thank Wendy McPhee and Al Gowans for their thoroughness, and for sometimes asking the question 'Why?'.

Of course, the in-house editor, secretary, coffee-maker and door-answering person, deserves the greatest thanks of all for keeping me on track.

Jodi, my editor, is great to work with, and I must also thank Jasper and his team at Joffe Books, Emma, Steph, and Nina, for their support and faith in me.

Thank you for reading this book.

If you enjoyed it please leave feedback on Amazon or Goodreads, and if there is anything we missed or you have a question about, then please get in touch. We appreciate you choosing our book.

Founded in 2014 in Shoreditch, London, we at Joffe Books pride ourselves on our history of innovative publishing. We were thrilled to be shortlisted for Independent Publisher of the Year at the British Book Awards.

www.joffebooks.com

We're very grateful to eagle-eyed readers who take the time to contact us. Please send any errors you find to corrections@joffebooks.com. We'll get them fixed ASAP.